Praise for *Geekerella*

"*Geekerella* has 'must-read' written all over it. A ⬚
comedy with coming-of-age sensibilities and authenti⬚
teens, this novel hits all the YA book-love buttons. *Ge*⬚
simply delightful."   —*USA Today*'s Happy E⬚

"Fairytale and fandom collide in this sweet, heartfelt, enter⬚
rom-com."
                                                        —⬚

"A legit love letter to geekdom."   —*Paste* magazi⬚

"With geekily adorable characters, a show that's part *Star Trek*
and part *Firefly*, a cosplay contest, and a food truck fairy
godmother, this is a love letter to fandom. Required reading for
geeks everywhere."   —*Booklist*

"A celebration of fandom and happily ever afters, this feel-good
reimagining hits all the right notes."   —*Publishers Weekly*

"The geekiest spin on Cinderella you'll ever read."   —*Hypable*

"Geeks and non-geeks will discover their inner fangirl when they
fall for this fan-tastic book that celebrates fan-doms, fan-tasy,
and 'shipworthy romance.'"   —*Justine*

"This geeky twist on a classic Cinderella story is honestly the most
adorable thing ever!"   —Her Campus

"This charming and funny twist on Cinderella is the perfect YA
fandom fairytale."   —*BNTeen* blog

THE
PRINCESS
AND THE
FANGIRL

A Geekerella Fairytale

By Ashley Poston

QUIRK BOOKS
PHILADELPHIA

Copyright © 2019 by Ashley Poston

Library of Congress Cataloging in Publication Number: 2018943035

ISBN: 978-1-68369-096-2

Printed in the United States of America

Typeset in Arkhip, Gotham, and Sabon LT Std
Cover design by Andie Reid
Cover illustration by Amy DeVoogd

Production management by John J. McGurk

Quirk Books
215 Church Street
Philadelphia, PA 19106
quirkbooks.com

10 9 8 7 6 5 4 3 2 1

For you, dear reader—
As someone once told me,
You're going to be amazing

THE
PRINCESS
AND THE
FANGIRL

THE FATE OF AMARA

By Elle Wittimer

[EXCERPT FROM *REBELGUNNER*]

AFTER A RECORD-BREAKING MONTH AT THE box office, *Starfield* has captured the hearts and minds of legions of fans worldwide, rocketing its young leads, Darien Freeman and Jessica Stone, to superstardom. Soon after the announcement of its third consecutive week in the #1 spot, the studio revealed plans for a sequel, to the surprise of no one who enjoys money.

Now, rumors are beginning to circulate: Who could the villain be in the sequel? Which new lucky lady will capture the Federation Prince Carmindor's heart? Jessica Stone has been silent about any sort of obligation to reprise her role as Princess Amara, and for those of us who have seen *Starfield*, we know this to be a near impossibility anyway.

The cast will come together for the first time since the success of *Starfield*, gathering at the twenty-fifth annual ExcelsiCon for panels, interviews, and meet-and-greets. The director, Amon Wilkins, will reveal the title of the sequel (and perhaps even our villain!) over the course of the sci-fi convention.

But as *Starfield* goes on, and the story continues where the television show left off, what does this mean for the legacy of Amara?

And what will *Starfield* be without our princess?

THURSDAY

"Is that how you greet your new ruler?
With a pistol and a sassy catchphrase?"

—Princess Amara, Episode 13, "The Queen of Nothing"

JESS

PRINCESS AMARA IS DEAD.

In a perfect universe, I wouldn't care. My character dies a noble and brilliant death at the end of *Starfield*, when she rams her spaceship into the Black Nebula (which is more like a black hole, but whatever) to save her one true love, the dreamy Federation Prince Carmindor.

In a perfect universe, I would've cashed my check and used *Starfield* as a springboard to more Oscar-worthy roles. Roles that *mean* something, roles that tell invaluable stories, that aren't me looking hot in a suffocating dress while running in heels.

In a perfect universe, I would be happy.

But this universe is not perfect and neither am I, although I've tried to be. I've tried so, so hard. And it all might be for nothing.

Because today I made three unforgivable mistakes.

The first one:

During a presser (a presser is basically a marathon of filmed interviews with different media outlets back to back to back . . . I can usually endure them for hours, but these nerd ones are a different beast entirely. How I long for questions about Darien

Freeman's new diet or my glittery pumps), held in a small room in a hotel, I accidentally let this slip:

"I certainly hope Amara doesn't come back."

Which, I *know*.

Bad answer.

The interviewer had been coming for blood for the past thirty minutes, poking and prodding at our airtight answers until *something* had to give, and the bright lights were giving me a headache.

So of course it was me who slipped first.

I wasn't paying attention. For hours Dare—Darien Freeman, my costar—had been entertaining the interviewers. He lived and breathed *Starfield*—he was a fanboy before he became Prince Carmindor, and that's stellar publicity. The world eats it up. It's adorable.

What's decidedly less adorable is Princess Amara, poor dead Princess Amara, played by a girl who's never even seen the show.

I don't make good press fodder.

Or, at least, I didn't think I did.

The interviewer's eyes widened behind her candy-apple-red glasses. She was petite and blond, stylish in a '60s pinup meets *Revenge of the Nerds* sort of way. "But thousands of fans would *love* to see you back! And your character, too. Have you heard of the #SaveAmara initiative?"

I shook my head.

Dare jumped at the chance to inform me. "Oh, it's a Twitter hashtag created to rally the fandom and save the princess from her fate."

The interviewer nodded enthusiastically. "The user who created it claims that Amara deserved better, especially in this reboot. She deserved to live, not to be fridged for Prince Carmindor's character development."

"Oh."

It was all I could say.

I curled my fingers tightly around the phone in my lap. It buzzed again. Another Instagram comment. Or Twitter. I wished it was neither.

The interviewer went on. "Natalia Ford, the actress who originally played Amara, whose shoes you stepped into, has already voiced solidarity for the movement, pleasing a lot of older fans. She has also recently criticized your interpretation of Amara, saying that you don't embody the spirit of the character. Does that bother you?"

For other people to not like you? The fandom to not like you? That's what she didn't say, but I saw it in her eyes. I was surprised, really, that it had taken this long for an interviewer to bring it up.

I'm a girl in Hollywood, I wanted to tell her. *I'm either too fat or too skinny or too pretty or not pretty enough. Nothing bothers me.*

But that would've been a lie, as evidenced by my death grip on my phone.

"Erin, right?" I said, when I should've not taken the bait. But I was too tired to stop, and I wasn't paying attention to Dare's signals to shut up. If you know anything about my overly enthusiastic costar, it's that he's never subtle about anything. I just didn't care. "Tell me, Erin, what has Natalia Ford done since she played Amara, what, twenty years ago? Another one-off *Starfield* special? Ms. Ford doesn't *have* a career. I do, in spite of what everyone says. That's all that matters—"

"I must be early," a calm voice interrupted. "That tends to happen to people without careers."

My blood ran cold.

In the doorway stood a woman with piercing brown eyes and peppery-gray hair pulled back into a bun. Her face was heart shaped, eyebrows dark and severe, her lips pursed. Though she was short, standing in that doorway she commanded the room. Trade her monochromatic pantsuit for a dress made of galaxies and starlight, and she was still the princess of the universe. In her arms sat a hairless cat who surveyed the room with narrow emerald eyes, looking almost as dour as his owner.

So, yeah, my second mistake was insulting Natalia Ford.

And my third mistake?

Well.

After that disaster of an interview, I needed to take a breath. Dare warned me that we had to be at a panel in ten minutes. It felt like every one of my days at this loud overcrowded convention was planned down to the second, squeezing as much of Jessica Stone out of my appearance as possible. But I needed quiet. I needed to breathe.

So I excused myself to the restroom to collect myself, and that was my third mistake. If I'd never gone to the bathroom, if I'd never left Dare's sight, if I'd followed him straight onto that stupid panel—

My phone dings, wrenching me out of my panic spiral. It is Ethan Tanaka, my assistant and best friend (only friend, if I'm being truthful).

ETHAN TANAKA (3:03 PM)

—*[pic]*

—*THIS ISN'T YOU.*

—*WHERE ARE YOU.*

—*JESS.*

—*JESSICA.*

Pulling down my black beanie in the hopes of passing unnoticed, I elbow my way into the ballroom, where the *Starfield* panel has already started. The one I'm supposed to be on. The lights are off and the audience is quiet—such a drastic shift from the thundering noise of the hundreds if not thousands of people in the Marriott hotel lobby. My ears are ringing with the silence; I can't even hear myself think.

My eyes slowly adjust as I gaze over a sea of anxious fans, panic prickling at my skin.

"I'm Jess—Jessica Stone," says a girl on the stage, but it isn't me.

This isn't happening.

This is impossible.

I stare at the girl sitting between Dare and Calvin. There, in *my* chair. Behind *my* name tag. She's exactly where I'm *supposed* to be. Where I *need* to be. But instead I'm in the audience, mute and invisible, and all the lights are on her.

And to my mounting horror, no one seems to realize that she isn't *me*.

IMOGEN

I must be dreaming.

That's all there is to it. I'm dreaming, and in like three seconds everyone's going to turn into Daleks and ANNIHILATE me and I'll have to run away with sexy David Tennant and help fight the Borg in a netherverse and duel against Sith Lords bent on conquering the empire, only to fall to the hands of the Nox King and—

Whoa, I'm getting ahead of myself. How did I even get here? On a *Starfield* panel when I am most definitely, one hundred and ten percent *not* Jessica Stone? Well, lucky for you, I can totally, *absolutely* explain this.

Yep. I can *definitely* explain this.

I can . . . *mostly* explain this?

Okay, you got me. I can basically explain only ten percent of this and none of it is my fault.

Well, maybe a little of it.

Oh, *starflame*, I'm dead.

Dead dead.

Like, I-am-masquerading-as-a-famous-actress-and-will-be-found-out dead.

I stare out at the crowd in the largest room of the entire con. There must be three thousand pairs of eyes staring back at me. It's standing room only. I can tell by the constant murmur—when you go to enough cons and sit through enough panels, you just know. You *know* that there are six thousand eyes staring at you like you're some god of fame and fandom. The audience is shifting in their chairs, the smell of the con so strong and distinct, it reminds me of a thirteen-year-old boy's bedroom.

I should know—thirteen was a rough year for my brother Milo. You never forget that smell.

Just like you never forget the sight of this stage from the audience. It's fifty feet long, set up with a white table draped in a cloth bearing the ExcelsiCon logo. There are three microphones for the five people on the panel, and paper nameplates at each chair identifying each star. (Although how can you *not* know who they are?)

No one notices that I'm not the girl whose name is on the card in front of me. They don't realize that I am not Jessica Stone. At least not yet. Because as the actors of *Starfield*—the same *Starfield* I saw fourteen times in theaters this summer (a fact I wear as a badge of honor)—go down the line introducing themselves, none of them calls me out.

They don't notice.

I mean, I do get the occasional "You know who you look like?" from strangers who feel the need to tell me that I look like Jessica Stone. And since *Starfield* came out, I've been stopped in Starbucks more times than I'm comfortable with. Which, come to think of it, is probably one of the major reasons I dyed my hair last weekend and basically killed my entire bathroom with neon pink. But you can't see my hair under my black SPACE QUEEN beanie—the same one Jessica Stone had on in the bathroom when

I met her—and with the way the stage lights are shining down so harshly, I probably look more like Jessica Stone than usual.

Oh, *starflame,* they actually think I'm Jessica Stone.

Cool, cool, coolcoolcool. Just roll with it, Imogen Ada Lovelace, drama is your favorite class in high school. Improv it.

Darien Freeman—ohmygod, *the* Darien Freeman, Federation Prince Carmindor, the love of my Tumblr life—leans into the mic we share (WE. ARE. SHARING. A. MICROPHONE.) and introduces himself, "I'm Darien Freeman."

Oh my God he's Darien Freeman.

. . . I know he is.

BUT STILL.

Cool, cool. Keep calm.

I thought today was just going to be a normal day. Just another Thursday at ExcelsiCon, helping my moms in their booth while drooling over the best cosplay. You know, the usual con stuff.

I think everything started going wrong when I decided to go to the hidden bathroom, the one on the second floor of the showroom's hotel, the Marriott, a really magnificent building in the middle of downtown Atlanta. Pockets of vendors are spread out over the four hotels that make up the convention center, all connected by sidewalks and skybridges. My moms just happened to get a booth in the biggest showroom in the main hotel (they should, they've been going long enough). That's how I know about the off-limits restroom. Technically it's reserved for special guests, but there's never any signs, so it really doesn't count as breaking a rule. Anyway, I'd done my business and exited the stall to wash my hands, humming the *Starfield* theme that Milo got stuck in my head earlier, when I saw her:

Princess Amara.

I mean, Jessica Stone.

She was just standing there, and for a second I thought her eyes looked a little red, as if she'd been crying. Which was odd, because I really never imagined Jessica Stone crying about anything. Her life is perfect.

When she saw me, she looked away and began rummaging in her purse for her signature rosy lipstick. I guess I felt sorry for her—I don't know—so I unpinned one of the buttons on my lanyard and held it out to her.

"Hi. I'm sorry for bothering you but I'm a really big fan," I said, which was one hundred and twenty percent true. "And I just wanted to tell you that I loved the way you portrayed Princess Amara. It really, you know, struck a chord. So, thank you."

I put the button in her hand: #SaveAmara.

It's from the initiative I'd started to bring Princess Amara back for the *Starfield* sequel.

She looked down and she just . . . got *really angry*. "*Save* Amara?" She shoved the pin back into my hand. "She can't save anyone—much less herself. She's better off dead."

Then she turned and retreated into a stall.

Honestly, I was too stunned to talk. I just pinned the button back onto my lanyard, checked my reflection in the mirror, and walked out.

I didn't know what to think. Maybe I thought she'd take the pin. Slip it among the dregs of her Prada bag and leave, forgetting it until years later.

Instead, I tried to act as if her reaction wasn't rude, or mean, or that I wasn't beginning to feel just a little bit angry too.

I'd just pulled down my beanie when I felt a tap on my shoulder. "Jess?" a volunteer said, looking at me. "It's almost time."

"No, I'm not—" I pointed back to the bathroom just as the

volunteer's earpiece started to chatter. Panicking, she did the one thing that volunteers were *absolutely not* supposed to do.

She grabbed me by the wrist and pulled me down the hallway . . .

And now here I am.

On the *Starfield* panel in front of three thousand people, standing room only. Displaced like a Yu-Gi-Oh! card in a Pokémon deck. Like a Nox in the Federation Court.

Like Princess Amara on the starship *Prospero.*

And I am in really, really, *really* big trouble.

Through one of the side doors slips a girl wearing a suede jacket and a black SPACE QUEEN beanie. The same beanie I have on. It feels a little like looking into one of those fun-house mirrors. You know it's you looking back, but it's slightly distorted. I mean, not in that wonky super-tall or super-wide way—it's just that something's off and you aren't quite sure what, and only you can tell. She and I have the same wide eyes and heart-shaped face, the same build, and I know she sees the same thing: a girl who looks a little too much like her, as if plucked from some impossible universe.

And right now, at this moment in this universe, *I've* been mistaken for *her.*

I remember what Jessica Stone said in the bathroom. The snarl on her lips.

Save Amara? She can't save anyone. There was no love in her voice for the character she'd played, or for the fans who loved her. *She's better off dead.*

"Jess?" the moderator says, and both Jessica Stone and I turn our gaze to Felix Flores, an internet-famous foodie and founder of the podcast SCIFI BYTES. He's looking at me. *Only* me. I don't think anyone notices the real Jess in the crowd. "Do you wanna take this question? Spoilers for all of you who haven't seen *Starfield* yet! How did you feel when your character, Princess Amara, died?"

I blink and my eyes dart to the fan who asked the question. He's tall and gangly, but I can't really make him out, blinded by the stage lights.

Darien hesitates beside me, looking from the moderator to me and then back to the moderator. He begins to lean in to the microphone, but then so do I.

I don't know why. I shouldn't.

Maybe because Jessica Stone is in the crowd, and I'm up here . . .

. . . something just shifts.

She's better off dead. Her voice echoes in my head and I can't stand it. My lanyard is laden with the burden of fifteen #SaveAmara pins and I think of those fifty thousand signatures from the petition demanding to bring her back from the dead.

The podcaster—and everyone else—is urging me to answer the question. I know *exactly* how Jessica Stone would feel. I hate it.

I take a breath, trying to remember the tone and crisp lilt of her soft Southern accent. "I was heartbroken."

In the crowd, Jessica Stone's face hardens.

Felix barks a laugh. "That we were—"

I cut him off. I'm not done. "She never should have died. She should have lived. She deserved to live."

The fan who asked the question stares at me, mouth agape, as if that was the most insane response I could've ever given to that question. It's no secret that Jessica Stone hates *Starfield*. That she can't wait to get out of the franchise. Like Robert Pattinson in his Twilight days, Jessica degrades the franchise every chance she gets.

But not now.

Not here.

I shoot a look at Jessica, who is glaring up at me with all the hatred in her bones. Good. Because Princess Amara is better off *alive*.

And I'm going to make sure everyone knows it.

JESS

I AM GOING TO KILL HER. I don't even know her name but I don't need her name to put her in an unmarked grave. I am going to chop her up into so many pieces that when alien archeologists find her bones in a thousand years they won't even realize that she was once human.

That is how hard I am going to kill her.

Spinning on my heels, my phone clenched in a death grip, I march out before anyone has even risen from their seats. I duck around the six-armed Zorine without so much as a second glance. She tries to say something to me, but I don't hear her.

All I'm seeing is red. I am *livid*.

"Wow, I thought Jess was super fake, but she was *so cool* on that panel," says a girl behind me as the ballroom empties. "And how she relates to Amara? I really hope they save her."

"Me too! I live-streamed the whole thing," replies her friend. "My comments section was going nuts."

I glance up at the two girls. They look like high school sophomores, neither one cosplaying anyone other than their nerdy selves—all faded jeans and tees with cute sayings or pictures of male figure skaters clutched in an embrace.

"She's so cool."

"Super!"

I turn away as they pass, but they don't even blink. They don't realize that I'm the real Jessica Stone. They just saw my doppelgänger on stage, so why would they even think it was me?

I'm . . . invisible?

To everyone?

I don't like this. I *can't* like this.

Breaking off from the crowd, I follow the signs to the backstage area. There's a volunteer guarding it, of course, but when I rush up and tell her someone's getting sick around the corner, she darts off to help and I slip into the hallway where the panelists had exited.

My anger is morphing into some sort of confused panic. The girls' conversation echoes in my head. How cool Jessica Stone was. How they related to the way that imposter felt about Princess Amara. They had to be joking, right?

Why don't they like *me*?

Starfield has only been out for a month, and I've gained close to a million followers because of it—which should be great, right? You want to be famous on social. But while Dare's touted for being one of the best character revivals of the decade, and *Starfield* as one of the best remakes in recent years, I am—

My phone vibrates again. And again. My assistant, Ethan, had said I should take the apps off, but then I'd be worrying what people are saying while I'm not looking. I'd be worried about what they *could* say.

My agent swore that playing Princess Amara would put me on the radar. It would make me a household name, like Jennifer Lawrence after *The Hunger Games* or Emma Watson after *Harry*

Potter. Well, it put me on the radar, all right. But *Starfield* wasn't a book series; it was an old sci-fi TV show. And that attracted a different kind of crowd. What my agent should have said was that *Starfield* would make me a household name like Kelly Marie Tran, or Daisy Ridley, or Leslie Jones, actresses whose biggest stories are not about their performances but about the trolls who chased them off the internet.

And now the trolls have set their sights on me.

Darien sort of got the same blowback when he was announced to play Federation Prince Carmindor—which is how he met his girlfriend, btw—but it died off as the fandom embraced him. Now they write love letters about his inky-black eyelashes and immaculate abs while I get entire dissertations on how the small mole on the left side of my mouth has ruined the beauty of Princess Amara.

So although I don't know what I'll say or how I'll say it, I know I can't let that *girl* wreck my image any more.

She played you better than you do, whispers a little voice in my head. *The fans like her better. Maybe she should just b—*

Shut up, shut up, *shut up*!

A boisterous laugh stops me dead.

I'd recognize it anywhere: Calvin. The panel must be coming this way, and that means my impersonator is, too. I glance around, nowhere to go. I curse. If they find me here with my "twin," I don't know what the director will do.

Will I be in breach of contract? There were too many witnesses for it not to make media rounds. Oh, that can*not* happen.

I can see the headlines now:

JESSICA STONE FAKING IT.

DOPPELGÄNGER PLAYS JESSICA STONE BETTER THAN JESSICA STONE.

I wince as the *Starfield* cast comes around the corner. Calvin, Dare, *her*—

But no director. Amon must be doing damage control after that disastrous panel. He'll scold me later, I just know it.

Dare is the first to see me; our eyes connect. It only takes a split second for him to slip an arm around Calvin's and Felix's shoulders to steer them in the opposite direction.

"You know, I think this is a shortcut," he says smoothly.

Bless Darien Freeman. Bless his tight jeans and his curly hair and his insufferable smile. Bless everything about that Hufflepuff.

I hear Calvin ask, "But what about Jess?"

"She has that interview, remember?" Dare says quickly.

"Oh yeah . . . "

Meanwhile, the girl is just standing there, looking at me with my fists clenched and my arms stuck at my sides. Just seeing her makes me want to murder her again. Like, meat-grinder murder. *Fargo* murder.

There's no one else in the hallway as I march up to her. The first thing I notice, in the steady flicker of the hallway halogens, is that she doesn't have my light-blue eyes. Hers are dark gray. And no one noticed?

"Look, I'm really sorry—" she says hesitantly.

I turn her badge to read the name on it. Then I look at her through my long fake lashes and tell her, "You will never say a word about this. You will never write in your little blog about it. You will never talk about it on Instagram or even subtweet it. And if you impersonate me again, *Imogen Lovelace*, I will see you purged from this con—and every other con—forever. Do you understand?"

She stares at me like I'm speaking parseltongue. "You know I didn't *want* to be you, right?"

"But you were."

"What else was I supposed to do?" she bites back. "Tell everyone you weren't there?"

A flash of anger burns in my belly. I let her badge drop, all those wretched pins clinking together. "You will never do it again. Got it?"

"But—"

"Jess!" shouts a familiar masculine voice behind me. I look over my shoulder and see my assistant, Ethan Tanaka, seventeen going on forty. His expression is pinched, no-nonsense. He stops a few feet away when he realizes who I'm talking to.

His eyes dart quickly between us. "So, that actually did happen."

"It'll never happen again," I clip in reply, and turn back to Imogen. "Why're you still here? It's VIP only, and you're *not*."

Her head jerks back as if she's been slapped, and then she scowls and shoulders past us on her way down the hall. I don't take my eyes off her until she's gone, and then I sigh in relief.

Ethan begins to talk but I raise a finger. "It was a misunderstanding."

He holds up his hands. "I was only going to say you were rather rude to her."

"She *impersonated* me, Ethan! She could've ruined my career—"

Ethan's gaze snaps behind me and he jerks upright. "Mr. Wilkins, it's great to see you!"

I bite my tongue and spin to face my director. Amon saunters up like he owns the hallway—he saunters everywhere, so it's no big deal—mirrored aviators pushing his thick blond hair over his head, a manila envelope tucked under one arm.

"Jessica! You did so great on that panel. It's like you were a different person!"

My smile strains a little. "You know, I'm sorry for anything I might've said—"

He waves a hand. "Nonsense! It was perfect. Any publicity is good publicity, and you definitely got the pot stirring. That reminds me." He hands me the manila envelope. "For you."

Warily, I take it. It's thick and heavy. My heart pounds against my rib cage because I know what it probably is. The contract extension that was detailed in my option clause, tying me to Princess Amara for another year, or two, or ten.

I—I feel like I'm about to vomit.

He winks and taps a finger against his lips. "Our secret, yeah?"

"But I don't think—"

A ringtone cuts through my words and Amon holds up a *wait a moment* finger, pulling his phone out of his jean jacket and looking pleased. "Finally! I gotta take this call—but read it over, will you, Stone?" He heads down the hallway in the direction that Imogen Lovelace went and shoves open the exit door, almost nailing the volunteer guard in the back of the head. He doesn't apologize, just bleeds into the crowd.

"I can't think about this right now," I mumble. "I can't think about anything that's happened in the last three hours." He takes the package dutifully and pushes his thick black glasses up the bridge of his nose. He's much taller than I am—five foot eleven—and lean, with short black hair gelled against his scalp, warm taupe skin, and a scar just to the left of his mouth. All of his brothers are tall, too, and every time I've gone over to his house, I only felt normal next to his grandmother, who is ninety-four and bent from almost a century of gravity, but she makes the best *onigiri*, a steamed rice ball wrapped in dried seaweed. Whenever Ethan visits home, he smuggles a few back on the plane.

"It wasn't as horrible as you think it was," he says. "She didn't do that bad."

Ignoring him, I eye his outfit: a crisp button-down shirt and slacks. "Why're you dressed up?"

He adjusts his cuffs. "This is my first time out in the wild as your assistant, so I have to look nice."

That makes me laugh. "Really?"

He nods seriously. "Plus it's part of my Angus cosplay."

"Ugh, *nerd*." I punch him in the shoulder, and he grins in delight.

Ethan Tanaka and I have been best friends since he was born, two years and three days after me. We went to the same middle school and kept in touch after I left for dramatic arts high school. Even as I became famous, our friendship just seemed to stick, although we couldn't have been more different. He wanted to go and do nerd things like write for video games, and I was, well, by then I was Jessica Stone. Then a few months ago, as I was complaining about my last assistant, who stole my expensive eyeshadow palette, Ethan—fresh out of high school and taking a year off before college—suddenly asked, "Is the pay good?"

"For what?"

"To be your assistant."

And that was it.

Ethan's the only person in the world who knows everything about me: that I'm deathly afraid of being forgotten; that every morning for at least three hours I comb through my Instagram profile, deleting the unsavory messages, only to have more pop up moments later; that I hate the mole on the side of my face that my agent, Diana, says is too iconic to get rid of; that I eat raw instant ramen straight out of the package when I'm stressed; that I'm not really twenty-three, but nineteen; and that I lied to a casting director to get a starring role in the indie film that got me an Oscar nod. I was fourteen at the time, but I told them I was almost eighteen.

We'd stuck with the lie ever since.

Ethan knows I'll do anything to keep my career. Even endure the trash in *Starfield*.

I know everything about him, too. That his favorite color is that god-awful yellow everyone hates, and his favorite band is some obscure indie-rock group that broke up eons ago, and he always selects Kirby in *Super Smash Bros.*, and he takes his peanut butter and jelly sandwiches without the crust, thank you very much. I couldn't ask for a better best friend. He's like a brother to me.

It's just a bonus he gets paid for putting up with my drama.

I keep waiting for him to figure out that he is way too smart, and way too nice, and way too talented to be my assistant.

I take a long breath. "If this is the extent of the fallout, I'm okay with it. Are you sure she was fine up there on the panel? Nothing'll come of it?"

"I don't know, Jess, but I didn't think it was that awful."

"Right."

His smartwatch beeps and he checks it. "Ah, crap, you need to be at an interview in three minutes. We better hurry."

"No rest for the wicked," I say, and follow him down the hallway. I trust Ethan knows where he's going. He has the nerd sense, or whatever it is, and can navigate ExcelsiCon despite never having been here before. I trail him like his shadow. I don't even try to remember where we are, what hotel we're in or what part of the convention center we're wandering through. It all looks the same. Bland hallways and people dressed up as characters and long lines and meet-and-greets.

We take an elevator up a few floors and step out into another long empty hallway. At the end, waiting patiently, is Dare. He's snacking on some sort of protein bar. Since filming for the sequel starts next month, he's back on his dreaded diet, which means he's just a little bit cranky and scowling at salads most of the time.

He sees us and waves.

"So, you get that whole thing sorted out?" he asks, inhaling the rest of his protein bar and tossing the wrapper in a trash can.

"Yeah," I reply. "Thanks for distracting Calvin and Felix."

"I figured it hadn't been planned. She looked scared to *death* up there. Who was she?"

"I think she's an exhibitor—at least, judging by her badge," Ethan says.

I roll my eyes. "She didn't *look* very scared when she went on that whole Amara tirade."

Dare shrugs. "She's probably part of the Save Amara initiative."

"Ugh, they're *everywhere*." I scowl.

The double doors swing open, and a woman in a Captain Marvel T-shirt greets us with a wide, plastic smile. "Oh, good! Darien, Jess, my name's Heather." She extends a hand for us to shake. "Thank you *so* much for taking the time out of your busy schedules. I'll be interviewing you for the next thirty minutes. Shall we?" She gestures back into the room, where I see a makeshift interview set, complete with photo lights, a green-screen backdrop, an ExcelsiCon banner, and three chairs. An expensive-looking camera on a tripod is off to the side, a cameraman in black standing behind it.

Ethan pulls out his phone and says, "I'll be out here catching Pokémon," and then wanders toward the elevators.

Nerd.

AFTER THE INTERVIEW, AS I FOLLOW con security across the sky-bridge to my hotel, I realize I'm still holding the package from Amon as I enter the hotel. *Our secret,* he called it. Must be the contract for the next movie, where I'll be relegated to melodramatic flashbacks. Or maybe it's panel questions for tomorrow, because that girl royally screwed me with her surprise performance.

Whatever it is, I'm furious that I even have it.

Ethan squawks as I lob the envelope into the nearest trash can, where it drops to the bottom with a satisfying *thunk*. If it's the contract, Amon's probably sent a copy to my agent. I haven't been officially brought on because no one knows if the princess will "return"—in a flashback or whatever—but either way I don't want to sign on for a sequel. I want to reiterate, *again*, that Amara is dead. Here's hoping she stays that way.

"Jess!" Ethan runs over to dig it out. "It might be important."

"Then Diana can take care of it," I say, a bit too loud. "That's why I pay her," I add, lowering my voice. Everyone in the lobby has begun to suspect who I am.

It always happens this way. First is the quiet, as people squint at me, trying to place my face; then they're googling or whispering to their friends; then—

"Amara!" someone calls.

And suddenly I'm not anonymous anymore. It's happening quicker and quicker these days. They call me that even though Amara's not my name and even though I don't turn around in response to whoever's yelling it.

I press the UP button on one of the elevators. Which, by the way, are breathtaking—pods of glass that rocket you up ten, twenty stories, some sort of meld between Willy Wonka's magical lift and a transporter in an '80s sci-fi flick. When we checked in yesterday I was awestruck by them, but now I can't look, keeping my head down, praying that no one recognizes—

"Princess Amara!"

That's *not* my name.

"It's just a fan," Ethan mutters. Then, in a kind but stern voice, he prods, "Jessica."

He's right. Of course.

I turn to the girl with a smile. "Hi!" She's about fourteen maybe, cosplaying as . . . something orange. She gushes about how big a fan she is and how much she loves me, and I pose for a selfie, biding my time until the elevator comes. More people have gathered around us.

Fortunately, before anyone else can take my picture or call me Amara, the elevator doors whoosh open and Ethan and I step inside.

IMOGEN

THE SHOWROOM FLOOR IS SPREAD ACROSS the second-biggest room in the main convention hotel. The space is massive, abuzz with hundreds of vendors selling everything from cosplay gear to mock weapons to T-shirts to dice to obscure tabletop games to books to trading cards, all arranged beside large exhibits hyping upcoming franchise films and obscure TV series. And in the back of the ballroom are three neat rows of artists in what we at ExcelsiCon lovingly call Artists' Back Alley. There are vendor halls in the con's other hotels, too, but this is where the magic happens.

In the distant corner, farthest from Artists' Back Alley, the Nox King has been hoisted to full mast, and I set my sights on him. It's one of those old plastic models that used to stand at the front of comics and gaming shops in the '90s. My moms bought it off a vendor before I was even born, and it's been a symbol of their business, Figurine It Out, ever since. The Nox King is present at every con they attend, and it's become a landmark for anyone who's lost their friends on the merciless con floor.

Here, this is where I belong. Not on some panel, being mistaken for Jessica Stone.

I'm no one.

I'll see you purged from this con—and every other con—forever. Do you understand? I still hear the icy warning in her voice, and it makes me wince.

I was basically born and raised right between the 200s and 300s aisles. I know every nook and cranny of this con, every shortcut across every skybridge, every back stairway, every rule, and every way to break them. I even know most of the long-standing volunteers. The con map is tattooed under my eyelids—I could walk it in the dark.

This is my kingdom, my home, existing as far back in my memory as the dawn of time. Well, okay, the dawn of *my* time, but time is wibbly-wobbly anyway—

"MONSTER! *MOOONNNSTERRRRR!*"

I glance over my shoulder in the direction of the voice.

A guy is pushing through a crowd of Attack on Titan cosplayers and stumbles out the other side—Milo, my younger brother, grinning now that he has my attention. He's broad and muscular, with curly brown hair that has a single dyed silver streak in the front, a child's Spider-Man backpack hiked high on his back. So you honestly can't tell whether he plays football or DnD on Friday nights. (Spoiler: it's both.) Last year, the twerp grew into his too-big feet. Now he's taller than me and he'll never let me live it down.

I glare at him as he approaches. "I told you not to call me that in public."

His grin widens. "Why, because it's true?"

It isn't true. I mean it kind of is, but only when there's one cheese-stuffed garlic roll left on spaghetti night. That last one is mine. I will spork your eye out for it.

Our moms began calling me Monster because, when I was little, my favorite pajamas were a *T. rex* onesie that I refused to change out of—ever. I went to kindergarten with it on, that's how much I loved it. I would stomp around and roar, and whenever someone asked my name, I'd tell them that I was a monster.

I guess my four-year-old self kind of trolled me from an early age. It doesn't help that Imogen shortens to Mo, which is, you guessed it, the first two letters in "monster." So it just kind of stuck. The fact that I sometimes get into trouble has nothing to do with my nickname.

It doesn't.

At all.

I scowl at Milo. "If you weren't my brother and I didn't love you, I'd strangle you with your own jockstrap."

At that he laughs. "Yikes, *someone's* had a bad day."

Oh, he doesn't know the half of it.

I dig into my backpack for a handful of pins and shove some into his hands. "Here, if you're going to walk beside me at least help me pass these out. Save Amara!" I add, forcing a pin into the hands of oncoming attendees. "Revive her! She deserves better!"

Most people take the pin and go on their way.

My internet friend Harper designed them. She draws the best *Starfield* fanart and designs the coolest merch and apparently makes delicious hotel ramen. We've never actually met in IRL, never Skyped or FaceTimed, so I honestly can't tell you what she looks like. But all that will change this weekend. We're sharing a booth in Artists' Back Alley, her selling her artwork and me hawking my petition and pins.

It's been fun imagining what Harper looks like, though. Her avatar has always been *Starfield's* fearless Zorine, so I kinda picture her as the six-armed green-skinned lesbian Llotivan who could strike fear into your soul with a single vicious red-eyed glare. She's so badass online that I'm pretty sure she *is* Zorine.

And she's talented on top of being rad. Harper is destined for greatness. Like my brother, Milo.

Like literally everyone I know. Except for me.

Milo quietly hands a passing Deadpool a pin before he says, "Okay, so I know this probably *isn't* the best time to tell you this, but I saw him."

I give another pin to a guy in a Dragon Ball Z cosplay—Goku, and he's definitely over 9000 on the hot-o-meter. "Saw who?"

"He-Who-Will-Not-Be-Named."

I try not to react when he tells me. I try not to look bothered at all. "What now?"

"I saw him today. On the YouTube Gaming panel. He's got some groupie following him around with a camera. You can't miss him. He's just *exudes* jerkoff."

"Oh," I say. My voice is small.

"You deserved so much better, Mo."

I really don't want to hear this right now. It's easy for him to say—he happened upon his perfect soulmate. They have the perfect relationship.

I take off walking but he catches me in two quick strides. I keep handing out pins, trying to ignore him.

"Look, Mo, I just wanted to tell you—"

"And you did. He's here. That's great."

But it's not.

So, a brief history of Imogen Lovelace's love life: I've only been in love once, and it was with—you guessed it!—He-Who-Will-Not-Be-Named. We'd been dating for about a year. It was long distance. He lived in Ohio, I lived in North Carolina, but we saw each other almost every month on the con circuit and we just kind of . . . hit it off. We loved the same horror flicks and laughed at the same scenes on *Galaxy Quest* and played *Over-*

watch together. We were supposed to go to the ExcelsiCon Ball last year (as the Tenth Doctor and Rose), and everyone knows what happened at last year's ball, but because he didn't show up I didn't get to witness the *most important moment* of *Starfield* fandom. The moment Prince Carmindor—I mean Darien Freeman, the actor, the stud muffin, the *legend*—fell in love with one of us.

A girl. A normal, everyday girl.

And I missed it, sitting on the curb bawling my eyes out because some guy I thought loved me decided to ghost me. I'd actually gotten dressed up for him—makeup! *Heels*! I never wear heels, I never put on mascara. But I did for him.

Because, stupidly, I thought I loved him.

I always had it in my head that love was kinda like two people passing each other on opposite escalators at the front of the convention hall as you hurry to your next panel, they dressed as Link and you as Zelda . . .

"Kick some butt, babe!" they say.

"I'll tell Calamity Ganon you'll be there shortly!" I'd reply.

That is love.

. . . but maybe I've spent too much time on the internet.

I reach into my bag and fish out a handful of pins for a group of Steven Universe gems. Milo quietly follows behind. We don't talk for a long while.

There's a big *Starfield* display near the middle of the showroom. If I didn't know better, it looks like the *Prospero*—the spaceship in the series. The back of it, with the cargo door down. Maybe it's a photo op? To one side there's an exhibit showcasing *Starfield*'s original costumes—one of the main reasons the original Carmindor (David Singh) and Amara (Natalia *freaking* Ford) are going to be here on Sunday, to talk about the original series and celebrate its twenty-fifth anniversary. On the other side is a larger-than-life Styrofoam mountain for a popular new fantasy TV series called *Blades of Valor*. All I know about it is that there's a hottie in the main role. You know the kind: big blue eyes, windswept blond hair, and a raging poison sword of doom aflame in his hands, ready to fight the coming apocalypse.

Exhibits rise up like skyscrapers from the art deco carpet. ExcelsiCon is known for its horrific hotel carpets, but the showroom's is the *literal worst*. Coupled with the often zany but dazzling installations, I don't think a year goes by that I'm not in awe of this place. People running around, arms full of swag and collectibles, trying to get to a panel or an exhibit or a restroom.

That's usually one of the longest lines. Which is why I went up to the second-floor bathroom in the first place.

In hindsight, that was the worst idea I've ever had.

I shiver, rubbing my hands across my arms. Jessica Stone was a total and complete b—

I shake off my thoughts and break the silence. "Have you heard from the coach yet?" I ask Milo. "About the quarterstaff position?"

"Don't play dumb," he chides, sending off a text and sliding his phone back into his jeans pocket. "It's quarter*back*, and not yet."

I kinda hope the big oaf'll get it. He's been practicing like mad since last year, and when the current quarterback busted his leg jumping off a rooftop into a pool, the coach had his two backup QBs try out against each other. Milo's going to be a junior, and he's tortured himself on the field long enough. He deserves it.

But I don't tell him any of that. Instead I just raise my hands and say, "Yay, sportsball!"

He laughs and elbows me in the arm.

"*Ow!*"

"Oh come on, that was barely a tap."

"I'm delicate."

He snorts. "Bull."

"Save Amara!" I yell, tossing a sexy Xenomorph a pin. She thanks me and hurries on.

He flips over a #SaveAmara pin. "Can I ask you a question without you getting mad?"

"Sure." I lie because we both know I always get mad because usually it's a clueless question, like "why do you dye your hair?" or "why didn't you date that cute guy in your trig class last year?"

"Why do you want to save a fictional character so badly?"

I stop in the middle of the busy aisle and study him. I know he's asking earnestly—my younger brother is nothing but sincere and well meaning. See? He's perfect. All my life I've been in his shadow, and I can't even hate him for it because he's so nice and caring and thoughtful. I'd feel like a brat if I did.

I can't exactly say that I want to save Amara because I want to prove I'm not a waste of space. I'm not *no one*. I might not be good at many things, I suck at trig and chemistry and grammar. But even though I'm not vice president of the student body like Milo, or salutatorian like his boyfriend Bran, I can still be exceptional. I'm not just a raindrop in a pond but a comet plunged into the ocean, and I can make waves the size of skyscrapers because I'm not just here, I'm *living*.

Just like Amara saying she didn't want to be a princess. She was terrible at it. She wanted to do something more, to make her father, the Nox King, proud.

So I started a hashtag and wrote articles and think pieces and put a #SaveAmara petition online that got over fifty thousand signatures. And I set money aside to split a booth rental. Last year's ExcelsiCon was moderately attended, but this year Harper practically had to beg to get us a booth in Artists' Back Alley. The movie just came out last month, and *Starfield*'s already broken almost every box-office record set by the *Jurassic Worlds* and *Avengers* of the world. It's kinda incredible.

Anyway, I want to save Amara to let her prove that she can *be* somebody outside of her father's or Carmindor's shadow.

Like me, I guess.

I can't really tell Milo the truth, so instead I say, "I'm just sick and tired of princesses being either damsels in distress or the foil for a male character's emotional growth, and I *know* people want her back."

I know because when I was Jessica Stone, no one booed me off that stage. Fans *want* to see her unfridged.

Amara is important.

Milo rolls the pin between his fingers, like he's trying to find a good reply, but I'm a little afraid to hear it. Maybe he'll think it's stupid. Maybe he'll not understand. Or, worse, maybe he'll agree with Jessica Stone—that Amara should stay dead. And that's the last thing I want to hear from my overachieving little brother.

"Hi, Pretzel Henry!" I call as we pass near the back of Artists' Back Alley, deciding to try to change the subject. An older gentleman—in his mid-fifties probably, with a peppery black beard to match his peppery black hair—looks up from a customer. When he sees us his eyes light up. He waves a salt-less pretzel.

Milo waves back. "He's literally here *every* year."

"Some heroes don't wear capes," I say, and shove another pin in the direction of a guy sipping a red ICEE. "Save Amara!" The guy scowls in disgust.

I stick out my tongue at him after he passes.

After a few more minutes of pushing through the showroom,

the crowds finally break and the Nox King stands triumphantly above us.

Under him is a booth displaying collectibles in glass cases and figurines still in their plastic packaging. Lounging on a throne made of FunkoPops is a gothic goddess of death, her bat-print dress spilling like blood onto the puke-green hotel carpet. She's tapping her maroon claw on the box of a Hulk Pop, her glittery eyeshadow sparkling in the fluorescent lights.

Minerva cracks open an eye when she hears us approach. "Ah, so my prodigious progeny returns," she purrs, although there's only one prodigious child between us, and it's not me. "Did you save the world or did you get lost?"

"Both?" I glance at Milo.

"Both," he agrees.

"Both is good," we say together. I sit in a chair while Milo dumps his Spider-Man bookbag in the storage area at the back of the booth. "Hello, Mummie. I see you finally finished your throne." I point to the outlandish FunkoPop construction.

"A queen must be properly seated," she replies. "And don't call me that."

"Mother dearest?"

"The All-Mother, if you will—"

"More like the lazy mother," says my other mom, Kathy, who appears from behind the booth wall. "Milo, put your bookbag where I *won't* trip over it, please?" She fluffs up her short frizzy or-ange hair, her patch-covered jacket jangling with metal pins. She's so colorful, she could be the spokesperson for Lisa Frank, that old psychedelic line of kids' school supplies. "Minnie, here I am doing all this work and you're just sitting around letting your nails dry."

"They are very delicate claws," Minerva points out, pawing at Kathy like a cat. "And I was just resting."

"Yeah, and I'm just breathing. I need you to put Captain America on the top shelf."

Minerva tilts her head. "I could've sworn he belonged on the bottom."

It takes everything I have to keep my mouth in a straight line.

When Kathy shoots her a long-suffering look, Minerva heaves another woebegone sigh and drags herself off her throne. It's situated on a pedestal, a little higher than the table, and she has to gently ease herself down to avoid disturbing the Funkos.

As Minerva puts away the Captain America, Kathy turns to me and asks, "And where have you been? That was a mighty long bathroom break."

"I kinda . . . "

"You said you'd be right back. We had a rush and really could have used you."

I open my mouth to tell her the truth—that I'd accidentally wound up onstage impersonating Jessica Stone—but then remember the threat to never talk about it, ever, unless I wanted to be kicked out of every con known to humankind.

I don't know if that's even possible, but recalling her withering look shuts me up anyway.

"That was our agreement, that we would let you do your own booth thing with your friend for the rest of the convention—"

"It's not just a booth thing, it's saving a fan-favorite character from being fridged for the rest of her fictional life!"

"—if you would be here today and help us unpack at the beginning and tear down at the end of the con. Milo and Bran gracefully covered your shifts."

I sigh. "I know."

"So where were you?"

I open my mouth again, then close it—I suck at lying. Especially to my parents.

Which is weird because I lied so well as Jessica Stone.

"She came to the panel with me," Milo interjects as he emerges from the back of the booth, pulling on a snapback hat. "You said we should do more things together, right?"

This answer seems to pacify Kathy. "I did. But I meant like school functions, not comic-con panels."

"You should've specified," Milo replies. But before she can chide him for back-talking, he turns and throws up his arms. "Bran! Right on time. We just got back, too."

"Nice to see you, babe." Bran Simons, Milo's boyfriend, stands on the other side of the booth, laden with three bags of collectors' items. He gives Milo a smile as bright as the sun, lighting a spark in his dark eyes. He is short, like me, and a little waifish, all ear-cuffs and close-cropped hair and bronze skin. He offers Milo the bags, careful not to disturb the meticulously stacked Sailor Moon collectible keychains. Milo takes them and heads to the back of the booth. Bran and Milo met last year in high school, in astron-omy lab, but I think they spent more time studying each other's astrological compatibility than learning about solar physics.

He slides behind the booth as Kathy attends to a customer. "So how's your con going?"

"It's going. You?"

Bran sighs. "I'm trying to convince your brother to go to a viewing of *Demolition Man* at three a.m."

"Yikes. You know he likes sleep."

"I'm hoping he likes me a little more. I like your hair by the way—is it fresh?"

"It is." A brightly hued lock sticks out from my beanie, which I sheepishly pull off. My hair is normally a mousy brown, like Milo's, but pixied. I dyed it just before ExcelsiCon. I like how the pink looks with my gray eyes. I don't really resemble either of my moms, although Kathy carried both Milo and me. I look like the sperm donor, apparently. My brother has Kathy's button nose, which I'm envious about.

Milo emerges again from the back, fixing his snapback. "Whoa, whoa, who's contesting my love?"

"He is," I say, pointing to Bran. "*Demolition Man* with your boyfriend at three a.m. or sleep?"

Milo wilts and looks pleadingly at Bran. "Uh, do I have to choose?"

"You can sleep in the theater."

"Deal."

My brother squeezes out of the side of the booth, nodding to a customer looking at the Dick Grayson/Nightwing collectible figurine—you know, the one with the really, really sculpted buttocks. Everyone who passes by looks at it. *I* look at it.

For hours.

Milo and Bran bid us goodbye, and my moms don't even ask where he's going or when he'll be back. They never do. They *always* ask me, but then again Milo's never in the wrong place at the wrong time, or delivering someone's homework to a house party when the cops show up, or getting in a fender bender at one in the morning without a driver's license, or—

You get the idea.

My phone dings and I take it out. To my surprise, it's Harper.

HARPER (4:55 PM)

—Can't wait till tomorrow!

—Should I wear a name tag? Dress in a certain color? Hold up a sign that says

—FANGIRL TRASH UNITE?

IMOGEN *(4:57 PM)*

—*LOL I think you'll recognize me!!*

—*AND I AM SO EXCITED TO SEE YOU!!*

—*Oh, I am also wearing your beanie so I'll be really easy to spot~*

—*And thank you so much for handing out those pins today!*

HARPER *(4:57 PM)*

—*Well duh. I want to save Amara too!*

—*BUT OH! Speaking of Amara—did you hear what happened on the panel today?*

I cringe and lean back against the booth's table, which starts to wobble. A $300 Supergirl tilts precariously, but I save her in time and step away from the figurines. My moms are talking to customers, blissfully unaware.

IMOGEN *(4:59 PM)*

—*Oh, no. What happened . . . ?*

HARPER *(4:59 PM)*

—*Jessica Stone said she loves Amara—even though we all know she's faking it.*

—*She must've gotten told off by her agent or something.*

—*It was weird.*

IMOGEN *(4:59 PM)*

—*You were there?*

HARPER (5:00 PM)

—I got someone to cover my booth. Couldn't miss it.

—Hey, suddenly got a line of customers—can't wait to meet you!

Ha, yeah. Except you kinda already met me but just didn't know it. I frown and stare at Harper's texts. I mean, of course people would think Jessica Stone's faking it, after she spent almost a year not caring one iota about *Starfield* or the fandom. I don't know what she had to worry about with me.

It's not like I can magically change her image.

Minerva sidles up beside me and gestures regally to the throne. "You should try it."

I put my phone away. "Building a throne of toys?"

"Sitting on it. It'd be a waste for it to go unattended."

I roll my eyes. "Yeah, maybe if I was ten. I have to go hand out some more buttons and help you with the booth and—"

Minerva stops me with a delicate maroon-clawed hand. "Monster," she says lovingly, "breathe, slow down, take your time."

But how can I, when everyone else is lightyears ahead of me?

"But—"

"Sit."

I shoot her a look that I hope means I don't *want* to sit, but she is unrelenting. Giving in, I climb onto the throne of boxes. It's a lot higher than I thought. I can see a few rows down, past the banners and the shelving and the booths, almost all the way to the life-sized *Prospero* display.

It . . . isn't half bad up here. Quiet. Not *actually* quiet, but kinda what it'd sound like if I was sitting on the Iron Throne, or looking out over Pride Rock to a kingdom where no kingdom should exist, here for four days and then gone.

This is my kingdom. This is where I grew up, where I cut my teeth on fan battles and shipper wars, and the sight fills me with . . . what?

Glorious, insatiable *possibility*.

Because I am a nobody, but I'm a nobody who wants to leave the world a little brighter than when she arrived.

Minerva was right, and she's looking up at me knowing she was right. "So? How's the view, Princess?"

Gloriously full of possibilities. I'll meet Harper IRL tomorrow and avoid Jasper (aka He-Who-Will-Not-Be-Named) for the rest of forever, get some kick-ass fan art and save Amara. I just know I will.

I hope I will.

I *have* to.

I sit up straight and languidly cross one leg over the other, then I quote Princess Amara in her familiar Noxian lilt: "The horizon's wide and I have a kingdom to rule."

Minerva cracks a smile.

JESS

THE STREETS BELOW ME THRUM WITH a strange Thursday night madness. It feels like the hours before a big concert, tension in the air so alive it's almost electrifying. Except a concert lasts a few hours and I'm stuck at this con for four days.

Four whole days.

I don't understand the allure of any of it. The crowds, the lines, the waiting. And I definitely don't understand dressing up like it's Halloween—*cosplaying*, as Dare often corrects me. Ethan's in the bathroom changing out of his mock-cosplay; he's shirtless, and sure he's pretty cut, but my eyes don't really linger. He'd be a catch if someone burns all of his nerd T-shirts and puts him in some jeans that actually show he has a butt.

As I sink onto the sofa my phone rings, startling me out of my thoughts. I quickly fish it out of my cross-body bag and check the caller ID.

It's my agent. My heart leaps into my throat. Diana doesn't call to ask about the weather, she calls when something has gone either terribly wrong or terribly right. She couldn't have heard about the panel, could she? No one even realized it wasn't me, did they?

Jess, breathe.

I answer the phone apprehensively. "Hello?"

A honeyed voice drifts through the speaker like a soothing balm, calm and collected like always. "Hi Jess, how's your convention going?"

"Ah . . . good?"

"Good. I heard about the interview."

Oh. In the stress of what happened at the panel, I'd forgotten about the interview. And Natalia Ford. "I—I'm sorry. It's just that I—"

"Don't worry, it's fine. Natalia's agent and I go way back. She explained to Natalia that you've had a difficult few weeks. Natalia is fine with it, but we have to make sure that when the interview releases, we have a statement prepared."

I close my eyes and sigh. "I'm so sorry, Diana."

"I know you've been stressed, and this is what I'm here for."

I nod even though she can't see me and anxiously worm a fingernail into my thumb cuticle. "I hate to ask but—have you heard anything about the indie film that I auditioned for?"

She gives a long sigh. "I was hoping to tell you after the convention, but I'm sorry. The shooting schedules for the *Starfield* sequel and *The Red Grove* compete too closely for the clause in your *Starfield* contract. You won't be able to do both."

Hearing that feels like a punch in the gut. "But I'm not *in* the sequel! As far as I've heard, the script's not finalized yet—and even if it is, I can't be in a lot of it, right? I'll be in a—a flashback or a—a—*something*. I can do both. It'll be easy—"

"Jessica."

My rebuttal freezes on my tongue. I sink into a cold, dread-filled silence. After a moment I ask, my voice tiny, "That's not the only reason, is it?"

Diana is quiet.

"It's because of *Starfield*, isn't it? Because it's doing so well—"

She tries to interrupt, "You have duties to the sequel."

"It *is* because of *Starfield*, then. Because it's doing too well, or because I'm no longer an indie darling, or because—"

"The director thought you were no longer a good fit for the role," Diana finally admits, and it feels like an arrow through my chest, puncturing my heart, and sliding out the other side, so painful I can barely breathe.

I feel my bottom lip tremble. *The Red Grove* was supposed to be my break back into real films, a lifeline to saving my artistic integrity. I've read the script. It's *decent*. What's more is that I know it'd be a lot better fit for me than playing some dead flashback princess in a subpar sequel.

"I know this feels like a huge setback, but I promise you'll have other roles. Everyone *adores* you in *Starfield*. Conan O'Brien loved you when you went on his show! Jimmy Fallon! We're even in talks to host *Saturday Night Live*. Amon thinks you were a great Princess Amara, Jessica."

Well, tell that to the comments piling up on my Instagram and my Twitter feed, I think bitterly.

I only signed that contract because I was told it would be a one-off. A nice popcorn flick to populate my repertoire, to show off my action as well as my acting chops. Diana wasn't wrong, but neither of us thought they would hold the sequel script this long without telling me my fate.

We never expected *Starfield* to be much of anything. And now it's my entire world. One that I can't seem to escape from, no matter how hard I try.

I'm about to spill everything—about the social media comments, the threats—when there's a beep on her phone. She says quickly, "Listen, I have to go, but please don't let any of this worry you. Try to have some fun! It's ExcelsiCon! Talk to you soon!"

The line goes dead with a *click* and I'm left listening to silence.

You didn't get the part, the self-deprecating voice inside me whispers as I drop the phone onto the bed. *You didn't get it because you're Amara, and you'll be Amara for the rest of your life.*

Ethan's been leaning against the doorway to the bathroom, adjusting and readjusting his smartwatch. He's washed his face and put on a plain white T-shirt, tucked into his slacks. He doesn't need to say anything for me to know that he heard—and understood—the whole thing.

Tears brim in my eyes, but I bite the side of my cheek to hold myself together. Ethan is my best friend, but Jessica Stone only cries when it's scripted. Yet the longer I sit there and the longer he messes with his stupid watch, the harder it is for me to stop my lips from quivering.

"I think we need coffee," he says, even though it's almost 6:30 p.m. He grabs his wallet from the coffee table in the living room—yes, our hotel suite has a living room—and heads out. "I'll be back in a minute. Chai?"

I nod.

It's only when he closes the door that I take out my phone, log onto my socials, and read the comments. All the bad ones, because those seem to be the only ones that get through. They stick to me like glue, clinging to my skin—

what a joke

she's the worst amara!! So glad she died

I can tell her where she can put those pretty lips

fixed her chest small titties lol [censored photo]

hope she chokes and dies on all the money she got

sell out

#notourprincess

That [censored] needs a cheeseburger

Jess's so fat must be the stress getting to her

Go ruin some other franchise, faker!

They are endless. And I am so tired of them already. I begin my daily routine of reporting and blocking, reporting and blocking, but my thumb stalls on the screen. What's the use? They'll just come back tomorrow, and bring their friends, and I will still be one girl standing in the mouth of the Black Nebula as it opens wide and they wait for me to self-destruct.

I won't give them that pleasure.

But I don't know what else to do. The contract might be in the bottom of the trash, but I'll still have to sign it. I'll still be *here*.

I drop my phone and grab a pillow, pressing it against my face, and cry.

IMOGEN

"Jessica!"

I look up at the barista, who slides a cup across the counter. My heart skips a beat until I notice Brienne of Tarth pushing through the line to get her drink. I exhale and turn my attention back to my phone, where I'm sending another furious tweet to a Twitter troll who can't seem to get his head out of his nostalgia hole. Jessica Stone *didn't* ruin Princess Amara's character, I want to type, but I know that if I reply to every one of these garbage cans, I'll find myself in troll hell.

The barista approaches the counter with four drinks in a tray and squints at the name. "IHM-OH-GEN-NE?"

"Well that's one way to say it," I murmur as I elbow my way to get my order. Two hazelnut lattes, an iced caramel macchiato, and whatever the hell Milo ordered. My phone must have dinged twenty times—can't he just be *patient?*

I shift the bag of vegan tacos to the hand that's holding my phone and grab the tray with the other.

One-handed texting, here we go.

Oh my God, he's not patient at all.

MILO (6:57 PM)

—*Got the grub?*

—*Hey, hey you.*

MILO (7:00 PM)

—*HAVE YOU BEEN EATEN BY A WOOKIEE?*

MILO (7:01 PM)

—*DO I HAVE TO GO SOLO NOW?*

MILO (7:01 PM)

—*COME BACK TO THE HOTEL TO LEIA YOUR HEAD DOWN.*

—*PS - I got some MEGA SUPER ULTRA WTF STAR-FIELD news to SHOW YOU*

MILO (7:07 PM)

—*No like really where are you do I have to release the hounds.*

Release the hounds is code for texting our mothers. Ugh, he's more dramatic than I am. Tray in one hand, vegan taco bag looped around the other, I reply—

IMOGEN (7:08 PM)

—*OMG CHILL OUT leaving now*

—*Also Wookiees don't eat humans, they'd be too chewie.*

MILO (7:08 PM)

—*this is bran pls bring food faster*

—*milo is about to go full super saiyan he's so hangry*

IMOGEN (7:08 PM)

—*OH MY GOD I'LL BE THERE SOON*

—*SHEESH*

I better get these tacos to the hotel before Milo starts eating his own arm off. If there's one thing about teenage boys that's absolutely true, it's that they are a freaking black hole of food. Like, I've never seen someone eat so much in my entire life.

"Monster?"

I freeze. I know that voice. That deep, captivating timbre. A lump lodges in my throat.

This can't be real life.

But when I turn, I realize that this is most definitely real life. He-Who-Will-Not-Be-Named is standing right behind me, a curious look on his adorable face. His brown hair is long and swirled back into a man bun and there's a little stubble on his cheeks, but it's patchy and doesn't quite pull off the hipster vibe I know he's going for. But otherwise he looks exactly the same—sporting a gamer T-shirt that barely covers his biceps, and jeans, and Vans, and God why does my heart unexpectedly feel so heavy and awful?

"It *is* you!" he says, and his curious expression quickly morphs into a smile that looks sincere.

The barista calls another name and a Ghostbuster squeezes past. We take the cue and step to the side. He pulls me into a hug and I prickle at his touch. I don't return the embrace, but he doesn't seem to notice.

"Oh man, Imogen, it's so great to see you!"

LIAR.

He lets go and looks me up and down. From my black jeans to my probably not-so-clean black hoodie to my black SPACE QUEEN beanie pulled over a pink pixie that *definitely* needs a wash.

For one inconceivable moment, I wonder if he approves—

APPROVES?

What am I, some heroine in a nineteenth-century romance novel?

Ugh, I hate my feelings sometimes. I hate the inexplicable way my brain works. And I hate the way he chews on his bottom lip, and the sea-glass-green color of his eyes, and the way his voice is always so soft and rich and tender, even when it's really not. I hate—

All of it.

Not in a secretly-love-him sort of way, but in a we-dated-for-nine-months-and-he-stood-me-up-at-the-ExcelsiCon-Ball-and-then-dumped-me-in-a-text-message sort of way.

I yank down my beanie, avoiding his gaze. "Hey. What do you want?"

He looks hurt. "I'm just happy to see you—I thought I'd see you this year. Your, uh, fandom thing is really something. Excited about the news that just leaked?"

I try to ask "What news?" but he just talks over me.

"You always go in with a bang, don't you, Monster?"

Every time he calls me that I feel like my skin is on fire, and I don't know whether it's because I still like him or because I detest him so viciously I want to raze his crops and salt his fields.

I look down at my #SaveAmara pins. "Yeah, I'm trying to keep Amara from becoming a fridged love interest."

"Fridged?" He grins. "But she went into the Black Nebula on her own. No one told her to go. Or forced her."

"But the writers had her die to further Carmindor's character arc and—"

"So every time a character dies it's automatically fridging?"

"No, but there were plenty of other ways for the series to end. And with her plot arc and development it didn't make sense for her to . . . "

He's laughing. Really and truly laughing.

At me.

I swallow my words and sink into silence.

"I love your passion," he says, and steps closer to me, the laughter still fresh on his lips like blood on a newly fed vampire. "I miss it."

He *misses* it.

I stare at him, trying—hoping, really—that he's just a figment of my sleep-deprived imagination. But the longer I stand here, the longer I realize that he is no figment. He's real, and he's doused in a very heady sandalwood cologne.

I clear my throat and look away. "Okay, so, you've been doing well. I mean, how many subscribers do you have now on your YouTube channel?"

His grin only widens. "Enough."

My phone vibrates in my hand. I know it's Milo. Has Bran Kamehameha'd the entire hotel in his hanger? I use the interruption as an excuse to exit this rotten situation. "Sorry, my brother's waiting for me," I say, holding up both the tray and the bag of tacos from the Magic Pumpkin food truck. "It was, um, nice seeing y—"

He takes me quickly by the arm, jostling the coffees, and says softly, "Wait, for a minute? We need to talk. *I* need to talk."

"*Now?*"

"No, I got an interview with another YouTube channel in a few minutes. How about tomorrow?"

"I have to be at a booth all day."

He frowns again. "All day?"

I nod. "Until the end of the con."

He frowns again, and I don't think he gets it. "Then what about after the con? Sunday, five o'clock? At the top of the escalators in the main hotel."

"The con closes at five," I say helplessly, as if that'll get me out of this.

He grins. "Perfect ending to a perfect con then, don't you think?"

Before I can say no, a guy in a backward *Five Nights at Freddy's* cap calls his name. Jasper leaves with a wave, the scent of his cologne lingering on me like an extra layer of skin. How dare he! Thinking he can just walk in all suave-like and act as though nothing happened? Like he didn't break my heart in the most cliché way?

And yet I know that on Sunday at five o'clock I'll be at the top of the escalators. I know I will.

Because I'm that kind of predictable, and even though he broke my heart, he was the only one who saw me. With him, I wasn't nothing. I was something.

I guess I just wasn't enough.

Grateful that Jasper's gone, I quickly turn to leave.

What I don't realize is that there's someone standing directly behind me—that is, not until I collide with the solid mass of another human. The two iced coffees on the front of my tray explode onto a tidy white T-shirt.

"*Starflame!*" I curse. "I am *so* sorry! Here, let me get some—"

"Jess?"

I look up and am assaulted by liquid brown eyes and amazingly long eyelashes. The human is tall and angular, like a lot of the

J-Pop singers Bran likes, with thick dark hair and black-rimmed glasses and . . . oh.

Oh *no*.

He is very *very* hot. Hot like I-want-to-be-stuck-in-an-elevator-with-you hot, not we-are-now-mortal-enemies-because-I-just-spilled-my-coffee-on-you-while-not-paying-attention hot.

He's holding a phone in one hand and a wallet in the other, and the front of his once-pristine tee and neat black pants is absolutely *drenched*.

Worse yet, I recognize him at the exact same moment that he recognizes me.

"*Really?*" is all I can say to Jessica Stone's assistant.

A subtle, almost vulnerable look crosses his face before his expression closes like a vault slamming shut. He scowls. "Do you even *look* where you're going?"

"You snuck up on me!"

"Snuck up? I was standing here the whole time!"

"Yeah, on your phone."

"The fact that I can stand and text and you can't see me isn't quite my fault," he snaps, picking his wet shirt off his stomach.

I grab a handful of napkins to mop up the floor. People are beginning to turn and stare. A barista armed with a mop and bucket is heading in our direction.

He crinkles his nose. "Ugh, *hazelnut* . . . "

I pause. "What's wrong with hazelnut?"

"Besides that it's all over me?"

"Trust me, it adds character." I stand up, tossing the sopping napkins in the trash.

We glower at each other. What an infuriating—awful—irritating—*ARGH!* The fury coming off us both is as thick as the Georgia humidity. You could try to cut it with a knife but it'd only cobble itself back together, like some *Scooby-Doo* slime monster.

And here I thought he was *hot*?

He opens his mouth to say something but then his phone rings. It's a generic tone—of *course* it is. White T-shirt, black glasses, skinny slacks, default ringtone.

Ugh, Muggles.

He's probably just as horrible as his boss. Like goes with like, as they say.

The barista pulls out the mop, which I take as my cue to escape. I grab my half-intact tray from the counter and beat a hasty retreat.

I don't stop until I'm back at my hotel, where I discover that, as fate would have it, I've lost my keycard.

MILO OPENS THE DOOR TO OUR room and leans against the doorframe. "Lost your key, eh, sister dearest?"

I scowl and push inside and he closes the door behind me. I dump the vegan tacos on the desk, put the remaining coffees beside it, and sink down onto one of the queen beds. Bran and Milo have the other one, but I doubt they'll be sleeping here. They're already packing for a night out watching *Demolition Man*. There are entire convention rooms where they play sci-fi and fantasy movies all night long.

Bran, sitting on the edge of the other bed as he scrolls through Twitter, looks up. And blinks. "Mo, what the hell happened to your shirt?"

It's only then that I realize I've got hazelnut latte trailing down my favorite hoodie. My scowl deepens into the bowels of hell. "I ran into this good-looking guy who turned out to be the spawn of Satan."

"The Hellmouth has opened." Milo nods solemnly and shoves a taco into his face. It's there one minute and then gone the next. Like Pac-Man chomping up those little white dots. I don't even think he tasted it.

"So," I go on, tearing my eyes away from Milo as he rips into yet another taco, "I accidentally spilled our drinks all over him, and the dude just went *off* on me. He was so nasty. I honestly felt like, if the last few years hadn't made me It's Fine fireproof, then I'd be a roasted main course of Imogen Lovelace."

Bran sighs and lounges back on the bed. "That's a pity. Sounds like it would've been a pretty memorable meet-cute. I've read it on AO3 at *least* a dozen times."

"Right?" I echo his wistful sigh. "But alas, true love has eluded me yet again."

"Oh merciful heavens," Milo moans from the chair, the wrapper carcasses of five tofu tacos littering the floor around him like tombstones in a graveyard. He leans back, one hand on his stomach. "I have been revived by tofu and fake cheese."

"I didn't take *that* long," I say, folding my arms over my chest, and my coffee stain, crossly. "Although I don't know why you wanted *vegan* tacos."

Bran rolls his eyes. "Because it's from the Pumpkin and your brother is extra."

"Hey, you're dating him. What's the Pumpkin?" I ask, handing him a coffee that he didn't order but I know he wanted. Americano with extra water.

"You are a goddess," Bran replies. "You know, the Magic Pumpkin?"

My stare must be brilliantly blank because my brother adds, "The food truck Geekerella worked at?"

I give him a surprised look. "*That* was that food truck?"

They nod in unison.

I remember a young woman with blond hair and purple glasses working the register while a green-haired woman prepped tacos in the truck's tight kitchen. No Geekerella in sight. "Huh."

Milo takes out two tacos for me and shoves the rest into his Spider-Man backpack. "All right. We got blankets. We got water. We got food. Got my eye mask," he adds, pulling a Carmindor-themed eye mask out of his back pocket and putting it on. The eye pads sit on his forehead, making him look as though he has a pair of Darien's dreamy peepers above his real ones. "Anything else we need?"

"What was the news you guys were talking about?" I ask.

Milo and Bran shoot each other the same unreadable look. "Didn't you see Bran's text?"

"No, I was carrying tacos and coffee, remember? What news?"

Quickly, Bran takes out his phone and shows me a tweet with a photo. A grin spreads across his lips and he says, "Monster, someone's leaking the *Starfield* script—and rumor is, it's *real*."

JESS

With an exasperated sigh, I fall back onto the bed, holding my phone and scrolling through the @s and RTs. The script has to be fake, but the internet is going *insane*. Again. And with more comments come more trolls and more fanboys bemoaning my existence. The first time the sequel script "leaked," earlier this year, it turned out to be a reject from the first movie. I got sent hateful comments for surviving at the end of the film. The three times after that they've just been fakes.

Honestly, though? I'd kill for one of them to be real just so Diana can finally confirm whether or not I'm in the damn thing.

@Fantasticwho
SOMEONE IS LEAKING THE SECOND STARFIELD SCRIPT
@sayjess @notthatdarien @calvinrolfe4real @dudebroamon

@Scifibytespodcast
A scene of the sequel script leaked!!! I AM SHOOK.

@starfieldscript337
EXCLUSIVE: photo of a page from the long-awaited sequel!

CARMINDOR fills the doorway, refusing to let the
NOXIAN GENERAL pass in the hallway. The tired
GENERAL gives him a dangerous look.

>   NOXIAN GENERAL
>   Your Highness, your treaty
>   with us is already thin.

>   CARMINDOR
>   The Black Nebula -- what's
>   happening to it?

The NOXIAN GENERAL draws herself up to full
height. She is unafraid of her answer.

>   NOXIAN GENERAL
>   It   has   opened   again,
>   u n s u r p r i s i n g l y .
>   Looks like your *princess*
>   didn't sacrifice enough.
>   Now get out of my way.

CARMINDOR's mood darkens. He stands rigid in the
doorway, like a sentinel. Just out of the NOXIAN
GENERAL's line of sight come two Federation
officers. They have their hands on their
pistols, ready to draw.

The NOXIAL GENERAL notices them and she whirls
back to CARMINDOR angrily.

>   NOXIAN GENERAL
>   You know this is war.

>   CARMINDOR
>   (to the Federation
>   Officers)
>   Arrest her.

```
For a moment, it seems like CARMINDOR won't
let her pass, but then he steps aside and the
General leaves.
```

Ugh, people.

From across the hall, the booms and murmured shouts of a TV show hum underneath the door. Dare and Calvin have been marathoning old *Star Trek* movies in preparation for the fourth or fifth one—I can't remember—coming out next week. They're up to the one with the whales. I recognize Leonard Nimoy's voice. My mom loves Spock—I think she had a crush on him, honestly.

Things were simpler back then, when Mom would catch the last thirty minutes of her favorite *Star Trek* movie before she bussed me off to auditions. Ethan would sometimes tag along, playing his Gameboy in the backseat while Mom and I played traveling games in the front. That was before I appeared in a commercial, which got me in front of a casting director for *Huntress Rising*, which nabbed me an Oscar nomination. Sometimes I wish Ethan and I could go back to Mom's VW bus, with the windows rolled down to catch the summer breeze, Led Zeppelin blaring from the speakers, the road wide and open and the stars spread out across the endless horizon.

I could be anyone I wanted.

My story was *mine*.

The door to my hotel room creaks open and Ethan appears with a dirty chai latte and chocolate Frappuccino. I quickly sit up, checking to make sure my mascara isn't runny from crying—until I notice a stain in the shape of Texas on Ethan's once-immaculate shirt.

"What the heck happened to you?"

He scowls. "It was that girl again—the one who impersonated

you. She's a total monster, but I survived." He marches over and gallantly hands me my chai latte and sits down beside me. He takes a long gulp of his Frappuccino.

I sip my chai, and it tastes like bliss. He smells like hazelnut creamer, but I don't say anything since he looks as annoyed as the time his older brothers put blue dye in his shampoo (they didn't know he used it for body wash, too).

"Thanks, Ethan," I say quietly, and lay my head on his shoulder.

"Don't mention it—"

"Not for the coffee, for everything. I don't know what I'd do without you."

"Call me every day and complain about your other PAs?" His spot-on guess makes me laugh. "You can complain to me any day of the week whether I'm your assistant or not, you know that, right? I'm always all ears."

"I've tried not to do it *too* often."

"But it's okay if you do. Everyone needs to vent sometimes, you know?"

I do know, but there are some things I can't even tell Ethan— especially not now. He reports to my agent, so it's his job to tell her whether I'm all right or if something is wrong in my life and how to make it better. But those are questions I don't know how to answer. He's my best friend and my secret-keeper, but it isn't his job to be burdened with all the self-doubts in my head.

He shifts slightly, a little uncomfortably, and says, almost in a whisper, "Hey, Jess? Are you . . . are you happy?"

At first, I don't understand the question. I blink once, twice, and the words sink in.

Are you happy?

Of all the interviews and online questions and magazine articles, this is one question I've never been asked. Perhaps because, in everyone's mind, it's never been a question. It's always been a statement:

Jessica Stone is happy.

She has to be.

I open my mouth to tell him the truth when—

My phone dings. Ethan looks at me expectantly but I wave him off. "Twitter notifications. Someone's leaking a fake script again."

"Again? Wasn't there one last week?" he asks. Thankfully he doesn't push the "are you happy" question.

"Yeah, they're being ridiculous—"

Suddenly, the *Jaws* theme shouts from Ethan's front pocket. We both glance down to it. The *duuuuuun-dun, duuuuun-dun* is so loud it would be almost comical if we didn't know who he assigned the ringtone to.

My agent.

But . . . I just talked to her. Why would she be calling Ethan so soon?

We exchange the same questioning look before Ethan pulls his phone out and answers. "Diana, good evening."

I sit quietly, straining to make out whatever Diana is saying. Ethan tries to keep his face impassive, and to most people it would look like he succeeds, but I know him better than I know anyone. I know that the left side of his lip twitches when he hears something he doesn't want to know; his breathing becomes even, deep, almost like a trance.

This is not a good conversation.

"Yes, she's here," he says, and hands the phone to me.

I have to talk to her; I don't have a choice. Is it about the script? Is she calling to say that I *am* in the sequel as some point-less five-second flashback? Or am I free?

Please let Amara stay dead, I think as I bring his phone to my ear. "Diana?"

"Do you still have the script?" she asks tightly.

What script? "Yes." I lie.

"Oh, thank God." She lets out a breath. "Because it's leaked, and as long as we know it isn't you, that's all we care about."

Dread slithers down my spine. *The tweets. Are they real?*

My heart is beating loud and ferocious. *Please let Amara be dead. Please let Amara be dead. Please let—* "So we know for sure? Am I in it? Am I free—"

"Jessica," Diana interrupts calmly, "the execs are thinking you leaked the script, but as long as you didn't then we're fine."

"Why would it be me?"

"Exactly. You're the most recent person to be given a physical copy, no one else in the cast has been given one yet. But if it wasn't lost in transit or anything, it must have been leaked from the studio—one of the interns, maybe, who got a hold of it when they shouldn't have. Anyway, I'll go ahead and tell the studio that it didn't come from our end. Just hang tight and sandbag *every* question about the sequel, do you understand?"

Oh no. I swallow the lump in my throat and nod numbly. "I understand."

"Good. Talk to you later with more details." She hangs up to call whoever and tell them that I am, in fact, *not* the villain in this story.

I exhale hard and hand Ethan his phone.

He quirks an eyebrow. "You don't actually have the script, do you?"

"Of course I don't. Why would I—oh." My eyes widen, and he must realize it at the exact same time. "Oh *no*."

"Jess . . . "

Oh no—oh no no no no no—

"The package. The one from Amon. The one I was supposed to open." My voice breaks and I can feel myself shaking.

Oh my *God*. I actually threw away a copy of the script for the *Starfield* sequel. And someone must've taken it out of the trash. And started tweeting it. This *is* my fault.

"Jessica!" Ethan looks more freaked out than I am. "*You threw it away?*"

"In the garbage, where it's supposed to be!"

"You don't mean that," he says.

"Of course I don't! I'm angry!" I bolt off the bed and dart out of the hotel room, Ethan instantly behind me.

Two minutes later, the elevator doors open into the lobby. I all but sprint to the trash can where I tossed the envelope, peering down into the dark crevice now filled with Starbucks cups and used napkins and candy wrappers. I have to dig through *that*? I reach in but Ethan grabs my wrist and motions for a clerk, who looks more than a little grossed out about someone trash picking in a five-star hotel.

Which is definitely not something Jessica Stone would do. But right now, I am definitely not Jessica Stone. I am a ball of anxious wet cats.

Ethan points to the trash and says to the hotelier, "I think my friend dropped her phone in here. Can we take this outside and dump it out?"

"Oh! Of course." She looks relieved. "You can go into the back hallway, Miss Stone," she adds.

I grimace.

Half the people in the lobby—the half who recognize my name—turn to look. Begin pulling out their phones. Clicking on their cameras at my arm elbow-deep in trash. I grab the lid with one hand and push Ethan toward the emergency exit with the other and we escape into an EMPLOYEES ONLY hallway that connects to a few offices and the laundry service.

"I hate this," I mutter as Ethan takes off the ornate golden lid and drags out the clear plastic bag. "It's at the bottom, isn't it? Isn't that it?"

He twists the bag and holds it up with one arm. "I think that's a fast-food container."

It is.

"Maybe it's more toward the middle?" he reasons, but I shake my head.

"No, I remember the *clunk* as it hit the bottom." I step back and press my palms against my eyelids. "Someone found it. Someone saw me chuck the envelope and then went after it."

I feel myself spiraling just as inevitably as a spiral galaxy.

Breathe. Think. Breathe.

I press myself against the wall and slide down until I'm sitting because I can no longer stand upright. I can't feel my knees.

"I am in so much trouble," I whisper.

Ethan puts the bag back in the garbage can and digs into his pocket, bringing out a small bottle of hand sanitizer. He squats next to me, squirts some into my palm, lathers his own, and stuffs it back into his pocket.

I take out my phone to look at the Twitter handle that leaked the scene. A faceless gray icon. Whoever it is posted a photo of the script. In it, the page is surrounded by retro green carpet. I know I've seen it before, but the longer I wrack my brain the less familiar it looks.

Ethan glances down at my phone and makes a face. "Looks like the hideous showroom floor. Well, I guess there's no accounting for taste."

"What did you say?"

"I said, I guess there's no accounting—"

"About the background in the photo. This is the con carpet?" I point to the art-deco pattern behind the script. "*This* carpet?"

Realization hits him. "*That* carpet."

All the color drains from his face—and probably mine, too. That confirms my worst fear. I tossed the script Amon gave me, I leaked it, and the worst of it is: this anonymous trash panda knows the future of my career before *I* do.

Never mind whether *Amara* is dead—

"I am so dead," I say. My voice is barely a whisper but steadily gets louder the more I panic.

"Someone must have known what you threw away," Ethan says. He presses the back of his head against the wall, looking up at the popcorn ceiling, but his brown eyes have a distant look. He's thinking. "And that same person must have known you had it to begin with—maybe the hotel clerk?"

The peppy girl who had looked utterly disgusted by my impromptu Dumpster dive comes to mind. I shake my head. "I think she's the same one from earlier," I tell him, "so she couldn't have taken that photo."

"Crap," he grouses.

Stay calm, I want to yell at myself. *Jessica Stone doesn't panic. She's cool and controlled and—and—*

Everything I am not at this moment. I clench my fists and force myself to suck in a lungful of air and breathe it out slowly.

Get my mind back on track. Think of what to do. First things first.

"I have to find that script," I say aloud, trying to keep my voice level. "Whoever took it is still here somewhere. I just have to remember who was in that lobby and . . . find them? Scour the con floor? When they post the next leak, try to figure out where they are and get there in time?"

"You're seriously going to do that?"

"I have to. The execs already think I leaked the script, and if they find out I threw it away? I'll be blacklisted for life. No one'll work with me after this."

Ethan pushes his glasses back up onto the bridge of his nose. "Jess, you can't be in two places at once. You can't be snooping out the culprit *and* be on panels and at signings and photo ops and . . . ."

His voice trails off as he looks down at his coffee-stained T-shirt, and then back up at me, and the idea strikes us at the exact same time. It already worked once, hadn't it? And no one noticed. No one even batted an eye.

"What if," I say, "I *could* be in two places at once?"

He groans. "Jess, no."

"Oh, Jess, *yes*."

IMOGEN

Someone pounds on my hotel room door.

I barely glance up from my phone. I'm in the Marriott—the con's official hotel—so it's probably some drunk Spider-Man or Goku or *Overwatch* cosplayer mistaking my room for someone else's. During the day, ExcelsiCon is pretty amazing, but at night, when the showroom floor closes, it gets wild. Already I've heard a conga-line dance party, led by Beetlejuice, sashay down the hallway to the Banana Boat Song *and* the last echoes of a flash-dance down in the lobby of the hotel almost a dozen floors below me.

So I decide to ignore the poor lost soul at my door and I roll over onto my stomach, scrolling through Twitter. So many people I follow were at the panel today, tweeting about Jessica Stone (*me*), saying that they supported her (ME!), and how they wished she would've spoken out sooner (definitely her). I try not to think about what could happen to my #SaveAmara campaign if Jessica Stone backed it. I got a taste up there on the panel, and I can't get the sweetness out of my mouth. *Starflame,* it was intoxicating.

People actually listened to me—to her. To us.

Imagine what I could do with a little more time.

I pause on a tweet by Darien Freeman, posting a pic of him kissing his girlfriend's cheek, him in his geeky *Starfield* T-shirt and her in what I assume is her costume for this year's cosplay contest—Princess Amara with a Cinderella twist. His caption reads *Ah'blena*.

It's a term of endearment in the *Starfield* universe. The closest translation is *my heart* or *my other half*, and for a moment I sort of wish I had someone to call me *ah'blena*.

"You don't have time for romance," I mutter to myself, and scroll on to the next tweet. Besides, I have a princess to save. I don't need some hunk-a hunk-a burnin' love clouding my head—

Someone knocks on my hotel room door again.

This time I glance up, and wait. Because instinctively that's what everyone does when they hear strange sounds at night, right? Like a dumbass, they wait for it to happen again instead of calling the police. Or the front desk.

This is why I'd die in a horror movie.

It's not Milo—I just got a text from him saying he and Bran are at a showing of *Galaxy Quest*.

Another three loud raps on the door. I crawl to the edge of the bed.

"Hello!" a voice calls from the other side. Female. Light, hon-eyed yet harsh, with the slightest Southern drawl. I know that voice. I *imitated* that voice.

Dread coils in my stomach like a snake.

Oh *no*.

"*Hello!*" she calls again and bangs on the door. I stumble out of bed, my legs still wrapped in the sheets. "I know you're in there! I have your keycard!"

Holy crap, how loud can she be?

Before she has a chance to wake up the entire hallway (including my parents, and I do *not* want to explain to them what a starlet is doing knocking at my door at ten p.m.), I unlatch the lock and peek through the peephole, but someone has their finger blocking it. Because *that* isn't murdery at all.

I'm going to die.

Maybe I can wait a few more seconds, maybe she'll leave and—

She knocks once more and I quickly crack open the door just a hair.

There in the hallway is Jessica Stone, her winged eyeliner alarmingly crisp, her lipstick bold and blood red. She's wearing the same black suede jacket and jeans from earlier but no beanie. Her hair is pulled up into a bun atop her head.

"I swear I didn't tell anyone!" I loud-whisper.

She gives me a once-over before handing me the keycard. "You dropped this in the bathroom earlier," she says, and pushes her way into my room.

"Okay, thanks?" I say uncertainly.

"I came here to set some ground rules."

"Ground rules?" I blink, making sure I'm seeing what I'm seeing. I *am* seeing this, right? THE Jessica Stone actually in my hotel room.

I blink. Yep, still here. I'm blinking and she's still here.

"Ground rules for what? I swear I didn't tell anyone!"

"I almost believe you."

"I didn't! Not a soul! Not even my brother, and trust me, he's *very* charismatic—"

"*You*," rumbles a deep voice from the hallway.

Oh, noooooooo.

I know that voice, too.

I turn to face the guy who is now taking up the entire doorway. Impossibly tall and gangly, thick black-frame glasses, with a swoop of raven-black hair gelled back. Jessica Stone's assistant.

And he looks about ready to kill me.

I groan. "Not you again."

"Trust me, the feeling's mutual."

Jessica shrugs out of her jacket and tosses it on the bed, flopping down beside it. "Oh right. You ran into each other, so we can skip the introductions."

I jab a finger at him. "He is possibly the worst nerfherder in the—" I say, while at the same time he says, "She's that monster of a girl I was telling you—"

We both stop midsentence.

"I'm what?" I ask.

"Did you just call me a nerfherder?"

I draw myself up to my full height. "It was either that or Muggle, and you don't deserve Muggle."

His eye twitches. It actually *twitches*.

From the bed Jessica calls, "Be nice to my assistant. Ethan, she looks like me, right? I mean her hair's a little *loud*, but we can work with that."

The anger inside me dissolves with a fizzle, replaced by a foreboding curiosity. "Hair? And work with what? I don't understand."

"This is a terrible idea, Jessica," Ethan sighs, massaging the bridge of his nose.

"It's the only one we have," she replies, "terrible or not."

"*What* is a terrible idea?" I ask them, glancing from Jessica Stone lounged on my bed to her assistant and then back again.

Instead, her assistant—Ethan—waves his hand toward my hotel room. He sounds tired—kinda like the Twelfth Doctor. Aged and haggard, having seen way too much to be optimistic about anything. "Aren't you going to let me in? And maybe put on some clothes?"

What? I look down.

Ohsweetbabyjesus, I'm wearing my ratty Sailor Moon T-shirt and ladybug pajama shorts and Starfield socks that come up to my knees. I look like . . . ugh. I am not dressed for company. Boy company. Any company at all, frankly.

I quickly cross my arms over my chest. Why'd I sling my bra onto the lampshade in the corner? Why did I think that was funny, like, two seconds ago?

"I—um—it's not, I'm not—"

"Just let him in," Jessica calls to me.

I open the door all the way. "Come on in. Don't mind the mess or . . . "

He takes two steps inside before we both realize there's a pair of my pink and white Superman underwear on the floor. Whether it's clean or dirty, neither of us knows.

Why.

Am.

I.

Like.

This.

I grab the underpants and shove them into my suitcase, which is half-exploded over the left side of the room. "Don't, uh, mind the mess. Don't even notice. Just be blissfully ignorant of it all."

And please don't look at the lampshade.

"I think I can manage," he replies cattily.

I find my cheeks heating up and avert my eyes to look at Jessica, who is now lackadaisically browsing through the pay-per-view channels on the hotel television. I hope she knows I have to pay for them. I begin to bite my thumb but she snaps her fingers at me.

"Nuh! No. That's the first rule. No thumb biting. It's gross and I never do it."

I quickly take my thumb out of my mouth, though I don't know why I'm listening to her. "It's a nervous habit."

"Pick another one. Second rule, *always* wear eyeliner. I'll show you how to wing it. It's one of my trademarks. Can't be Jessica Stone without the trademarks."

"But I don't wear makeup."

She rolls her eyes. "Are you one of those girls who thinks girls who wear makeup are vapid?"

Yes. "No."

I can feel her disapproval.

"I don't see the point of tricking people into thinking you have bigger lips or higher cheekbones," I admit. "I just don't think it's worth the time, is all. Unless you're cosplaying."

She sits up on the bed and turns to face me. "Look, makeup is anything you want it to be. It *can* make you look like you have more defined features or more perfect skin, but to me it's like armor. Eyeliner as lethal as daggers. Lips red like men's heart blood. It's more than a mask, makeup is protection in battle."

"But what does Jessica Stone need to protect herself from?"

At that, she quickly glances away. "Rule three—"

This is too much. I can't think straight. "STOP!" I yell, forming my arms into an X. "Pause. Back up. Why are you here, Miss . . . ?" It feels weird calling her Miss Stone, and she scowls at the title, too.

"Call me Jess, please," she says, turning back to me. "And I'm here because I need your help. Look, I fail at being me. Especially in this . . . *environment*. But you? You're perfect at it, and I need to appease the masses. So. You *do* still want to be me, don't you?"

This feels like a trap.

"Who doesn't want to be Jessica Stone?" I say hesitantly.

She spreads her arms wide. "Then here's your golden opportunity! Let's trade lives!"

She can't be serious. I wait a heartbeat, then another, expecting her to cave and expose this elaborate joke, after which a cameraman busts out of the closet and *surprise!* I've been punk'd!

And yet . . .

I don't think she's joking.

Everything about Jessica Stone is perfect, from her manicured nails to her artfully messy topknot. Even in an unassuming blazer she looks like a movie star. It's weird how some people just *shine.*

Is it really that easy? Can I just step into her shoes and become her? I've seen people don cosplays all my life, becoming space princesses and starship captains and robot mercenaries and Vulcan Jedis. Assume other lives, other names . . .

And here is Jessica Stone offering up her name to me. Does she know what I could do with it?

I narrow my eyes. "What's the catch?"

She falters. "Catch?"

"Yeah. Why would you let me be you? What's so bad about being you that even *you* don't want to be you anymore?" By the tightening of her lips I know I've struck a chord.

Why would someone like Jessica Stone want to trade places with a nobody like me?

Her blue eyes slide to her assistant, and a silent conversation passes between them, like two best friends who don't need words to communicate. I feel my stomach drop, as if I'm watching something intimate, and avert my eyes.

Finally, Jessica replies, choosing her words slowly and carefully, like she's stepping on slippery rocks across a river. "Because I need to be someone else for a little while, and I figured I'd ask you. It's the chance of a lifetime, right? To be Jessica Stone."

Not only to be Jessica Stone, but to be a Jessica Stone who cares about *Starfield*. Maybe I can use this opportunity to my advantage. Do I feel horrible scheming about this?

Sure.

But sometimes you need to think outside the box to accomplish your goals, and thanks to the thousands of signatures on my petition—and the reaction at the panel—I know I have a community of fans who'll back me up.

I just need the actress who plays Amara to be one of them.

I clear my throat, not wanting to sound overly eager. "It sounds too good to be true, being you."

"I promise it isn't. No strings attached. Oh, and rule three: don't talk about Amara. About her death. Wanting her to live. Whatever. That thing you did on the panel, you can't do it again."

My face pinches. "Why don't you want to save Amara—your *job*?"

Jessica waves her hand dismissively. "It's none of your business."

Ugh. I chew on the inside of my cheek. I'm not going to stop just because she can't see a good thing right in front of her. Amara deserves to be saved—and what Jess doesn't know while she's off being me won't hurt her. Besides, she'll thank me later. I'm sure of it.

"Fine," I lie, crossing my fingers behind my back. "I won't."

She lets out a sigh of relief. "Perfect. Besides, Ethan will be with you the whole time."

The nerfherder and I give each other the same look—a glower that could cut straight to the soul. I really, *really* dislike him. Like to a degree I don't think I've ever disliked anyone.

"And that brings me to the fourth rule," Jessica says, looking between the two of us. "Don't flirt with anyone."

My cheeks redden. "I—what?"

"Don't flirt. With anyone."

"Why would you—but I wouldn't—"

She levels a look at me. "And you won't. Understand?"

"Fine! I don't know who I'd flirt with anyway."

"Darien," she says, "Calvin, the volunteers, Ethan—"

"I would never flirt with *him*," I say at the same time as he says, "I'd never flirt with your two-bit clone."

"*Clone*? Well that's rude," I say.

He clicks his tongue admonishingly. "And I want to keep my job."

Jessica snaps her fingers to draw our attention back to her. "Children, children. I need you two to play nice. Rule five, be nice to Ethan."

I jab a finger at him. Again. "He started it!"

"Rule six"—she holds up six fingers, as though I need a visual aid—"you will wear contacts at all times."

I laugh. "Sorry. I don't do contacts."

"My eyes are blue, so now you will," she says matter-of-factly. "Rule seven, you will be nice to my fans but you will *not* take selfies with them outside of photo ops. Rule eight," she brings up the finger count again, "no interviews without my consent, no signing things, no nothing. Rule nine is no soda. I don't drink sodas."

"They're gross; I agree."

She looks happy at that and holds up all ten fingers. "Rule ten: you are only allowed to be me at this convention. And only for this weekend. We'll swap back on Saturday evening. No going out after the panels, no dinners with costars, no nothing. *And* you'll never speak of this again."

"That's hardly fair—what if someone invites me out?"

"No. It's my image, not yours."

"And what about *my* image?"

She gives me a once-over as if I'm barely worth her time, and I feel *very* affronted. "I'm sure your image will be just fine."

"But I have con obligations, too."

"So is that a no, then?" She cocks her head. "I didn't figure you as someone to refuse something like this."

Oh, she has me pegged. I huff, folding my arms over my chest. "You aren't . . . wrong," I say.

"All right then." She smiles and outstretches one of her manicured hands for me to shake. This is a bad idea. I can think of ten ways to Sunday why this would never work in real life. Only in K-dramas. Only in animes. Only in YA novels. This sort of thing doesn't happen in real life, and it most certainly doesn't happen to me.

And yet . . .

And yet here is Jessica freakin' Stone on my bed, stretching her perfectly manicured hand toward me.

What are the odds?

Almost impossible.

"What do you say?" she asks. "Will you be me, Imogen Lovetrue?"

What other choice does my Gryffindor heart have? Who boldly goes? Who leaps before she thinks? Who rushes in? Me. Because I can still feel the shadow of everything that I'm not looming over me, and I can still hear Jasper laughing when I told him I wanted to save Amara. And here is Jessica Stone, unwittingly giving me the chance to do exactly that. To change the course of my community, of my fandom, of Princess Amara.

Of me.

And when I meet Jasper Sunday at 5 o'clock, I'll enjoy seeing his face once he realizes I did the impossible. I hashtag saved Amara.

"It's Lovelace," I correct, looking down at her hand. "But you can call me Mo. And even though I'm not *important* like you, I also have responsibilities. So if we're trading places, you have to pretend to be me, too. I'm sharing a booth with a friend in Artists' Alley, and I promised I'd be there."

Jessica pulls her hand away. "I don't agree to that. I don't have time to sit in some booth."

So she *is* hiding something.

"Well then, no deal," I say with a shrug and begin walking to the door. Counting the steps. I know she won't let me just boot them out. She needs me for some reason. She needs to be no one. "Now please, I have a lot to get done tonight, movies to watch and Netflix to chill, so I'd kindly ask you to—"

"Fine," she snaps and marches up to me. "*Fine*."

This time when she offers to shake on the deal, it's not in comradery. She looks almost pained. I smile and accept her outstretched hand.

"I think this is the start of a beautiful friendship, Jessica Stone."

DAY TWO

FRIDAY

———

"*Starflame*! I am not a Noxian Princess
for you to save. I will be Queen, and you
will kneel before me."

—Princess Amara, Episode 43, "From Amara with Love"

JESS

AT NINE O'CLOCK ON FRIDAY MORNING, Ethan and I are dragging ourselves to the space-age elevator, still half asleep. I sip a double-shot dirty chai latte, hoping it'll give me some sort of kick. I can't remember what time I went to bed last night—I was up pacing and scrolling through *Starfield* hashtags, hoping no one's realized that the leak is real or that it's *my* script, before Ethan woke up and took my phone away.

"Go. To. Bed," he enunciated and flopped back onto the couch.

I guess I did, eventually, but I don't remember falling asleep.

We crowd into the elevator, squeezing between green face-painted witches and home-sewn Viking warriors.

I should still be sleeping.

Though, miraculously, my social is quiet this morning. Blissfully so. There are some rude or derogatory comments, but nothing I can't swipe away with a swift DELETE.

It's very cathartic.

Maybe the rest of the weekend will be this easy. I'll find the person who stole my script and I'll put an end to it, and then Diana will call me and confirm that Amara is well and truly dead.

The elevator dings to a stop on the eighth floor. Imogen's room is at the far end, just beyond the flickering light.

I raise my hand to knock when Ethan stops me and pulls me away from the door. "Are you sure you want to do this?' he whispers. "Think about it. She could ruin your career."

"More than I'm ruining it myself, you mean?"

He frowns. "You're being too hard on yourself."

"I have to find that script, and I'm counting on you to make sure she doesn't do anything stupid, okay? You've babysat me my whole life. You can take care of one nerd girl for two days. It won't be that hard."

He rakes his fingers nervously through his thick black hair. "Okay. If you're in this, I'm in this—but at the first sign of trouble, we're out. Swear?" He holds up his right pinky finger.

I hook mine through his. "Pinky swear."

We kiss our thumbs and the deal is sealed.

Ethan marches over to the door. He gives it a knock and Imogen appears. She gives him one quick look before diverting her eyes to me. Oh that's harsh.

She really does detest him.

Though the feeling looks pretty mutual.

"Oh thank *God* last night wasn't a dream!" she blurts out in relief. "I was kinda afraid you wouldn't come back. Not that I think I'm imagining things but my moms do say I have a pretty good imagination and some of my dreams recently have been super whack so—"

"You're babbling," Ethan interjects.

"*Anyway*," she says tightly, "come in."

I follow her inside. It's clear that someone else shares the room with her—two other someones, by the looks of it—but just like last night, they're not here.

She sees me staring at the two suitcases and says, "My brother and his boyfriend won't be around much this weekend. They might come in to take a shower or something, but Bran's a film nerd so he'll be in movie showings all weekend or at panels, and my brother's dedicated to him."

"Ah."

I glance around at her suitcase strewn across half of her bed. Again, just like last night. Clearly, she's not a *tidy* person. But she seems to like space operas and fantasy shows, by the looks of the graphic T-shirt collection strewn on the ground. And she wears Converses.

I pick up the SPACE QUEEN beanie on the nightstand.

"It's kinda weird, right?" she says. "How we got mistaken because of that beanie? It's funny, I got that beanie from my—"

"Artists' Alley," I interrupt. "Ethan got mine there, too."

"*Oh.*" As if Ethan even stepping into that area of the con seemed unbelievable to her. "Well, I was thinking we could just keep using it. Since it worked the first time?"

"Someone's bound to catch on," I reply dismissively, "which is why we brought a wig." And as if on cue, my assistant produces a plastic bag out of his satchel. "It's brown, almost the same color as my natural hair, a good enough dupe if you don't look too closely. I had my housekeeper overnight it from LA."

Imogen blinks at the wig Ethan's holding. "You just have a wig lying about? That's convenient."

"I bought it to disguise the awful Amara-red I had to dye my hair," I reply.

"And what about you?" Imogen says. "Will you cut your hair to look like me or something?"

"*I'll* wear the beanie," I say.

"Can you imitate my voice?"

"I don't see why that's necessary—"

"Because you're going to be me," Imogen says, startling me with the sound of my own voice. I'd forgotten she could mimic me so well. "So you need to be convincing," she says, sounding like herself again.

"To who?"

She stares at me, blinking, and then looks away. "Never mind. You're right."

I roll my eyes and fish an extra pair of Ethan's glasses out of his bag. I'd popped the lenses out of them (promising him I'd pay for a new pair). I put them on. "See? I barely look like myself."

It's not like she has anything to worry about. I'm a fantastic actress. I'm Oscar worthy. Pretending to go along with Imogen's side of this switch should be easy enough, and I can just casually dip out of that Artists' Alley booth and find my script.

I swirl my hair up inside the beanie. "Okay, now let's make you me."

IMOGEN

THIS IS SOME SERIOUS *Twelfth Night* meets *The Parent Trap* kind
of weird.

Jess Stone and I are roughly the same size (I definitely I have
bigger boobs) so most of her clothes fit me, even her shoes. She
opts to keep on her boots, and though I'd rather stick with my de-
pendable sparkly Converses, she won't let me. Instead she shoves
a pair of two-inch heels in my direction.

"*Heels?*"

She gives me a testy look. "What about them?"

I decide not to bring up that time she faceplanted on the red
carpet. It was the GIF seen round the world.

Instead, I take the shoes and pray that there's an ER nearby in
case I accidentally wipe out on the stairs.

We exchange everything—con badges, schedules, ward-
robe—agreeing to change back by Saturday evening, before the
ExcelsiCon ball. Although Jess doesn't think we'll need to switch
places that long. She puts on my makeup and wipes hers off. The
assistant—Ethan Tanaka is his name, apparently—reminds me of
an overbearing German shepherd, the kind my neighbors used to

have. Eager to please whoever feeds him and overprotective to a fault. He would totally be hot if he wasn't glowering at me the way the Rebel forces look at Kylo Ren.

Jessica checks her phone and says, "So the panel isn't until two, and it's in the big ballroom, wherever that is."

"The main stage," I say automatically, lacing up my shoes. "I mean—I didn't mean to correct you."

"Whatever. I don't know the lingo for these things."

"That's kinda condescending," I murmur.

"No, it's not," she shoots back.

Oh, I can already see this is going to be a problem. I clear my throat and continue, "Okay, just stay away from my moms' booth because they'll know you're not me in two seconds flat. It should be relatively easy to spot—just look for the obnoxiously huge Nox King, and that's it. The con floor can be a little harrowing. It's not as big as San Diego or New York, but ExcelsiCon has its own set of problems—"

She cuts me off with an "I'll figure it out."

I hesitate because, well, color me shocked but I highly doubt she will. "Should we exchange numbers at least?"

With one hand on the door, she turns to look at me, conflicted. "I don't think either of us will be hard to find," she replies, and then says goodbye and heads out.

Leaving me with her jerkface assistant.

Whatever did I do to deserve this torture?

He turns to me and says, "I want to be frank with you because I think you deserve it. You seem like a . . . *nice* girl, but if you do anything—"

"Nice," I echo, not even letting him finish his sentence. "That's not condescending."

He blinks. "It was a compliment."

"Like the weather is nice, or your new pair of shoes are nice? I'm sorry, but I kind of take offense to that word. I'm not nice."

"I can see that."

"Good. I'm glad we're on the same page. Listen, I think we got off on the wrong foot like ten times yesterday. I'm Imogen Lovelace. Nice to meet you, Gryffindor." I extend my hand cordially. Minerva taught me this move for jerks like him. Extend the hand first, act like the bigger person, grip tightly, and then punch your fist through his sternum—no, wait. That's a *Mortal Kombat* move.

To-tal An-ni-hi-la-tion.

He looks down at my hand, then back up at me, then down at my hand again, as if expecting me to replace it with Edward Scissorhands' finger blades.

I narrow my eyes. "You're a burnt Hufflepuff, aren't you."

He takes the plunge and squeezes my hand firmly, bending a little so we're eye-to-eye. "How dare you compare me to that marshmallow trash. I'm Slytherin born and bred."

"Ooh, you missed a good joke there."

He lets go of my hand and shrugs. "I'll slither it in some other time."

I try not to smile, because that was *not* funny—and, I keep telling myself, think of rule number *whatever*—but he's already gathering up the con ID and hotel keycards. I finish putting on my other heel.

"To be fair, I didn't mean to insult you," he says as he slips the hotel keys into his back pocket and hands me Jess's VIP badge. "I just don't want to see you throw away her career. And don't have any hard feelings about her not giving you her number. Unlike her costar, who seems to enjoy chatting with strangers on the phone, Jess has had a much different experience."

"Stalker?"

"Well, let's say that someone found her number and put it up on an unsavory message board, so . . . "

My eyebrows fly up in surprise. "Eesh." He hands me the badge and I slip it on over my head. "Okay so we have everything, but I think we forgot to . . . "

He picks up the bag with the wig from the bed and holds it out to me. I can now see that there's also a satin pouch—a contact lens case? "You know how to put on a wig, right?"

"I've dabbled in cosplay," I say, then I make a face. "I hate long hair."

"Jess has it, so you do, too."

"Can't Jess shave her head?" I ask. "I'll shave mine in solidarity—"

"*No.* Now go." He points to the bathroom, checking his smartwatch in the process. "Hurry up. We should probably be at the con by one at the latest."

"You're one of those on-time-is-late people, aren't you?"

"You're one of those always-late people, aren't you?"

"I'm *mostly* on time," I mutter as I trudge into the bathroom and lock the door. I'm beginning to regret signing up for this scheme. I'm not sure what I thought it would be like—that I'd magically morph into Jessica Stone? Moon Prism Power Make Up and throw some glitter and just . . . be a celebrity? *Don't be ridiculous*, I chide myself.

I start with the contacts first. I hate contacts. Fortunately, I've worn them enough for cosplays so I don't need hours to put them in but, *starflame!*, that's going to take some getting used to. It's like condoms for my eyeballs.

Remember why you're doing this, I think to myself as I blink the lenses into focus. You're doing it to save Amara and—who knows?—maybe even Jessica Stone's career.

True, I did not expect a sorta hot but bossy Slytherin (I still think he's a burnt Hufflepuff) to hover over me like a helicopter parent the whole time, but I think there's a way to fix that.

One thing at a time.

I wiggle the wig over my neon-pink pixie, flip it back, and comb my fingers through the brown strands. It seems like a pretty expensive wig. The hair feels real. *Starflame*, it might even *be* real. I smooth it out until it looks like my own hair—well, what I guess my hair would look like if I grew it out this long, though I never will. I hate the way it feels on my neck. Plus the whole bit about long hair being more feminine is Noxballs. Social constructs can go take a hike.

I gather a section at the front and braid it like Princess Amara's hair in the thirteenth episode of *Starfield*, when Prince Carmindor first meets her. It's a subtle nod, but fans will recognize it. I used to braid Minerva's glossy black locks like this all the time when I was younger. Then I twist the braid behind my head, pinning it with one of the bobby pins in the bottom of the plastic bag.

But I still don't feel like Jessica.

"Hey, uh, dude," I call from the bathroom, realizing that I can't remember his name. "Do I look enough like her now? I still feel a little weird. The wig doesn't look too *wiggy*, does it?"

He looks up from his phone, clearly about to snark at me again, but whatever he was going to say falls from his lips. I shift on my feet, self-consciously.

He tries to speak, closes his mouth. Then tries again.

Wow, he must really love Jess—I mean, of *course* he does. He's only babysitting me because he loves her so much.

Finally, he says, "Jess doesn't wear her hair like that."

I stand up a little straighter. "Then I guess it's time for her to try something new. Besides, the braid hides some of the wiggy-ness."

He eyes the braid, not liking it at all. "It will do."

"Good."

"Fine. Let's go."

"After you," I reply, flourishing a bow as he wrenches the door open. I grab Jessica's purse from the edge of the bed and we head out down the hallway. Once inside the glass elevator, he pushes the button for the ground floor. As we descend, the mythical land that is the showroom floor slowly unfurls underneath the transparent elevator floor. People are already cosplaying, milling about in clusters on the three levels of the lobby. No matter how many times I see this spectacle, I am constantly in awe. So many nerds coming together to celebrate the things we love.

It's magical.

Meanwhile, Ethan—Ethan! that's his name!—clears his throat, startling me out of my thoughts. "Hmm?" I ask.

"I *said*, give me your phone number. In case we get separated."

I hesitate.

"You're not leaving this elevator until you give me a number."

"So you can keep track of me? Can I have yours, too?"

"I don't see a reason why, I'll be with you the whole time."

That doesn't seem very fair. With my phone number he can track my device if he wants to. Bran taught me about some of those programs. I take his phone and put in the number I know best—the local pizza joint back home in Asheville—and hand it back with a smile. "There."

"Good, now—"

Before he can finish, the elevator doors open to the lobby flooded with fans and paparazzi and journalists. They turn their bright camera lights and cell phones to me.

"Jess, is it true?" someone shouts, and a camera flashes.

Ethan quickly takes me by the shoulder and steers me toward the door, but my lips are curving into a smile. Oh my *God.*

"Jess, I love you!"

"Please look over here!"

"Will you marry me?"

We're only halfway across the lobby and all eyes are following Ethan and me like we're the center of the universe. Is this what Jessica Stone comes out to every day? People shouting how much they love her? How much she matters?

Who would want to give up something like this?

"Miss Stone!"

"Jess!"

"*Ah'blena!*"

With each step, with each shout of her name, I fall in love. With the moment. With the feeling. With her life.

"Don't listen to them," Ethan whispers into my ear. But how can I not? It's wonderful. "They're trying to distract you. Let's just get to the panel and—"

"Ethan." I mimic Jessica's voice so well that he jerks back in surprise. "Don't worry. I'm fine."

And then I do the most audacious thing I have ever done. I don't know what comes over me. Maybe it's the wig, or the weird contacts that turn my eyes a sort of oceany blue, or the fans in the lobby or the paparazzi snapping photos or the journalists asking questions about the script, which is no doubt fake, right? Or maybe it's that, deep down, I'm not only going to help Jessica Stone.

I'm going to save Amara. Not with petitions, not with pins, not with harassing Twitter trolls. But with my own words. My actions.

Jess'll thank me later.

So I wink at my new assistant and boop his nose and head in the direction of my first panel of the day.

JESS

IMOGEN'S BOOTH IS WEDGED BETWEEN an artist hawking sexy pinups of burly men and a mustachioed gentleman selling carved wooden blocks with famous people's faces on them—Ruth Bader Ginsburg and Edgar Allan Poe seemingly the most popular. Her booth is located toward the middle of the aisle and is decorated with glitter, with a display of fanart in saturated colors on the back wall.

I can only guess that belongs to Imogen's friend—and then I realize her friend will know I'm not Imogen. Did Imogen plan this as some sort of humiliating stunt to—

A young woman ducks out from behind the artwork and sits down and my mind just—

Well.

It blanks.

My mind *never* blanks.

She is very pretty, with delicate features, brown skin, and natural hair pulled into twin puffs on the sides of her head. She's wearing a yellow dress with some sort of star design—when I look closer I realize it's the *Starfield* logo.

Can't *one* person not like this franchise? Based on the fact that she's Imogen's friend, I want to think she's Team Save Amara, and so she likes me—I mean, Jessica Stone. But what if she doesn't?

What if she says she does but she's really one of those people leaving hateful comments on my posts—

She gives a start when she realizes I'm standing in front of the booth like a weirdo. "Oh! Sorry! Wow, hi!" she says, putting down her breakfast burrito. "It's so nice to finally meet you in person! It's Harper—I mean, I know you know I'm Harper, but . . . This is so nice, you know, meeting in person. Anyway, I'm babbling!" She laughs, loud and sweet, and smiles at me, her hand outstretched. Each of her long fingers glitters with midi rings and normal rings, her nails a polished and pointed teal. "Hi."

Oh.

Imogen and Harper have never actually met. That must be why Imogen wasn't afraid of me meeting her. They're internet friends. It's like a balloon pops in my chest and I can breathe again.

I grab her hand and shake it. "It's nice to meet you, too. I'm—I'm Imogen."

She smiles, as if my hesitation is just nervousness. "I know." She sits back down, and I take the chair beside her. "Burrito?"

"Um, no thanks." I push up my glasses self-consciously.

"You sure? I got them from the Magic Pumpkin. I just *had* to see what it was all about. It's pretty good, you know, for vegan."

"Ah." Dare's girlfriend's food truck.

"Oh! And I've given away a ton of your pins," she adds, nodding to my side of the table.

"What?"

"Your pins."

My pins?

That's when I notice them on the table, along with an iPad to sign a petition and ribbons to stick on the bottom of your con badge, all sporting the same phrase: #SaveAmara.

A cold feeling grips my stomach. I grab the iPad and navigate to the petition page and feel myself spiraling. The Save Amara initiative.

"She started this . . . ," I whisper. Harper hears me and leans over.

"Oh yeah, you've got, like, fifty new signatures."

I quickly flick off the screen. Imogen Lovelace is the creator of the Save Amara initiative and didn't even tell me? It all makes sense though. Her giving me that pin yesterday in the restroom. Speaking out on the panel.

Wanting to be me.

Everything's fine, I remind myself. *Ethan won't let her do anything.* But the other half of my brain is screaming that my worst enemy is running around pretending to be me. And I can't do anything about it. Not right now.

Because at any moment the next scene could be leaked, maybe a page with my name in the corner and an irreparable spoiler that will get me blacklisted from every studio in Hollywood. Not to mention that I'll get sued for violating my NDA, doxxed by angry nerds. And I'm stuck here wasting time at her ridiculous #SaveAmara booth!

What if Diana drops me?

What if I never—

Stop. Breathe.

After she finishes her burrito, Harper looks over at me. "Are you okay? You seem a little . . . "

Weird? Different? Not who you thought your internet friend was?

I wonder briefly how Imogen and Harper met in the first place.

A pretty big clue is the copious amount of fanart of Princess Amara in the arms of various characters—men and women—that hangs on the corkboard behind us. The prints on the table tout pairings from *Steven Universe* and *Voltron* and Harry Potter and some video-game artwork with a guy in a twirly mustache and bull-looking humanoid creature. And me. Have I mentioned there are drawings of me? Well, me as Princess Amara, but still. I'm sure I don't understand any of it. Why is everyone into these bizarre pairings?

"Okay, so fess up. You're secretly a Caruci shipper, aren't you?"

"A what?"

"Carmindor and Euci. *The* slash. Don't play coy. I've been watching you check out my artwork. I thought you were a Carminara girl."

A . . . what?

"Carine?" she goes on. "Zoruchi? *Amaruci*? Zomara? Oh please say it isn't so." And then, as if a secret question, "*Sondara?*"

Is she speaking in tongues?

"I . . . ah . . ."

"You can hide behind your Carmindor and Amara, but I see you." As if that settles things, she pulls out a sketchbook and a mechanical pencil from her bag and then turns to a page with a half-finished drawing of two men in Sailor Scout uniforms. She looks up, her dark eyes rimmed with kohl and gold. I feel naked without my makeup. Unprotected.

Come on, you're an Oscar-nominated actress. Play your role!

"I'm Carminara all the way," I reply smoothly, pushing Ethan's glasses up the bridge of my nose like I'd seen him do a thousand times when he's confident about something. "I . . . stan Darien."

I hope Dare never hears me say that out loud.

She laughs, and it sounds like honey.

I sit there for a few more minutes while people browse Harper's art selection. A girl stops and looks at one of the prints, which shows Princess Amara and Zorine (Zomara?), her childhood best friend, holding each other in a loving embrace—with all six of Zorine's arms. She points and asks, "How much?"

Harper says, "It's ten for one, three for twenty."

The girl scrunches her nose. "Ugh, never mind. I'll just print it off the Web."

"Hey, before you go," Harper says. "Save Amara!" She grabs a pin from my side of the booth and hands it to her. "It's free."

The girl brightens. "I'd love to," she says, and takes the pin.

The nerve of this girl!

Harper seems unbothered. "A lot of people do that."

"And you just let them?"

"What can I do about it? Even if I offer my prints exclusively at cons, someone'll scan them onto the internet and people will just get them that way."

"Shouldn't they want to contribute to the creators?"

Harper rolls her eyes. "Not when everything online is free," she says sarcastically.

I lower my gaze to the print. I guess I can kind of relate. My signature being sold for hundreds of dollars, photos of my life being pawned to the tabloid with the highest bidder, my story confiscated bit by bit until nothing is mine anymore.

I look through a few of her fanarts and stop at one of me—the real-life me.

It's from when I took that spill on the Oscar red carpet, and she has all of the details eerily perfect. The way I styled my hair into a half bun, the cut of my evening gown. My utter lack of grace has been GIF'd so many times I get sick to my stomach just seeing it. My hands flailing, the dress caught on the heel of my shoe—

Just looking at it makes me angry.

I had a bruised cheekbone for a week while I listened to everyone make fun of the disaster, as if my mortification was entertainment. I guess sometimes it is. I thought that was the worst that would happen to me. But then I became Princess Amara.

I flip the portfolio closed.

"Aren't you going to hand out the pins?" Harper asks. There's a few scattered on the table and another big box under my feet.

I pick one up and realize that I should, even though it pains me. Imogen is being me—and promised not to mention this pointless initiative—so I guess it's the least I can do. Until I get a lead on the person who stole my script, and to do that I need to wait for another post.

I hold the pin out to a passer-by. "Save Amara," I force out.

The person doesn't even acknowledge me.

I try with the next group. "Save Amara!"

Again, they pass without even looking in my direction.

I frown and look at Harper. "Why aren't they paying attention?"

"Because you sound dead, Mo," she says with a laugh. "It's like you've never done this before. Here, watch and learn. SAVE AMARA!" she cries, throwing the pin into the crowded aisle.

The next person—a World of Warcraft cosplayer—stops and takes one. "Oh, cool! I heard about this."

"There's a petition to revive her—"

"Although it's not official," I interject. There's no way I could see the studio ever acknowledging something like this. Harper shoots me a strange look, so I quickly add, "But please can you sign it?"

"Sure!" They sign without so much as another word, buy two of Harper's fanarts, and move on their way.

After they're gone Harper says, "See, it's easy. Just, you know, make it sound like you care."

"I do care!" Not.

"Mmm-hm. Are you okay, Imogen? You seem a little—"

The phone in my pocket dings.

I set an alert for tweets by the person who stole my script. Another ding, and then another, and another, and people begin pulling out their phones. Even Harper takes out hers.

Frightened, I do too.

Another page from the script:

Looks like we're in for some stormy weather ;)
PS – Can you guess where I am? A surprise might be coming if you can find me!

I feel the urge to vomit. They're taunting me.

```
[INT. THE NOXIAN COURT -- late evening]

A group of soldiers push CARMINDOR, tied up and
beaten, into the middle of the council. CARMINDOR
stumbles and collapses onto the dais. Blood
drips from his mouth, where he has been punched
repeatedly. The NOX KING's throne sits empty, and
beside it PRINCESS AMARA's.

Her empty seat is bittersweet, and her voice in
CARMINDOR's head returns --

                AMARA (V.O.)
           Look how you've fallen,
           ah'blen. I warned you
           not to play with fire.
```

CARMINDOR struggles to his knees in front of the
council.

                    CARMINDOR
          Let me go or you'll face the
          wrath of the Federation --

                    MYSTERIOUS VOICE
          Oh, my dear brother, can
          we not talk peace? We
          have both suffered such
          a tremendous loss at the
          hands of the Black Nebula.

                    CARMINDOR
                (through gritted
                teeth)
          You have suffered *nothing*
          of the same.

A figure steps out from behind the throne, clad
in threads of gold that glow like the sun. At the
sight of him, the council bows as if to a god.

CARMINDOR cannot believe his eyes.

                    CARMINDOR
          You?

Now's my chance. I have to find this trash human before the
worst happens.

The script is being held up this time, the background is blurry.
I squint, trying to focus it. It's colorful, with lines? Drawings?

I can see people in the shot. The backs of heads, cosplayers—
and then I see the World of Warcraft guy who just stopped by our
table.

They're *here*. In Artists' Alley!

I quickly look around, but my peripheral vision is constantly blocked by these nerd glasses. I shove them onto my head but of course don't see anyone suspicious. Everyone's looking at their phones, gossiping about the script. I couldn't care less. The only thing I care about is who is leaking it.

I don't notice that Harper is looking at me until I've already decided to leave and look for the thief. She doesn't stop me, and I lose her booth in the crowd.

The photo was taken somewhere nearby—that much I know. There's the purple in the banner in the background, and the retro carpet, and the narrow aisles . . .

I spin around, trying to gauge where the thief would have been when the photo was taken. I pass another aisle, glancing down at the tweet, at the background around the script page, up at the sea of cosplayers and fans. I feel like I'm suffocating.

How can so many people congregate in such a small space for . . . what? A bunch of vendors that only want one thing: their money? Don't they realize that most of this stuff doesn't really matter?

It's just make-believe. A bunch of adults pretending that their love for a TV show or a movie or a game means more than it actually does.

I just don't get it.

I walk along the aisle until I think I come to the spot where the photo was taken. The thief was here, overlooking Artists' Alley. I had been less than fifty feet away. I grip my phone and scan the masses of humanity, but I don't recognize anyone from the hotel lobby.

Blond hair, biker jacket, pink nails, lip gloss, mole-on-cheek, bunny, I recall the lobby scene in my head. The girls on the sofa, the guy at the desk with his back turned. None of them are here.

I approach a girl behind a row of anime plushies. "Was some-one standing here just a few minutes ago?"

She looks up. Her hair is streaked with pinks and purples and greens, her glasses are large and round. She blinks at me, and then slowly shakes her head. "I haven't seen anyone."

But then I notice that she's playing a game on her phone. I doubt she'd have noticed someone standing here, anyway. I turn away from her but then she says, "Hey, you kinda look like Princess Amara—that girl."

That girl.

In alarm, I pull on my glasses. "Thanks, I get that a l—"

"MONSTERRRRRRR!"

I look up, along with half of the crowd, and see a particularly tall and muscular guy coming toward me, his brown hair almost contained in his backward snapback, a curl twisting out of the opening. His arms are flapping in the air, as if he's waving some-one down. He's looking directly at me.

"Hey! Monster! You wouldn't believe what just happened!" he shouts again.

I glance around to see if anyone is responding.

No, no they are not.

That leaves only one possibility.

The girl selling plushies looks at me and says, "I think he means you."

"I was afraid of that," I reply. Imogen *definitely* didn't tell me about him, or the person with him—ebony skinned, slender and waspish, dressed in a half cape and pointed witch's hat, an umbrella resting on his shoulder. He's cosplaying as *someone,* but hell if I know who.

And I am definitely not going to stick around just so they and the plushie seller can find out that I am most certainly *not*

"Monster" and am, in fact, that girl who plays Princess Amara.

I slip my phone into my pocket and take a step backward, and then another.

"Monster! Monster?" the muscular guy shouts. His thick eyebrows furrow. He's about twenty feet from me and—

All right. I'm leaving.

I take off out of Artists' Alley as fast as I can, pushing through a group of people dressed as angels, and to my absolutely awful luck, Imogen's friends pursue.

Here's the thing: I'm terrible at running (especially in heels—hello, I tripped on the freaking *red carpet*). Never mind sports. Tennis, softball, track. I am horrible at literally every form of exercise. I'm even bad at the elliptical, which is something no human being in the world is bad at, except me. And that is why I never do my own stunts. It's just not something I'm good at.

So when I take off running out of Artists' Alley, I am praying that my knees don't buckle and I am able to worm my way between enough people to lose Hunky and his friend in my wake. I'm lithe. Just have to pretend I'm a dancer and swirl through the crowd. Plus, it's *much* easier to run in flats.

My shoes slap hard against the tiled floor as I turn onto a skybridge, dodging under a cosplayer with a six-foot wingspan.

They call again, "Mo! Mo, watch o—"

I'm hanging a left at the end of the skybridge when my foot slams into the long purple tail of someone dressed as the Nox King (of *course*). I pitch forward and slam into the ground.

IMOGEN

THIS MANY PEOPLE SHOULD NOT BE able to fit inside a room this size, although I know, from being a plebian squeezed into the back row last year, that indeed they can. I was smooshed between a Deadpool and a comics collector when the cast of the fantasy series *Blades of Valor*, starring the dreamy Vance Reigns, played an impromptu game of Never Have I Ever onstage. Vance had put a finger down for "Never have I ever had a crush on Ron Swanson." ("We're all on a sexual spectrum, and mine is girls and Ron Swanson," he clarified later.) I thought that was going to be the highlight of my life in this room.

Alas, I was gravely mistaken.

I peek out between the black stage curtains, pulling at the high collar of my—well, Jess's—dress. It's navy blue with white trim, and my hose is a shimmery black. The blue isn't the right *Starfield* shade, the hose is demonic, and don't get me started on the heels. Given her history with these torture devices, you would think she'd have sworn them off long ago.

Apparently Jessica Stone is one of those people who double down.

So now I have to worry about tripping in front of three thousand people. How nice of her.

Is it hot in here or is it just me? I'm trying not to sweat too much and keep my arms chicken-winged from my sides so I don't leave pit stains.

Starflame, how does she operate under these conditions?

Her grumpy assistant sits down in one of the reserved seats in the front row, shrugging into a casual dark-gray suit jacket. Ugh, doesn't he know he's at a con? The only people dressed in suits are Men in Black, any of the butler *shojo* and *shonen* anime, and occasionally a Doctor, depending on the season. Clearly, Ethan is cosplaying as a douche with a giant stick up his butt. But I can't let some too-cool-for-school wannabe Bond ruin what'll be the best days of my life.

"I'm probably going to complain—this is *ridiculous*," a voice behind me, well, complains. It's male, all-American. Calvin Rolfe. I look over my shoulder and there he is with a Starbucks cup, wearing a brown bomber jacket, his ginger hair swooped up into a wave. The freckles on his nose look more prominent without movie makeup, and they draw together when he scrunches his nose. "A panel *every day*?"

"It's ExcelsiCon, which started as a *Starfield* con. What else do you expect?" Darien replies—*the* Darien Freeman. Prince Carmindor. Now that I'm not looking at him in the spotlight, he looks a lot more . . . normal? I don't know how that's possible since he looks like freaking Carmindor even in real life—curly black hair and smooth brown skin and eyelashes that go on for days. But there is something decidedly nonchalant about him. Also, he isn't as tall as I thought.

Or maybe I'm just a giant in these heels.

Calvin rolls his eyes. "Yeah, yeah, and your girlfriend's tied to it, so of course you'll take the con's side."

I've never seen Darien Freeman glare more ferociously.

Calvin raises his hands in defeat. "All I'm saying is that we should only do one panel at a thing like this. We're busy people with busy lives. Our time is money and, uh, we're not getting paid nearly enough."

"They're our fans. It's the least we can do."

"Can you get your fanboy head out of your fanboy a—"

"I think it's really cool," I interject before my common sense can reel me in and tell me *it's a trap*.

Darien and Calvin look over at me, surprised either that I spoke up or that I'm defending Darien and this con, I'm not sure which.

I clear my throat and tug on a lock of wig hair. "I mean, they're all here to see us, right? And this panel's about villains in *Starfield*. It should be fun."

"Except our Nox King super isn't here," Calvin points out. "Why isn't Robert coming again?"

"The great Robert Thomas Eddington is shooting *King Lear* in Scotland as we speak," Darien says begrudgingly. He gives me a curious look. Oh no, did I do Jess's voice wrong or something? Remember the tilt, the toneless accent, the drawl.

Calvin sighs. "Ugh, why am *I* here, wasting this perfectly good Friday? Euci isn't a villain."

"Actually, in episode—" I stop myself before I can recite the exact episode in question, because Jess wouldn't know "—in *an* episode, I think, when you nearly get everyone killed. With, like . . . a lightsaber or something."

It pains me to say *lightsaber*. In the episode, Euci becomes possessed by the Balu'atho, an ancient Noxian blade, and goes absolutely bonkers on the ship. What we don't find out until the end is that the artifact only channels the darkness that's already inside a person's heart. Euci is terribly jealous of Carmindor—sometimes so much that he does become a villain.

It's only fair. I mean, I get it. Carmindor is damn near perfect—like my brother, I guess. It's impossible to live up to that.

"She's not wrong," Darien adds, giving me another unreadable look. "And I'm here because I'm the only one of us who actually watches the show, but apparently . . . "

"Oh no, I haven't watched it," I quickly lie. "I read the *Wikipedia.*"

"Ah."

Calvin slaps him on the shoulder. "Thanks for taking one for the team, buddy!"

Our moderator—a chipper older woman with pastel rainbow hair—calls us over, telling us that we can make our way onto the stage. Calvin goes first, and I begin to follow, but then I feel a hand on my shoulder.

I jump.

It's Amon Wilkins.

He grins, all Hollywood-white teeth and dashing surfer-bro swagger, looking like he could be in the next remake of *Point Break.* "So, how're you enjoying the con so far?" he asks, putting his phone into his back pocket. The moment he does, it dings with a notification.

Then again, and again—and a shadow of annoyance crosses his eyes, until he decides to ignore it. His gaze settles on me, prompting me to answer.

I snap out of my stupor. "Um—yeah—great! Much great. Very fine. Wow."

Oh, *starflame,* I'm supposed to be acting like Jessica Stone, not Doge.

Amon laughs and squeezes my shoulder, and a weird feeling reverberates through me as his phone lets out another series of dings. He *is* going to silence that before the panel, right? No one likes those people. "Hope the reading material was to your liking. I have a feeling today is going to be great. I've got a killer surprise," he adds, and follows Calvin up the stairs to the stage.

Reading material? Was Jess—I mean me—supposed to read something for this panel?

Darien lingers on the steps, waiting for me. I quickly put my hands on my hips, elbows out, praying that he doesn't notice how badly I'm sweating and that this is just . . . a pose I struck. Just to strike it. Because Jessica Stone doesn't sweat. She barely *breathes*.

Oh *starflame*. My cover is *so* blown.

But as I make my way up the stairs, he does the weirdest thing—Darien Freeman loops his arm through one of mine. "You'll be fine," he whispers, and leads me onto the stage like . . .

Like we're friends.

I know a lot about Darien Freeman and Jessica Stone and Calvin Rolfe. I follow the gossip blogs and watch TMZ. But somehow it never crossed my mind that Darien and Jessica could be friends. Well, that anyone could be Jessica's friend. Not because she's mean or curt or aloof (though she is kind of all of those things, but who can blame her?) but because . . .

I don't know.

Of course they'd be friends.

And for a moment I feel like an imposter again—someone who's stepped into someone else's life undeserving.

Why am I so nervous?

I wasn't nervous yesterday, when I was pretending to be a girl I only knew from interviews and rumors on Twitter and Insta comments. But now I'm supposed to be *her*—not a caricature—

only better. The Jessica that everyone wants Jessica to be.

The one who would sign the #SaveAmara petition.

Remember your goal.

I have a job to do, and a career to save, and a princess to rescue. Or, at least, an argument to make for the princess to rescue herself.

I might not know who I am sometimes, but I know who everyone wants Jessica Stone to be. I know who I want Jessica Stone to be. Someone in whom every girl can see herself.

I *am* Jessica Stone.

The din of the room just a few moments ago goes deathly quiet as we all take the stage. Darien lets go of my arm as we reach our seats. I take the chair between Darien and Calvin—the one with Jessica Stone's name card in front of it—and sit down, brushing my fake brown hair behind my shoulder in what I hope is a cool, aloof Jessica Stone way.

I breathe deeply and raise my eyes to the crowd. Three thousand pairs stare back, the stage lights almost blinding me as they rise to illuminate us.

The moderator introduces herself as Laurel Brinkley, a columnist for a sci-fi magazine, and asks us to introduce ourselves and name our favorite villains.

Amon leans into the microphone, mulling over the question with a dramatic pause. "That's a tough one. Oh! By the way, I'm Amon Wilkins, the director of *Starfield* and the upcoming untitled sequel. I want to say *I'm* my favorite villain because who on earth would do what I did to poor Amara?" He winks at me, and I am really regretting my decision to like him. "But I digress. My favorite's the Nox King. Robert sends his regards, by the way. He's sorry he couldn't make it."

The crowd cheers, and he gives them a quick wave.

"You took mine," complains Calvin. "So I guess probably

Darth Vader if we're sticking old-school. He's super scary. I'm Calvin Rolfe, also known as Euci. Hi everyone, thanks for coming!"

There's a steady cheer from the crowd.

And then it's Darien's turn. A chorus of squeals erupts and outlasts all the other welcoming applause. He waves, disarming the screams of lust with a dashing smile, and the audience quickly quiets down. "I'm Darien Freeman, and I'd probably have to be the odd fish out and say the xenomorphs from *Alien*. They are *terrifying*."

"That they are," agrees the moderator, and then all four of them look down the panel to hear my answer.

Well.

I squint through the glare of the lights to the front row. To Jessica's assistant, who crosses his arms and shifts in his seat like a bored four-year-old at a movie, as if he's already predicted exactly what I will do.

Well, think again, bucko.

"I think everyone knows who I am," I begin in Jessica's sweet voice, turning my gaze to the audience, "and the most terrifying villain is, without a doubt, m—"

The stage lights flicker.

A crackling *boom* erupts from the speakers.

And a masculine voice, low and soft, purrs:

"*Me*."

I jerk back from the microphone. What's happening?

Everyone twists around, craning their necks to glimpse the source of the voice. Darien and Calvin look over, as if I'm the one doing it, but I shake my head. The lights flicker brightly again and then go out.

Something catches the corner of my eye.

A figure is coming up the back stairs to the stage, a golden robe billowing behind him, glimmering like the sun.

My stomach flops.

Me, I was going to say. *Amara.* But I'd forgotten about one villain. He was in only a few episodes but sent invisible spiders crawling across my skin the second I first saw him. The Nox King may be scary, but he's nothing like *this guy.*

The figure in the gold costume stalks in front of the panel table; in the darkened room, his uniform shines like it's made of the sun itself. Lights embedded in his cape blink and sparkle, neon-yellow piping underneath his crisp Noxian uniform glows. But he's not Noxian, not in the least, with long white-blond hair braided down one shoulder and his pointed yet human cheekbones. He wears fear on his sleeves like precious cuff links and tugs at them as he stops center stage.

Is he here to interrupt the panel? Darien and Calvin don't seem to understand either. They're looking back at the volunteer behind the stage and then at Amon.

Who is smiling.

Oh. I get it.

This is part of the program.

The golden man outstretches his arms, and in the darkness I can hear the murmur of the crowd, the click of cell phone cameras, the rustling of bodies to get a better view.

He says, "My brothers, have you missed me?"

The crowd is silent.

Then everyone who has seen the show, anyone who knows who this golden knight is, collectively *loses their minds.* Like the christening of a champagne bottle against a new ship, I hear a thousand Tumblr stansites being born. The noise is so loud my waterglass vibrates, as if this guy's the second coming of Loki at San Diego Comic-Con.

He holds up two white-gloved hands, lowers them gently, and

the crowd quiets again, under his spell.

My heart races. Darien leans over and whispers, "Did you know?"

I subtly shake my head. How could I? I'm an imposter of Jessica Stone—I know less than anyone on this panel. Except for maybe Calvin. I don't think Calvin realizes what is happening at *all*.

I didn't prepare for this. I hadn't even thought this could be a possibility. And also, this prick interrupted me. He could've waited until after I'd answered.

Or maybe this is symbolic of how Princess Amara and Jessica Stone are old news?

Whatever it is, it is very, very bad for me.

"I have woken from an endless slumber, brothers," the golden knight says, addressing the audience, "and I know some of you are not quite sure what to make of me yet. But you will, I promise. All will become clear within the guiding light of the Sun. You will be saved, my children, my brothers, my . . . *friends*." He says the last bit slowly, oily, and a tremble races down my spine.

He turns his head slightly—to me—and leans back against the table. He slowly raises a hand and runs his finger along my jawline. My brain turns to putty.

"All you must do," he says, as if we are two lovers whispering intimately, "is conscript your fate to me."

I stare into his face, which is lit from the glow of his costume, and see the thin mic headset clipped to his ear, the slope of his nose, the thin curve of his lips.

He slides the tip of his finger to the edge of my chin, following the contour of my face, before turning back to the audience. His smile imitates that of the original actor—the late Arthur Boise— down to the slight uptick on the left side of his lips.

His voice, languid and commanding, slithers across the crowd.

"Any volunteers?"

Everything I know about *Starfield* changes in an instant. Of course no one wants to be conscripted to the Path of the Sun—it's like watching Patrick Stewart be assimilated into the Borg—but honestly I don't think anyone's thinking straight. I know I'm not.

In that moment, I admit I'm kind of fantasizing about how long that conscription would take.

The crowd explodes like the Death Star after Luke hits the sweet spot.

Amon stands as the lights rise and then walks in front of the table. "Vance Reigns, everyone!"

Vance Reigns.

Ohmygod. The heartthrob who stole MTV's Hottest Actor award from Darien Freeman last year. The face of Chanel advertisements. The magic-sword-carrying hero in the *Blades of Valor* TV series. The guy I watched play Never Have I Ever and cop to "had a crush on Ron Swanson."

That Vance Reigns.

I swallow thickly.

Amon grabs him by the shoulder and grins, pleased as a peacock. "And Vance, can you tell me who you'll be playing?"

The golden knight sneers, still in character. "General Sond, you plebeian."

Vance Reigns is playing *General Ambrose Sond.*

A villain who somehow got into the hearts and minds of half the *Starfield* fandom and became a reoccurring character. A problematic fave if I've ever known one. An antihero. Not quite evil, but not all good either. A zealot of the Path of the Sun who believed in harnessing the Black Nebula to become a god. But Princess Amara saved everyone in that three-episode arc because she couldn't be conscripted to the cult due to her half-Noxian

He puts a finger to his lips and his eyes flick to a nearby volunteer. Right, people could overhear us. *You're being real smooth, Imogen.*

I whisper, "She's fine. Did you—did you know? About . . . " I motion toward the film star in his golden cloak as he and Amon come into the green room.

Darien lifts an eyebrow. "No. I mean, I assumed there'd be another villain besides the Nox King, but we were told it'd be a surprise."

"I wish it was a different surprise. I *hate* that guy," Calvin interjects, coming between Darien and me. He grabs a sandwich from the snack table. We're all staring across the green room at Amon and Vance laughing it up, feeling like we're the old toys in a playroom. "No one asked *me* to go onstage in costume."

"Or me," Darien adds, and his voice has a weird edge.

"Didn't Vance beat you for best stud of the year or something?" Calvin asks, earning a glare from his co-star.

"Thanks for reminding me," Darien deadpans.

Calvin shrugs and chomps into a tuna melt.

My stomach growls. Jess didn't tell me a rule about not eating in public, but I'm pretty frakkin' sure she'd chase me down and stuff me in a hundred sardine cans if I blew tuna breath on everyone. I'm so hungry even Pizza the Hut sounds delicious right now.

"Crap, act natural, here they come." Darien quickly turns toward me as Amon and Vance saunter over. Darien gives me a half smile, but it's a weird one. Like he's encouraging me that I have this. Why wouldn't I?

Amon and Vance join us, but I can tell it isn't because they want to shoot the breeze. *I shouldn't be here*, I realize, looking around to see if I can escape. Jess's assistant finally dips into the Green Room, making a beeline for me, but security stops him

lineage. She brought Carmindor back from its depths, and
ended up trapping General Sond in a cryogenic chamber, never
be woken again.

And I realize as I glance over at Darien, who seems to come
the exact same conclusion at the exact same moment:

Princess Amara is very much *dead*, and if they wake Genera
Sond, there will be no one left to save the Federation Prince.

———————

As we leave the stage, I train my mouth to stay in a straight
line. Amon slaps Vance Reigns on the back for a job well done
with one hand and slides his phone into his back pocket with
the other. I can't help but give both of them a wary eye. I *guess* I
could have predicted General Sond as the new villain. You know,
if they hadn't killed Amara at the end of the *Starfield* reboot. So
now I'm beginning to wonder, will someone else be immune to
General Sond's conscriptions? Will that just eliminate the impor-
tance and agency of how Amara defeated him to begin with?

Princess Amara is supposed to be unique in that way—she
can't be swayed or conscripted. She can barely be told no, for
starflame's sake.

I don't like this.

I follow the rest of the cast down the private hallway and into
the green room, which is little more than a hotel meeting space
with a few chairs and a measly buffet. Darien grabs a water bottl
and offers it to me. "You okay?"

"Hmm?" I don't realize I'm chewing on my thumbnail unt
it's too late, and quickly pluck it out of my mouth. "Oh. Yeah.

"Is *she* okay?" he adds in a quieter tone, and my bre
hitches. He means Jess. So he knows—like yesterday, he know

"Listen, Jess was—"

and asks for his badge. He pushes up his glasses as he assesses my situation.

"Help," I mouth.

His eyes dart to the real actors—and then he shrugs and mouths something that looks suspiciously like "Don't do anything stupid."

Thanks, buddy.

"Jess, did you hear me?"

My ears prick as I whirl back to Amon.

"I, um . . . no."

Amon laughs. "You're always a breath of fresh air, Jess. I hope everyone enjoyed the panel. As I said, the script leaking is real. But we've been told by the higher-ups to sandbag every question—"

Say it now. You didn't have a chance to on the panel. Bring up the #SaveAmara initiative.

"Actually," I interrupt, "wouldn't it be a good time to talk about some of the fan movements, especially the Save Am—"

"Amon," Darien interrupts, giving me a strange look. "You said you needed to talk to me about something?"

The director claps his hands. "Right! Jess, can you excuse us? Just put a pin in our conversation and I'll be back later." He takes Darien by the shoulder and steers him away.

The strained smile across my lips falters. Why did Darien interrupt me? Does he do that in real life? Just interrupt people?

I guess being a movie star has gone to his head.

Calvin also slinks off, back to the snack table, where he picks up another tuna melt.

So now I'm alone. In the green room. With Vance Reigns, like, ten feet away.

General Sond. It's still so weird. I'm not sure whether I'm

absolutely terrified of him or really digging the long white-blond hair. He looks like Orlando Bloom as Legolas, and my childhood *Lord of the Rings* trash self is low-key screaming right now.

Okay, maybe not low-key.

My moms say I don't do anything low-key.

Vance approaches me, sipping a cup of water.

"Where did everyone go?" he asks in a surprising English accent. I did not realize he was English.

"To, ah . . . they went . . . "

Brain, you have failed me for the last time.

"I don't think we've been introduced. I'm Vance," he says. "I didn't mean to interrupt you earlier. It was just my cue, and you know how we Brits like our queues."

I think he's trying to make a joke about standing in lines, but all I can do is stare at him.

I thought being flabbergasted by Darien was the extent of my fangirling, but this is insanely different.

One, Vance is single (and straight, with the exception of Ron Swanson), which means my inner monologue can't scream *but his girlfriend/boyfriend/partner!* Thus the unoccupied part of my brain is already marrying him and having his children and—

Two, being in the same room with him is like being next to the sun. He is face-meltingly hot. His shoulders and chest are broad, his torso tapers down to thin hips and sturdy legs. I mean, not that his legs *wouldn't* be sturdy, but you know the kind of legs where you just know, under the molten-golden trousers, that he can basically smash watermelons between them? Yeah, that's the kind of thighs I'm picturing, and I think my knees have gone numb and oh dear god he's way too close. He clasps his hands behind his back in this unassuming, almost boyish way and gives me a smile that exudes warmth and honesty and long walks on the beach, causing the system-wide meltdown of Imogen Lovelace.

Mayday. I am in trouble.

He's playing the *villain*?

"So," he says languidly, almost in a purr, and that coupled with the English lilt of his voice makes me remember how much I love accents. His, specifically, the way it forms around his lips. "You're the infamous Jessica Stone."

What are words? Who am I?

I think my ovaries are exploding.

"I . . . ah . . . " I have absolutely nothing in my head. It's a blank slate. His smile renders me absolutely and ridiculously incompetent.

I didn't think I was this kind of girl. I've never been speechless before.

Lies! my emergency reboot program howls. *All lies!*

He goes on, oblivious to my distress. "I know we kind of got off on the wrong foot. I honestly didn't want to interrupt you, but Amon thought it would serve the best dramatic effect. I want to get off on the right foot, so . . . do you have plans tonight?"

What are plans?

I am a puddle of human flesh who can't even form words because his eyes are the prettiest shade of blue I have ever seen and his eyelashes are long and his eyebrows are well groomed and his face has just enough stubble to make his General Sond cosplay believable and terrifying and . . .

So hot.

"Plans?" I squeak.

He smiles, and my melted brain goes into overdrive, launching a thousand OTPs. Sond and Carmindor. Sond and Euci. Sond and the Nox King. Sond and Amara. Sond and Zorine.

Sond and *me*.

"I was thinking we could get dinner." His laugh jerks me from my stupor.

"I . . . we . . . ummm . . . "

Think, Monster!

But it's no use. I am now made of idiocy, my brain launching ships that *I shall go down with*—

An arm loops under mine and pulls me to the side. Sweet cologne, a starchy suit jacket. *Ethan*, I realize. "Sorry, but we have plans," he says.

Vance's face falls slightly. "Oh, that's a pity. Well, all right then. If you do end up free tonight, I'll be watching reruns of *Parks and Rec* in my hotel room here at the Marriott if you need me."

"*I'm* here at the Marriott!" I gasp. We have so much in common already!

"Good. Maybe I'll see you there." Then he leans in and murmurs in my ear so Ethan can't hear, "And maybe we can talk about saving Amara. I'll call you tonight."

He knows about my initiative?

He will call me tonight?

Au contraire, he can call on me anytime he—

Imogen, *breathe.*

Before I can muster up the brain power to say anything, Ethan clears his throat. "It was a pleasure, Vance. *Jess*, we have to go."

He drags me away from my hunka-hunka-evil-space-general-Englishman-lover and doesn't let go until we are well out of the green room and in one of the off-limits stairwells. He whirls to me, his lips set in a thin line.

Ruh-roh. That's not a happy face.

"You will *not* get away with this," Ethan snaps.

I blink. "With what?"

He takes out his phone and shows me my profile on Twitter, @OhSparkleMonster. "Jess might not have done any digging, but I sure have. *You* started the Save Amara movement. That's why you were so willing to trade places with her. Your outburst yesterday on the panel makes so much sense now—" This he says more to himself than to me.

My mouth falls open. I don't know whether to be offended or to applaud him for figuring me out.

He puts his phone away. "You don't understand what's at stake. I won't allow it—and neither will Darien."

I scoff. "Allow me? What can you do to stop me?"

"You'll ruin her career."

"*Ruin* it? I'm going to save it! If the world knows that Jessica Stone backs the movement, maybe the producers will think twice about killing her. Or having her stay dead."

"Maybe she doesn't want to get behind the movement."

"Maybe she should. Maybe she should stop being Burr and start being Hamilton."

He blinks. Of course that reference went straight over his head. He's the pencil-straight, button-up-shirt kind of guy who probably listens to smooth jazz while reading a Stephen Hawking book. Which is fine, no shade there, but ugh. Of course I have to be stuck with the most uncool person at the con—

He steps up to me, looming like the five-foot-eleven beanpole he is, and says in a soft rumble, "She is. She just doesn't want to waste her shot."

Gooseflesh ripples across my skin.

"You know the rules," he says. "And that thing you just tried to pull with Vance? Yeah, smooth move, criminal."

"I wasn't actually—that wasn't—I had it under control."

"Right, 'under control.'" He puts it in finger quotes. *Starflame,* who does that anymore? "Jess would never have given him that much face time. Not to mention he interrupted you."

"It was a great entrance!" I defend. "And it was a crowd-pleaser. Besides, he apologized."

"Get the lovesick out of your ears, Imogen."

I grit my teeth as I feel a blush redden my face. "I am *not* lovesick. I just had a minor brain fart, okay?"

"A brain . . . " He pinches the bridge of his nose and mumbles under his breath, "I should get a raise for this." Then he pushes up his thick black glasses. "Jess—you—have a meet-and-greet in"—he checks his watch—"twenty minutes. We should get lunch, and I'll teach you how she signs her name, and you need to fix your makeup and—"

"Chill, dude."

He shakes his head. "Jess's career is already on the line and I'm here to make sure she doesn't screw up her chances because of some rapscallion look-alike." He stands a little straighter, as if needing the extra height in order to call me names, even though he is *already a full head taller* than me.

Which, point taken. He does. Especially after *that* name-calling.

"Rapscallion?" I echo, keeping my voice even. "That's all you've got? Rapscallion?"

He hesitates, unsure whether I'm just so angry that I've lost all inflection or I'm about to burst out laughing. "It—it sounded fine in my head."

And he looks so uncomfortable and so embarrassed but trying so hard to keep his cool that I just sort of . . . lose it.

Laughter bubbles up through my chest and I double over in hysterics, gasping for breath. "Ohmygod, rapscallion! It's like you're from some eighties fantasy cult classic or something! Ohmygod, my spleen. Where did you get that—your mother's regency novel? 'Hark, you dastardly rapscallion!' What do you say when you're *really* pissed?" I straighten enough to twist my voice into that of a crotchety old man: "'Oy, you rascally kids, get off my lawn!' Oh, you and Pretzel Henry would get along so well!"

And then I bend over into another gasp of laughter.

"It wasn't *that* bad," he mumbles, but there's definitely a red tinge to his cheeks. He folds his arms over his chest and looks away. "And who's Pretzel Henry?"

When I'm finally able to calm down, I wipe the tears from my eyes and blink at the ceiling. "Oh my God, I haven't laughed that hard in ages. My mascara isn't running, is it?" I ask, batting my lashes at him.

He looks into my eyes, and oh—he *is* blushing. He quickly looks away. "No, it's fine. Come on. We should get lunch."

"But shouldn't you text Jess about this first?"

He pauses midturn. "I already did. She'd want to know about Vance—"

"No, I meant about you secretly being an old man in a young body," I say, at which he frowns again.

+10 Disapproval.

"Ha ha. Come on." He turns abruptly and marches out of the stairwell, and I feel a grin tugging at my lips before I can stop it.

"Whatever you say, old man."

He tosses over his shoulder in a startlingly awful Yoda impersonation, "Master Ethan it is to you, young Jedi."

Five minutes later, he peels me up off the floor because I've died and become one with the Force.

And then it hits me—

If the script is real, then Amara is truly, *truly* dead. And that means I've failed. I failed, like I always fail, and our princess is never coming back—

No.

Just because there's a script doesn't mean the fate of the character can't change. Like Agent Coulson in the MCU! Darth Maul in *Star Wars*! Spike in *Buffy*! Freaking angel Castiel in *Supernatural*! Axel in *Kingdom Hearts*! I can go on. It's not unheard of, and I still have time.

I have to.

JESS

"Here," says the muscular guy with the gray lock of hair, handing me a rag full of ice he got from a nearby vendor selling water bottles and shaved ice. I'm sitting against a wall, close to where I bit the ground. "You hit your head pretty hard."

I take the ice pack gratefully and press it against the side of my face. I don't think I have a concussion, but this is *exactly* why I don't do my own stunts. I hiss as the cold cloth touches the growing bruise on my cheek.

How am I going to explain this to Ethan, or Diana, or at the pressers I have after this convention?

Thankfully, I have makeup. I guess.

My pursuers had quickly helped me up from my faceplant and are now squatting beside me. Well, the waifish guy in the witch's hat is leaning on his umbrella, looking down at me as if he can't quite figure out who I am. But I am most definitely not "Monster."

I hate conventions.

"What happened to the Nox King?" asked the burly one to his friend.

Umbrella Guy shrugs. "He jetted as soon as she bit the floor."

"Typical."

I hate conventions.

At this rate, I'm more likely to blow Imogen's cover than find the jerkoff who stole my script, and that has me very annoyed.

PS – Can you guess where I am? A surprise might be coming soon if you can find me!

It's like this person *wants* to be found, and I'm afraid if someone does find them, they'll reveal that the script was mine. Do they want to publicly humiliate me? Sic every living *Starfield* fan on me and drive me off the internet à la Star Wars? They're already on the road to doing that if my Instagram comments are any indication. I can just imagine some greasy dirtbag riling the masses to get me annexed because how dare I even *try* to live up to their dear, beloved Natalia Ford?

Was that their plan all along?

My fingers curl tightly around the ice pack. I can't let these strangers see me lose it. *Breathe.*

The broad guy with the curl of silver hair studies me. "So . . . it's clear you're not Mo . . . "

"But she looks familiar, doesn't she, babe?" asks Umbrella Guy, giving me a long look. He has a jade earring in his right ear and strikingly dark eyes. He twirls his umbrella around his wrist. "You know, if I didn't know better, you kinda look like—"

"I'm no one," I interrupt.

"No one's no one," replies the muscular guy.

"Then it's none of your business," I snap and rise to my feet, gathering my strength even though my cheek is still throbbing and all I want to do is crawl back into my hotel room and watch reruns of *Project Runway*.

Maybe all of this is just one horrendous nightmare, and I'll wake up soon and not have to worry about any of it. The stars will align and I'll be Jessica Stone again, hating *Starfield* but solid in my career. Or maybe *Starfield* will be the nightmare, and I'll wake up—

Someone touches my arm gently, and I whirl around.

It's the burly dude, looking worriedly at me. "Do you need help?"

"Help?" I try not to laugh. "With what?"

The two guys exchange a hesitant look, and I play with the idea that they know what I'm looking for, can magically identify who's leaking my script, but I quickly shove that thought away. As soon as they "help" me, they'll want something in return, guaranteed. Everyone always does.

"Sorry," I tell them, "but I don't even know you. Thanks for the ice pack, I'm fine."

"Wait!" The one in the witch's hat calls after me, and as I turn around to give him a really good tongue-lashing, he holds out Ethan's glasses. They're a little bent, but not broken. "You might need these."

I snatch them out of his hand, slide them on, and leave, the ice pack still pressed firmly against my face.

———————

I FIND I'VE WANDERED TO THE other side of the showroom, where it's a little quieter. I scroll through the Twitter timeline, trying to find a clue who the thief might be. But I'm at a loss. I'm just lucky they haven't yet posted a page with my name on it.

I sink down beside the bathroom near the corner, where a guy with a pretzel stand is humming the *Starfield* theme song.

Of course.

I can't seem to escape *Starfield*, and looking at the latest tweet gets me angrier and angrier the longer I sit here. The *Starfield* side of the internet is exploding with news of General Sond as the new villain.

Vance Reigns.

His agent had been trying to set us up on a date for a while, and I guess now I know why. It'd look like a trading of the mantle, of sorts, from one *Starfield* villain to another.

I'm being replaced—by a *golden knight* no less.

Why do I care? I shut off my phone and drop it between my folded legs. Why do I care so much that *Starfield* announced their sequel villain? It wasn't like I was holding out hope it would be me.

That's silly. I don't *want* it to be me.

I'm Jessica Stone, an Oscar-nominated teenager. I am a serious actor. I am cool, I am coveted, I am professional.

I . . .

What else am I?

"You look like someone who could use a pretzel," says a voice to my right. I glance up to see the pretzel vendor looming over me with an unsalted sample of his wares and a pack of cheesy goop. He motions to the ice pack still pressed against my cheek.

"Oh." I pat down my jeans and realize with a sudden jolt that I don't have any money. Or ID. *Nothing.* I can't remember the last time I didn't have at least my AmEx on me. "I, ah, I'm sorry, I don't have any cash . . . "

"It's free."

"But I'm not that hungry—" My stomach growls and my cheeks get hot. I accept the pretzel. I can't remember the last time I had one. I can't remember the last time I ate in public without a storm of paparazzi on me. It feels surreal, a warm pretzel in one hand and a container of delicious plastic cheese in the other. I ask the man, "Is there any way to repay you?"

"Nah. I don't need the money." He looks out across the showroom. His face seems familiar, but I can't place from where. With that god-awful peppery beard, I can't tell if he's homeless or cosplaying as a lumberjack. "You know, it feels pretty peaceful on this side of the convention."

"I don't understand these people."

He laughs and puts his hands in his pockets. "Haven't you ever loved something so much, you introduced it to your friends?"

I cock my head. "Does Groupon count?"

He laughs again. "Sure, but any TV shows? Video games? Movies?"

"I really liked *Sailor Moon* when I was little, but I grew out of it. These people," I gesture to the crowds, "clearly haven't grown up. *Starfield. Stars Wars. Star Trek. Battlestar* whatever. *Firefly.* I just—I think I'm a little too old for silly sci-fi shows."

"Or," the man says, no longer laughing, "you aren't old enough. Perhaps, young miss, you're still trying to find out who you are, and seeing these fans so adamant about what they love makes you feel like you're missing out on something, but you're too headstrong to admit that maybe you want to be a part of it, too."

"Yeah, sure." I slide up the wall to my feet and stubbornly push up my glasses. "Thanks for the pretzel, erm"—I look at his battered nametag—"Henry. I hope you get a lot of business. Bye now."

He gives me the *Starfield* salute. "Look to the stars!" he calls after me.

Which gives me an idea.

I whirl back around and ask him, "How many years have you been here?"

"Enough," he answers carefully. "Why?"

I take out my phone, and he comes out from behind his pretzel cart. I show him the photo of the leaked script. "Do you recognize anything in the background?"

He frowns and strokes his beard. "No, but . . . " He leans closer and squints at the image. "You know, that kind of looks like Amara's dress. The one in the exhibit." He points to the blurry image of purple glitter in the top corner of the photo.

Holy shit. It *does*.

Hope flickers in my chest. I return the phone to my pocket and with a swift "thank you" I'm speed-walking in that direction, clawing con-goers out of my way. I toss the melted ice pack in the trash and set my sights on the exhibit—the one with the fake *Prospero* ship you can take a photo in and the original costumes from the show.

I keep an eye on the Nox King towering above the booths near the other end of the showroom, where Imogen's parents supposedly are. As long as I stay away, I should be fine.

People crowd inside the exhibit, taking photos of the costumes, murmuring to themselves how magnificent they are, how well kept after twenty-five years. Natalia Ford and David Singh are supposed to do a panel on Sunday to celebrate the anniversary—

And I remember my mortifying run-in with Natalia and I wince.

He's here. I know the thief is here.

I take out my phone once more and begin comparing the angles of costume boxes. There are lines of people waiting to take photos with the costumes, and I think I'm photo-bombing the majority of them.

But when I get to Amara's costume, it makes me pause. It's

mine—well, Natalia's. The dress that launched a thousand cosplays. From one angle it reminds me of Cinderella's dress, but from another it's all points and angles, metallic stitching on the shoulders and across the corset. The folds of the skirt are supposed to billow when the wearer walks—swirling around her feet, full of blues and purples and reds. It is a dress with an entire galaxy sewn into the seams.

I stare a little longer than I should.

And I think—I wonder . . .

How was I ever supposed to live up to that?

The thought startles me, and I hate how true it feels. So many people at this con are passionate about Amara, about the TV series, about the movie. They love it and connect with it in a way I've never connected with anything.

In Hollywood there's two types of films: popular ones and meaningful ones. *Huntress Rising*—the Oscar contender—was a gritty tour de force adapted from an obscure comic book. No one went into that film with any sort of emotional baggage. And even if they did, it was an art film on a low budget. They are award-worthy but not *viewer*-worthy. But being here, hearing these fans celebrate popular films and favorite characters, makes me second-guess that. What is it about those art-house movies that makes them better than *The Last Jedi*, *Black Panther*, or *Starfield*?

I thought all I needed to do to be Amara was read lines and put on a pretty dress, but I failed to see how this princess transformed people's lives in a way my Oscar-nominated role never will.

There were so many expectations woven into this dress before I ever accepted the role.

I tear myself away, angling the phone just so so that—

"Here, kitty kitty," someone calls behind me. I spin around

and come face to face with—

"Amon!" I say, startled, forgetting that I'm supposed to be Imogen.

He glances at me briefly and then looks away. He's rubbing the back of his hands, where there are angry red scratches. "Sorry, can't sign right now. Have you seen a cat?"

My own director doesn't recognize me.

It takes a moment to realize what he asked. "A cat?"

"Yes, yes," he replies impatiently. "Hairless? Looks like some ungodly demon spawn? Never mind. I'll find it." He resituates a stack of papers I assume is the con program under his arm and wanders off. Then I remember that Natalia Ford had a hairless cat when she walked in on my interview. Could it be the same one?

But what would Amon be doing with her cat?

Anyway, I don't see the hairless nightmare *or* any sign of my thief. They're probably long gone by now. But knowing they were *here* helps me feel a little better, even though this is beginning to feel like an impossible quest.

I stand in the exhibit for a moment longer, my gaze finding Carmindor's original uniform. Huh, Darien was right—it *is* a different shade of blue. This one, the original one, is deeper somehow, more plum than navy, so rich that even after twenty-five years it hasn't lost its color.

I bite into the top of my pretzel as I study the uniform when a kid comes up to me. He can't be much older than nine, maybe ten, dressed as Carmindor, and he squints at me with a deep frown.

"You look like Amara," he says decidedly.

My eyebrows jerk up.

He turns to his dad and says, "Doesn't she look like Amara?"

At the sound of the character's name, half the people in the exhibit turn to look at me, and I swallow my mouthful of pretzel with a dry gulp. "No, I'm not—"

"Ah, your meta cosplay of Jessica Stone is amazing!" adds a woman, grinning at me as she takes out her phone. "You even have a SPACE QUEEN beanie on, that's adorable! What do you call your cosplay?"

I hesitate, knowing that if I flee they *will* think I'm—well—*me*, and if I play it off then . . . "Oh, this? It's just Jessica Stone on Vacation."

The woman barks a laugh and snaps a selfie of us. "Love it! Look to the stars!" she adds as she leaves through the exhibit, shoving up the *Starfield* salute. I smile and nod.

Right. Okay.

Time to leave.

Before anyone else can take a photo, I quickly disappear from the exhibit, looking for somewhere to sit and eat my free pretzel, but every bit of the wall is taken by tired con-goers. I shoulder my way to the back exit and out the side of the building, into what looks like a hotel courtyard—a barren space with grass and a sad-looking tree. I find an unoccupied bench and sit down in the quiet to snack on my pretzel and check the texts and emails I missed.

Oh, Ethan texted me a few minutes ago.

ETHAN (5:15PM)

—*Vance Reigns is playing the new villain, if you haven't heard.*

—*All's fine here. Keeping her in check.*

—*Do you have any leads yet?*

"I wish," I murmur, putting my phone back into my pocket. I pry open the container of warm plastic cheese.

About twenty feet away on the grass are two dozen or so cosplayers dressed as Princess Amara (all different kinds, even a Black Nebula version, who seems to be leading the horde). I've heard about these get-togethers—meet-ups, I think Ethan calls them.

How many of them are like Imogen and want to save Amara?

You don't understand, I want to scream at these Amara cosplayers. What about me? How come no one is trying to save *me*? The negative comments on my Insta and Twitter are so loud, I can barely hear anything else in my life. The strangers calling me ugly are so much louder than my own parents telling me I'm beautiful. My mother once said the only thing that can ever truly be *ugly* about a person is how they act, who they are on the inside—whether they're good or rotted to the core.

It seems like there are a lot of people who're rotten.

I wonder if, to some people, I'm one of them.

I twist my lanyard around my fingers, looking across the loading docks to the patch of green on the other side, and the gathering of Princess Amaras. The girl dressed as the Black Nebula Amara shouts the catchphrase "Look to the stars!" and the others shout "Aim. Ignite!" and thrust their hands in the air with the *Starfield* sign.

I once asked Dare why he thought *Starfield* needed a sign— like the Vulcan "live long and prosper" salute, or the Sailor Senshi "I will punish you" hand signs, or that weird *Naruto* run—and he said because everyone needs a universal greeting sometimes.

Starfield's is "You and I are made of stars."

It's a hand sign that says we are the same.

What a novel thought. I wished I believed that.

The cosplayers are part of a photo shoot, absorbing the best thirty minutes of the day just before sundown. They strike all the poses I've had to meticulously learn for the movie's promo images while trapped in a studio in front of a green screen, a fan blowing at my face to feather out my bleached-and-dyed crimson hair as a photographer told me to push my shoulder forward, lean back a little bit. I hated every minute of it.

Or I want to think I did.

But there is this strange, small part of me that wants to know what it's like to be them. These girls who love an image of Amara in their heads. Girls who don't have to worry about conforming to a producer's or a director's or the fans' image of her, or run in heels even though she lobbied—in vain—to wear boots.

I want to know what it's like to . . .

It's silly.

I finish off my pretzel, scooping out the rest of the delicious cheesy goop and shoving it into my mouth. Not having a napkin, I brush my greasy fingers on my jeans. I turn to go back inside the con, but then feel a tap on my shoulder. I turn around, my mouth full of pretzel. It's the girl organizing the photo shoot— Black Nebula Amara—and she smiles when she sees me.

I recognize her now that I can see her face, even without her black glasses.

"I thought that was you sitting on the curb," she says and nudges her head back to the Amaras. "I know this is kind of weird, Jess. Don't worry, I won't tell"—she adds when I give a start of panic—"but would you mind taking a photo of us? I need one for an article I'm doing, and there's no one here and the light's almost gone . . . "

The sunlight is beginning to dip below the Atlanta skyline. I should say no, because if any of those girls finds out that I'm me while I'm supposed to be at a photo op, but . . .

I finish chewing my pretzel and swallow. "Sure. Let's hurry before the sun sets," I say, taking her camera.

"Thank you!" She twirls around and hurries back to the group. They each strike a pose again and I lift the Canon to my eye, through the viewfinder, with the dusky light painting their glittering dresses and armored suits and polished military jackets in the perfect shade of blue, I think I see what Imogen was talking about. There are two dozen Princess Amaras smirking back at me, all of whom look different—different skin colors and body types and sexualities and gender identifications. Princess Amaras who have gone through the Black Nebula and those who led the Nox King's military and those who fell in love with Carmindors and Zorines and Eucis. But they all have one thing in common:

They love who they are as Amara. They love themselves.

I click a few photos and quietly hand the camera back to the organizer. She fixes her crown before pulling the camera strap over her neck as the sun dips below the buildings.

"Just in time—thank you so much. I forgot to bring my tripod and I was kicking myself," she says with a laugh. "You're a life-saver. Really, thanks!"

"My pleasure, Elle," I reply, and head back into the showroom.

———

I RETURN TO ARTISTS' ALLEY. THE showroom hasn't closed, but artists are beginning to pack up and the steady stream of attendees trickles away. I find the aisle with the purple Princess Amara banner and sheepishly walk up to the table.

Harper slams her hand against her chest. "Oh my *God*, you

came back!"

"Um . . . yeah?" I push up my glasses again.

"I thought for sure I'd run you off." Her dark eyes linger on the bruise on my cheek, and I quickly look away. "Did something happen to you?"

"I tripped over a Nox King's tail."

She winces. "That's about the worst way to go."

"Tell me about it." I sink into my chair behind the booth. There are only a handful of Save Amara pins left. Harper's been handing them out all day while I've been gone. That was very . . . nice of her.

I guess she must be good friends with Imogen—or was, before I stepped in. I've been nothing but cold or dismissive to her.

I've been mean and cold to everyone at this con, I realize.

Since when did I start acting like such a witch?

Harper's packing up her things, zipping her pencil case closed and tossing it into a clear bookbag. I pick up one of her prints. It's of Amara and Zorine in a heartfelt embrace, and I can't help but blush seeing a girl with my likeness kissing the likeness of Fiona Oro, who plays Zorine. I hand the print back as I realize she's putting them all into a box under the booth.

I bite my lip. "Can I ask you a question?"

"Sure, why couldn't you?"

"Why do you draw these fanart?"

She shrugs.

At first she doesn't say anything, but then she takes the print of Amara and Zorine out of my hand. "You really don't know?"

"I mean, I might but I've forgotten. Sorry."

She tilts her head and studies me, as if I've surprised her again. It's the same look she gave me earlier, the kind where she isn't sure who she's looking at, but it isn't who she thought. I self-consciously tug on my beanie.

Crap, I'm not good at this Imogen thing at all.

"I mean, you don't have to answer—"

"Mo, it's because I think it's nice to see ourselves represented. If not on-screen, then maybe in an OTP in fanart. Fanfic. It's important to show that people like us exist. That we can be happy."

That we can be.

We.

I'm reminded of Ethan asking me if I was happy. I haven't allowed myself to be in a long time. I've dated who I was told to, and flirted with people who would get me on the cover of magazines, but I've been too busy and too worried about my career to think much about—

Well . . .

Anything else.

"Oh," I say, lacking a better response.

"So," she grins, still so near to me. I'm tempted to lean away but I really don't want to. "Can I ask *you* a question, Imogen?"

I don't know if I want to answer. I don't know if I can. Because I'm beginning to realize that I definitely don't know enough about Imogen to pull this off. I don't even know where she was born. Is Planet Weird too mean? I clear my throat and say nonchalantly, "Yeah, of course."

"Why do *you* like *Starfield*?"

I don't, I want to tell her, but I bite my lip to stop myself from saying that. Partly because I'm Imogen right now, and partly because . . . I remember the feeling I had earlier when I looked through the camera's viewfinder at all of those Amaras just being themselves. The best version of themselves through a character they love and relate to . . .

And I wonder what that's like.

For some inexplicable reason, I want to tell Harper the truth. That I've pretended to be someone for so long, I don't know how to be myself anymore. And maybe I just wanted to stop pretending for a little while. I wanted someone else to squeeze into the name Jessica Stone.

Because it feels wonderful to be in Imogen's shoes. To be anonymous. To be able to sit down on a bench in a hotel courtyard eating a pretzel, alone, without paparazzi snapping photos and the internet asking if I've gained weight. To not have to worry about where my next job will come from, whether it'll be the one to sink my career or if I'll be the dead Princess Amara, like Natalia Ford, for all eternity.

Will I be typecast as one thing for the rest of my life? How many other dead space princesses can there be?

I bite my lip so hard, I feel it going numb. I can't answer her. I don't know how to.

But I can't stay silent either, so I begin to think up a lie when I see a gremlin head poke out from under the booth tablecloth across the aisle. It stares at me with its narrow green slits for eyes—

And then it disappears again.

So Amon *was* looking for Natalia Ford's cat—what was its name? She never goes anywhere without that gremlin-looking thing in her arms. She takes it with her to interviews, she even took it onto *Hello, America* a few weeks ago to promote the re-release of the original *Starfield* series.

Harper glances over, but the cat's already gone. "What?"

"Natalia Ford's cat! Demonlike creature with glowy-green eyes."

"Oh, Stubbles! He's here?"

"Someone was looking for him earlier. I think he's lost," I add, and pop out of my chair, hurrying across to the booth that the cat disappeared underneath.

The artist in the booth glances at me, her long blue hair pulled over her shoulder and spilling down onto her sketchbook as she draws a weird-looking alien from what *appears* to be a video game she really loves.

"Excuse me," I say awkwardly, and point at her booth, "but I think there's a cat under your table."

She gives me a strange look, but then draws up the corner of her tablecloth and gives a start. "*THAT'S A CAT?*"

At the same moment, with a yowl that I can only describe as warlike, Stubbles leaps onto the next booth's table and squirrels across it, knocking over displays and posters as it hops onto the next one, and then the next one, eliciting horrific screams from each unsuspecting artist.

"Stubbles!" I call frantically.

It tears across the aisle, hopping from table to table, and I dodge through the crowd after it.

Then it turns, diving between the aisles, and I quickly run to the other side. Harper has already cut over and blocks the cat from heading the other way. It turns around, skittering under a Cersei Lannister's robes, and pops out the other side with a hiss.

Stupid freaking cat.

As it darts left, I cut across to head it off. It stares me down like the evil green-eyed gremlin it is—

Until a guy adorned with ram horns, wearing nothing but boxers covered with hearts, scoops up the hairless beast with a pillowcase. It jerks and yowls, hissing and spitting in its fabric prison. He holds it out frightfully.

"This, uh, is this yours?" he asks.

"Close enough," I say and gingerly take the pillowcase. I can see claws poking through the fabric. How in the *hell* am I going to get this thing out of this pillowcase?

As if knowing my question, he says, "You can keep the pillowcase."

"Um, thanks."

"No problem," he replies, and leaves me with a squirming bag of angry cat. But now that I have it, what the hell am I supposed to do with it? Natalia Ford hates me!

No, she more than hates me.

If there is a level even lower than hate, the slow and simmering rage of a thousand exploding suns, *that* is how Natalia Ford feels about me.

Harper seems to have the same question. "So, um, do we know where Natalia Ford is?"

"I have no idea—"

Another artist leans over from his booth and says, "Isn't she in the photo ops right now? Jessica Stone's supposed to be over there, too."

Great.

Stubbles howls again, but this time it sounds strangely pitiful. Harper shrugs and says, "I've already started packing up, so I can close down my booth and we can head over there."

"Really, you don't have to go—"

"Are you kidding?" she says with a laugh. "This might be my only chance to see Natalia Ford in the flesh. It's going to be amazing."

I don't want to burst her bubble and tell her that *my* run-in with Natalia was a good deal less than amazing, but I just smile and say "okay" before I follow her back to the booth to close up shop. She finishes putting away her art pieces and thanks her neighbor—a guy who looks the part of a starving artist, all gaunt face and jutting bones—for looking after the booth while she was gone. After throwing a thin blue blanket over her table, she turns to me and says, "Okay, let's go find Princess Amara."

It doesn't take long to find her. In the photo-ops area there are standing posters with the names of who is in which black-curtained area, and lines that wrap around half of the large room. My—I mean, Jessica Stone's—is one of those lines. I hope Imogen can handle it. *Ethan's with her, of course she can.*

I don't have to worry about her not sounding like me, either. She's eerily talented at mimicking my voice.

The meet-and-greet begins in a few minutes. Good. I can just keep my head down, pop over to Natalia's line, and then pop out again long before anyone notices that I might look slightly too similar to the girl who plays the new Princess Amara.

No one has recognized me yet, at least. People have taken a second look, but I think my disguise is well behind the shield of *Jessica Stone Wouldn't Be Here.* Which I am grateful for, but also . . .

It wouldn't be so bad, you know.

If Jessica Stone *was* the kind of person you'd see here. I mean, at a nerd convention, not being in two places at once. That would still be awkward no matter what universe I'm in.

Natalia Ford is gathering her purse to leave, her meet-and-greet over, when Harper and I find her.

A security guard stops us before we can get in—her private security, I might add. Tall, burly guy. Very mustached.

"I, um, I think you lost something," I shout to Natalia.

She stops and turns around, her eyes narrowing. I hold up the pillowcase. As if on cue, Stubbles lets out a low growl of discontent. Natalia gasps and rushes to me, pushing past security, to plunge her arms into the pillowcase and gather up the cat. The creature begins to purr the second she clutches the furless night-mare to her chest.

I don't understand this animal at all.

"I know, I know. I've missed you, too," Natalia coos to the rumbling demon cat, and then she says to Harper, "Thank you for bringing her back." She doesn't even look at me, even though I'm the one who delivered the cat. "Amon was supposed to be looking after her, but all he ever looks at is his phone, apparently. I don't know what I'd do without her, so thank you."

Then she finally gives me a glance—strange, almost like she can see right through my disguise—and turns away, disappearing underneath the black curtain in the back and out of sight. Her assistant, a harrowed-looking college girl with large pink glasses and pink-tipped blond hair, quickly thanks us and follows her boss.

Harper and I stand there for a long moment.

I look at the claw marks on my arms.

Stubbles is a demon cat, there are no two ways around it.

And then Harper starts to laugh. A loud, echoing guffaw that makes her clutch her sides. "We actually chased a cat! That has to be the most ridiculous thing I've ever done at ExcelsiCon," she says, wiping the corners of her eyes so her mascara doesn't start to run. "Well, now that *that* drama's taken care of, what do you say to a party?"

I start. "A what?"

"A *party*. My friends call it the Stellar Party. It's space themed. We do it every year in a hotel room. We drink a little, sing some karaoke, stuff like that."

"Oh, no. I don't do karaoke."

And also, I need to find the thief who stole my script. The Twitter account has been quiet for a long time, and I'm beginning to worry.

Besides, what if my cover got blown at this party? I'd end up on the cover of every national newspaper in the country—or at least every gossip magazine. I realize I'm not important enough for, like, the *New York Times* . . .

Am I?

"Come on," Harper eggs, and she's smiling in this way that makes my stomach twist. "You can stop trying to save Amara for two seconds. Take a breather. Enjoy life. You deserve it. Our princess can fend for herself for an evening."

I hesitate.

If I don't go to the party, there is a definite chance I'll just be sitting around my hotel room, waiting for the next tweet. Maybe if I hang out with a bunch of *Starfield* geeks, I could ask around to see if anyone's heard rumors of someone leaking the script.

Yeah, that's a good reason.

It's a lot better than the other one in my head: that it feels nice to talk with someone who doesn't see me as Jessica Stone, who doesn't want anything from me, who is nice and honest and very pretty. And I don't even want to think about the way she puts her hands into her dress pockets, leaning back as if to get a better look at me, or how she didn't have to come with me to herd the cat but she did anyway. And how, even though I was kinda dreadful to her in the beginning, she's still sticking around.

It's because to her you're Imogen, her friend. She's being nice to you because you aren't Jess.

That makes my stomach twist further. I clear my throat and cross my arms over my chest. "Well, as long as you don't make me sing."

She crosses a pinky over her heart. "Hope to die," she says

with that same smile, and for the first time I realize why it's so enthralling. Because there's adventure tucked into the corner of her mouth.

The kind of adventure I want to go on.

"Okay," I say, "count me in."

IMOGEN

WE ENDED UP STEALING SANDWICHES FROM the Green Room and eating in a vacant stairwell. The tuna melts weren't that bad, actually, and Ethan had mints to cover up our dreaded fish breath. He also had a pen in his pocket, and a small notepad, so I could practice Jessica's signature.

"Are your pockets bigger on the inside?" I tried to joke, but he just rolled his eyes.

"I don't have *that* much in my pockets."

"Maybe you're a magician—Merlin, is that you, old man?"

"Shut up and practice the J again. Loop it more—no, like *this*," he instructed, scooting close to me. He took my writing hand into his much larger one. He guided the pen into the perfect loopy J. "There, see?"

His hand was very warm, and he was very close, leaning against my shoulder. Much closer than he'd ever been to me before. Too close, really, for someone who hated me. He noticed a moment later, and quickly let go of my hand and scooted to the other side of the step. "We should go back," he said gruffly, standing, and even though I hadn't perfected my loopy J, we returned to the showroom. He didn't know where the meet-and-greet area was, but I did, so I led him to the bottom of the Marriott and into one of the bigger ballrooms, and that's where we find ourselves now. My head's beginning to itch under my fake hair. "My wig's hot and I hate it," I say.

"Tough."

"And the hair's sticking to my neck," I whine.

Ethan rolls his eyes. He's worriedly twisting a silver ring on his left middle finger and peeks out from behind the curtain. After a moment he pulls his head back in and curses. "There's a long line."

"Well, it *is* for Jessica Stone."

"What if someone realizes you're a fake? Your contacts slip? Someone pulls on your wig—"

I put a hand on his shoulder. "Relax, old man. I'm a professional."

He closes the curtain and levels a glare down at me. And I'm reminded of the moment in the stairwell when we were this close before, and alone, and it is *bad*. Because beneath his thick glasses, his eyelashes are dark, and underneath those eyelashes are his eyes, which remind me of puddles of black ink, the kind that gets on a writer's fingers. His hair is now messy from being run through too many times, and I detest that thin set of his mouth, how it makes him look so self-righteous and—

How can someone so infuriating be so handsome?

The thought repulses me, and I quickly avert my eyes. The volunteer operating the camera hurries into the photo booth, pulling back her dark hair. "Sorry, sorry! Hi, I'm your volunteer, Savvy. Are you ready to start?"

"Yes," I quietly reply, relieved that there's someone else in the booth with us.

Ethan shoves his hands into his pockets and leans on a stool in the corner, looking down to his . . . superhero shoes. No, like, literally. They have the Captain America shield in little dots all over them. And then I'm just thinking of Ethan punching Nazis, and that's kinda hot, actually.

Nope, don't go down that road. He and Jess are probably a thing, which is why he's so mean to me. Because he'd rather be with her and—

WHY AM I EVEN CONSIDERING THIS?

"Just remember," he tells me quietly, so the photographer can't hear, "sandbag any questions you don't know. Be polite. Do *not* talk about yourself. Say only 'Oh, thank you for coming! It was so nice to meet you! Have fun at the con!'" he says in a terrible falsetto, and I grimace. "That's it."

"You know, I—I mean, Jess—don't sound like that, right?"

"I'm making a point."

"I get it, don't worry."

Then the volunteer handling my line lets the first person into the booth, and I pull a smile over my cherry-gloss lips—and clam up. I don't know how to pose with fans, and I'm not sure which side Jess favors—

"Left," Ethan reminds gently after the first fan. "Always left."

"Like Captain America."

"Dork," he murmurs, but I catch him fighting a smile before the next fan comes in.

Victory.

So I pose to the left, and smile, and after the twentieth fan my cheeks are beginning to hurt. But I become a little more confident. And with each photo it gets a little easier. The hour is a whirlwind of dudes leaning too close, fangirls flipping out over meeting their princess, and cosplayers asking me to strike ridiculous poses and laughing over *Starfield* jokes. It's both wonderful and terrifying. I don't want to slip up. I don't want to make a mess of things.

I soak in every moment.

There are girls wearing my #SaveAmara pins and guys flashing me the *Starfield* salute and begging me to Nox-conscript them and *duh*, you *know* I will. I meet fan after fan just like me, and I want to reach out and tell them that I'm just like them. That we are more alike than they think. I try to tell them in my smile, in the way I pose, in the handshakes and the hugs . . .

How can Jess not like this? How could she want to trade this—this feeling—for anything else in the world?

After the last fan leaves, Ethan ducks into the booth and hands me a water bottle, but my head is still buzzing. I drink half before I say, "That was amazing. Did you see the cute little girl in Carmindor cosplay?"

"Mm, she was cute, yeah," he replies.

"And the guy who proposed to me! I tried so hard not to laugh, but *starflame!* does he need to work on his delivery."

"Mm-hmm."

"And the Disney Princess Noxians and the Jedi Amara and—it was all so cool! I've never done anything like that before in my life!" I laugh and twirl around. "I haven't been this happy since season six of *Voltron*! What?" I realize that he's watching me with a strange look in his eyes. Not, like, a bad strange, but definitely not Old Man Ethan, either. It almost looks like . . . "What's that look for?"

He doesn't realize he's staring at me until I speak, and then he clears his throat and turns away. "Nothing. I was—nothing. You look like a fool twirling around. Jess doesn't do that."

"Oh, right." I pass my hand in front of my face; one moment I'm smiling and the next I'm wearing Jess's nothing-makes-me-smile look. "Is this better?"

"Much." When we get to the end of the hallway, he says, "May I request a favor?"

"Why yes, old man, you may."

He glares at the nickname but then sighs in concession. "There's a panel starting in ten minutes over on the main stage. I'd like to go to it."

"Oh, you mean the D&D live podcast?"

His eyes widen. "You . . . know what the panel is?"

"Oh come *on*, I'm like the queen of ExcelsiCon over here. I know everything happening in my domain." I throw my hand out across the hallway, indicating the rest of the con. "Everything the nerd funk touches is my kingdom—"

"That's gross."

"But true," I point out, and he agrees. I sigh and shrug, unwittingly crossing my fingers behind my back. "Fine. Just leave me to go back to the hotel *alone*. Have fun with the tres horny bois."

He brightens so much that he almost looks charming—almost—before whirling around and shouting "Thank you!" as he runs down the hallway. "And *please* don't stop for the paparazzi!"

And then he's gone.

I uncross my fingers.

And I smile.

Because without any sort of supervision, I can finally break a rule, and if Vance Reigns is gonna take me out tonight, I have to look pretty for it. No, I have to look *Jessica Stone* pretty.

And he wants to talk about the Save Amara initiative.

With him on my side, I'll have double the star power.

Turning happily on my heels, I head out onto the skybridge. Besides, Ethan definitely likes Jess. I can tell by the way I caught him looking at me while I was posing for pictures with a seven-year-old Carmindor, the softness of his gaze, the curl of his lips upward ever so slightly. He must've forgotten for a second that I wasn't the real Jess. Those looks are probably only for her.

That makes me strangely bitter, and I'm not sure why.

He's right about the paparazzi, however. They're waiting on the skybridge when I get there and attempt to ask me questions, but I ignore them and walk into the hotel lobby. Are they going to follow me all the way up to the room?

But then a tall, broad black man steps between me and the two trailing paps. In a deep rumble of a voice he asks them to leave. They begin to give him trouble until they see the PRIVATE STAR SECURITY patch on his shirt; then they do a quick U-turn out of the lobby.

"They giving you trouble, Miss Stone?" he asks, as if I'm supposed to know this towering goliath of a man.

I open my mouth, close it, open it again.

I'm saved, thankfully, by a familiar voice. "Hey, Lonny!" Darien calls. "Sorry it took us so long. Elle didn't know what color Converses to wear."

He and his girlfriend, Elle Wittimer, cross the lobby when Darien recognizes me with a soft smile. "Hey! Nice to see you again. This is my friend, Lonny Johnson, head of Private Star Security," he says, motioning to the muscular man. "He's the one in charge of ExcelsiCon's security this year. I probably owe my life to him a few times over. He used to be my bodyguard."

"Still miss it sometimes," Lonny replies.

"Really?"

"No." The big guy checks his watch. "And we're going to be late if we don't get going. Antonio will kill me if I miss dinner again."

Elle laughs. She *is* really pretty—those online smear campaigns lied about absolutely everything. Her hair is box-dyed the perfect shade of Amara red, and her eyes are hazel behind clear glasses. She's wearing a subtle *Starfield* T-shirt dress and sparkly Converses. She looks over at me and says, "Would you want to come?"

Yes. But then I remember Vance Reigns asking me to dinner, and it feels like the Hulk has split me in half. *Starflame*, I wish I had a body double right now.

I put on a plastic smile. "Oh, no, I can't," I tell her, trying not to sound like part of my soul has been ripped out of my body. "Thank you, though."

"You can always call if you change your mind," Darien replies, folding his fingers through Elle's, and they follow Lonny out of the hotel and onto the Atlanta street, where they get into a black car and drive away.

I stand there, wishing I'd gone with them and simultaneously missing Milo and Bran—and *Harper.* I've known Harper for years on the internet and what do I do? Let Jess pretend to be me and meet her IRL. I hope Jess didn't bungle it. I hope Harper doesn't hate her—um, me. They'll be going to the Stellar Party tonight, and I wish I could go.

But you have that rad date with Vance, I remind myself. Even though I don't know how to contact him. Could he just call the hotel phone? Yeah, surely.

Right?

I force a pep back into my step, telling myself that I'm coming down with a case of the con crud; it's not that I'm missing my friends and having massive FOMO while I dig around my purse for my keycard. It's fine. I'll just go back to my room and, I don't know, watch episodes of *Starfield*? Browse Tumblr's #sheith and #carmindeuci tags? Play Pokémon Go! around the lobby? I have a few lures left . . .

I press the button to summon the elevator and glance down at my phone. Nothing. I thought someone would've texted me today at *least*. The #SaveAmara tags are old. No one is talking about it right now.

I make it back to my room, plop down on the bed, and stare at the hotel phone. Vance will call me. Yeah.

I know he will.

JESS

THE PARTY IS . . . NOT WHAT I EXPECTED. I'm not sure what I was thinking when I agreed to go with Harper, but it definitely didn't involve a gender-bent Elsa and Captain Marvel rapping to the *Pokémon* rap, or a green-haired fashion designer and her girl-friend modeling cosplay on a wiener dog. Sure, I thought some-one would be singing "I'm Looking for a Hero" while everyone else tried to ignore them, but this is different.

There isn't a bouncer at the door or a DJ spinning sick tunes. There aren't fancy shrimp cocktails or caviar toasts making the rounds on platters balanced by dour-looking servers. This party is in a hotel suite—I don't know whose, but hopefully it's some-one Harper knows—with about twenty people. There's colorful ribbons strung across the walls and plastic wrap over the lights to make them different colors and glowsticks hanging from the ceiling. One of the lamps has been replaced by a blacklight that makes my shoestrings glow, and on the kitchenette bar is a wall of liquor bottles and sodas.

I'm not old enough to drink, I think, and then I realize that neither is anyone else.

This isn't a party so much as a gathering of friends, and I know absolutely no one. Harper invited me but we're not really friends, and I'm praying that none of these people know Imogen.

I am incredibly out of my element.

If I would've told my morning self that I'd be going to a con party that evening, I would have laughed. I can't remember the last time I went to a party that wasn't black-dress or cocktail appropriate. Or a party where I wasn't expected to be Jessica Stone, hugging the arm of some up-and-coming star to bolster his fame (and perhaps his ego). Or the last pool I floated in where I didn't have to suck in my stomach or make connections over finger foods or dodge paparazzi on the way out.

This feels like . . . a dream. Whether it's a good or a bad one, I honestly have no idea.

My phone vibrates in my back pocket, and I look at the name. Ethan. Probably to ask what I'm doing, whether I'd lost a screw, what my plan was, why I shouldn't do this—and maybe if I answer him, I won't regret this later.

Will I regret this later?

Harper turns to me and arches a single eyebrow—why is she so good at that? It's a look that makes gooseflesh ripple across my skin. I want to study it. I want to trace the curve of her brow and the slight uptick of her mouth.

She is curious, and I am Alice falling into the rabbit hole.

"You look like you've never been to a party before." She leans against my ear to be heard above the ear-bleeding karaoke. "Relax, you're with friends."

"*My* friends?" I ask, trying not to sound too alarmed.

She shrugs. "Maybe? Were you in the Carminara circle on Tumblr?"

"That still sounds like an Italian recipe to me."

She giggles, and her breath across the small hairs on the back of my neck sends a shiver down my spine. "Come on, let me introduce you."

"No need to introduce me, I already met her," interjects a soft voice, the timbre warm and rich, and a young man steps up to greet us. Oh, no. Pointed witch's hat. Umbrella. Long flowing red robe. His hair is painted now with a shock of gold that accentuates his ebony skin. He was with the beefcake earlier. The one who thought I was Imogen.

Oh *no*.

He outstretches a hand. "But we didn't have a chance to trade names. Bran."

I accept it with a little hesitation. What do I say?

What *can* I say?

"This is Imogen," Harper fills in.

He cocks his head a little, and then smiles, as if he knows my secret. No, he *does* know my secret. "Hey, babe," he calls behind him to the muscular guy—the one who called me Monster. The room is beginning to spiral. "Your sister's here—"

"Brother!" I cry forcefully, taking Bran's shoulder to force him around as I go to greet the tall guy. This is Imogen's *brother*?

I shepherd both guys into one of the back bedrooms and slam the door.

Bran pushes his hat out of his face and sips loudly from his SOLO cup. Not the red plastic kind, but a SOLO movie cup, with Alden Ehrenreich's and Chewbacca's faces on the front.

I exhale a calming breath and try to explain: "Look, I'm filling in for your sister while she does something for me, okay? Can you two play along?"

Bran and Beefcake exchange the same look, and then Beefcake says, "You didn't murder her, did you?"

"What? No. Why would I—"

"Because that would be really uncool."

"I didn't *murder* her," I reinforce, "but I will murder you two if you blow my cover." I give Beefcake another look. "Or *try* to. Listen, just trust me and play along, okay?"

"Then what's my sister doing for you?"

Ah. Of course he would ask that. I try to think up a good excuse, but I'm running on four hours of sleep and am lacking all creativity. They'd probably see through it, anyway, and then text Imogen to get the real story.

Defeated, I pull off my beanie and glasses. "I'm Jessica Stone."

Bran whistles low. "Have you been rehearsing that?"

"What?"

They exchange another look before Beefcake says, "We kinda knew who you were since our run-in earlier. I mean, the glasses and beanie obviously work, but I know Monster. She's my sister. And she definitely doesn't wear glasses. But she *does* look a lot like you."

I stare at them, thinking of nothing but the insurmountable horror of them telling everyone they know. Because who wouldn't? "Did you tell the paparazzi?"

Beefcake looks stunned. "Why would we do that?"

"It'd be the story of the week."

"We're not like that," Bran says. "We'll keep your secret, and I know for a fact that Harper doesn't know you're, well, *you*."

"But you should tell her," adds Beefcake.

This can't be that easy. I look at the two of them, but they seem sincere enough. Could my secret really be safe?

Then Beefcake stretches out his hand and says, "Let's start over. I'm Milo Lovelace, Monster's younger brother, and this is my boyfriend, Bran Simons."

"You are very muscular for a Milo," I comment, and shake his hand. His grip is strong, like Dare's.

"I'll take that as a compliment," Milo says with a laugh. "You shouldn't keep Harper waiting. And, before you worry, the shiner on your face doesn't look that bad."

"Thanks?"

We rejoin the party. Bran offers me a drink in a red Solo cup. This is like a scene straight out of every teen movie I've ever seen. "Drink? It's Kara's specialty—she's the one hosting the party. We call it the Oh No."

"Oh no," I comment, dreading it more than a little.

Harper laughs. "That's the point!"

"I'm good," I say, pushing the cup back toward Bran. "I, um, don't drink."

His black eyebrows—dusted with glitter—shoot up. "Seriously?"

"It's a personal thing," I amend, because in truth I wouldn't mind a drink to calm my nerves, but I don't know any of these people.

Even though my secret is safe with Bran and Milo, my PR senses are tingling. Every one of these people has a phone. With a camera. They can snap a picture and send it to the highest bidder, and then I'll wake up to the headline JESSICA STONE INTOXICATED BY THE NORMAL LIFE? or some such nonsense.

I'm lucky that the room is dark and no one actually thinks *the* Jessica Stone would be here. I just look like someone who *looks like* Princess Amara, too strange to be Imogen but not quite Jessica Stone either.

Somewhere in the middle, that's where I teeter dangerously. One slip and everyone will find out.

"Well, then you'll be great company with Harper. She also

isn't drinking tonight. Meanwhile," Bran says, then downs the drink he offered me and thrusts up his hands. "Whoo! ELSA! YES, YOU!" He turns to the gender-bent Elsa and Captain Marvel as they finish their Pokémon rap and challenges Elsa to "The Story of Tonight" from *Hamilton*.

Harper shakes her head. "Oh No is way more vodka than common sense."

"Why aren't you drinking?"

She gestures to the rest of the party. "I've learned my lesson: don't drink unless you want to wake up with regrets, and I have *way* too many commissions to do tomorrow. Come on, let me introduce you to some people."

And she does. I'm used to memorizing faces and names quickly, since most of my social outings involve a lot of meet-and-greets and work-related introductions. Harper's friends are people who'll probably never wear Gucci gowns or get endorsements from ridiculously fake diet-pill companies, but their fingers are ink-stained and their smiles are genuine, and I wish they were the kind of people who *did* get those endorsements instead. They're people I couldn't have met if I were Jessica Stone, because they would think they didn't need to talk with me to know me. They would just assume they know me already. Jessica Stone.

"Are you the one who chased Natalia's cat earlier?" asks the green-haired fashion designer.

Harper laughs. "Guilty as charged."

"So it *was* Stubbles?"

"Sadly," I mutter into my cup of water and the green-haired girls laughs.

"Oh! I was wondering, Harper. Do you still have that print of Darielle at your booth? I keep meaning to buy it and I swear I will this time."

"Please don't call them Darielle, it's weird," says her girlfriend, who's holding the wiener dog. He looks happy in a sparkly pink tutu and spandex leotard, his tongue lolling out as he tries to taste whatever's in her drink. "Frank, *stop*. You don't want Oh No."

"What's wrong with Darielle, love?" the green-haired girl asks, sounding wounded.

Her girlfriend pushes her purple glasses up her nose with the hand holding the Oh No. "Stop trying to make fetch happen."

"I'm *going* to make it happen."

I agree with the girlfriend. Darielle is *very* weird. Almost as weird as Carminara. Why do people smoosh couples' names together, anyway?

Harper laughs. "I think I have a few prints left—stop by tomorrow? I'll reserve one for you. What do you want that print for anyway?"

"Because their anniversary is tomorrow," the green-haired girl says, "and you really did my costume design justice. You have no idea how many times I pricked my finger sewing that dress together on the way here last year. Elle might be a lot of things, but a good driver she is not."

The girl holding the dog agrees. "Elle failed her driver's test twice."

"How do you know Elle?" I ask.

"Oh! Sorry," Harper says. "I forgot to introduce you." She points to the green-haired girl. "This is Sage. She sells custom nerdy T-shirts."

"We are right beside the huge Nox King statue this year," Sage says, grinning. "Imogen, your parents are so cool."

"They're pretty rad," Harper agrees. I just nod because I guess they are. Next, Harper stretches her hand to the blond-haired girl holding the dog. "And this is Sage's girlfriend, Calliope. Cal is

Elle's stepsister, right?"

"Yeah, married in. I'm a twin, so I'm *not* the one from all the Geekerella drama last year." She pushes her purple glasses up again, adding, "I'm the *good* stepsister."

"I wouldn't want to meet the bad one," I say with a laugh because I've heard the stories from Dare.

Apparently she's a monster—and not in the Imogen sort of way.

"Trust me, she's sworn off cons for the rest of her life after what happened last year," Cal assures. She lifts the fat wiener dog just enough for him to look at me with his pitiful beady black eyes. "And this sir here is Mr. Frank. He's our model."

Frank shakes his head, ears slapping the sides of his face, and sticks out a pink tongue. He tries to nose into Cal's drink again, so she sighs and excuses herself, saying that he must be thirsty. "It was nice to meet you, Imogen."

I smile and reply, "You, too."

"Swing by our booth and we'll give you a shirt. Oh, and honey?" She gently touches Sage on the shoulder. "Stay as long as you want, but I'm going to take this boy and retire to our room. This music's too loud for both of us, I think." Cal stretches up on her tiptoes and plants a kiss on Sage's mouth.

I don't mean to stare but their kiss is so simple and easy, like saying *see you later*, that I don't think any thought was put into it.

I wish I knew what that was like.

We spend a few more minutes talking with Sage about her first year in college and her big plan for a clothing line—geeky with a dash of the eccentric. I've heard Dare talk about her a few times, but I never paid attention. Maybe I should have.

I never paid attention to a lot of things. It wasn't part of Jessica Stone's image.

I try to picture Harper in one of my settings, gilded parties and stuffy cocktails, but the image is blurry, like a camera lens that doesn't want to focus. Meanwhile, I feel like a weed in a flowerbed, somewhere I don't belong, afraid I'll be found out and plucked away. Harper . . . she looks happy.

Happy.

I look away, remembering Ethan's question.

Sage and Harper are gossiping about some YouTuber they both know, someone who is bad news, but I can't get a read on why before Bran calls Harper's name over the karaoke speaker. The entire room quiets, and she turns expectantly toward the stage.

Bran jabs his finger at her. "I challenge you!"

Harper puts her hands on her hips. "To *what*?"

He extends the mic and wiggles his eyebrows. "To a duet-off."

She rolls her eyes. "You can't handle my talent, Bran."

"Chicken!"

"You know that's a lie. I've already beaten you three times."

Bran gives an aggravated sigh. "Then duet-off with your friend!"

This time Harper barks a laugh. "No way, she wouldn't—"

"I'll do it."

Her eyebrows shoot up.

I'm not this bold, am I? No—yes. Maybe. Once upon a time. Before I had to fold myself into Jessica Stone. And now that I'm not, my bent edges are beginning to unfurl as slow and steady as a butterfly's wings.

The view seen through the lens of Elle's camera haunts me.

Are you happy? Ethan's question reverberates in my head.

I want to find the answer.

I take Harper by the hand and pull her across the room to the karaoke corner, between a throng of cosplayers dressed as gender-bent Disney princes and princesses (Elsa is among them). Bran hands us two microphones.

"Are you sure about this?" Harper asks, hesitant. Her eyes dart around the room.

"Are you scared?" I challenge, and moment by moment, Jessica Stone unravels like a piece of yarn caught on a snag. The room is loud and I can hear all of the songs in my head—

No. One song.

Bran hands me an iPad; I quickly select the tune and hand it back.

Harper eyes me curiously. "What did you pick?"

I smile at her. "You'll see."

The sweet trill of a violin rushes over the karaoke speakers. The view through the camera lens sharpens. I'm not supposed to really know this song. I'm not supposed to care. I don't, do I?

Her eyes glitter. "I knew you'd pick this."

I want to believe it's true as the words to a song filled with perfect notes begin to spin over the TV screen. I don't need to look at the lyrics. They're as familiar as the fit of Amara's corset, and the pinch of her heels, and the heavy tiara in her hair.

As the music begins, I remember the Amaras posing on the grass, and the passion in Imogen's voice as she spoke of saving a lost princess, and the familiar exuberance in Dare's face whenever he talks about this stupid show . . .

Most people only know the opening thirty seconds of the *Starfield* theme song, "Ignite the Stars," but in a secret all my own, I've turned up the song a thousand times in my dented bumblebee-yellow Volkswagon Beetle and let the lyrics spill out from the windows into the infinite expanse of sky and clouds and stars—

I've never seen the TV series, but I've most definitely listened to the soundtrack.

But what if someone finds out? What if someone is filming? whispers that voice in the back of my head, and I miss the first word, but Harper saves it, singing in that brash and bold way she seems to do everything. She glances over, daring me to join in.

At the first bridge, she mouths, "Chicken."

Like *hell* I'm chicken.

When the second stanza starts, I catch the words first, singing about all of the constellations and stars in the night sky, and being brave, and seeing your friends until the end of the line. Living boldly. Burning bright and lighting a way in the dark.

Igniting the stars.

I mean, I wish I could tell you it's like *High School Musical* where we absolutely slay karaoke but . . . well. By the end of the song, we're almost in tears because neither of us can sing and we've about broken everyone's eardrums, but we howl the last note and mime the slick drum solo at the end—

And then the song dies, and the room crashes into silence. I've never done that before—just let myself have fun. Be uncool.

I'm wheezing so hard, I can't even laugh anymore, holding my sides because it hurts to breathe.

"That was SO BAD!" Bran cries from the crowd. "You should feel ashamed!"

Harper presses two fingers to her lips and blows a kiss to the crowd. I mimic her and we drop our microphones, quickly vacating the stage before someone throws something at us. She wipes her eyes with the back of her hand as we escape to the balcony and close ourselves outside.

"We were horrible!" she gasps, unable to stop laughing.

"But it was worth it," I reply.

We're grinning like two idiots.

Oh God, how I want to just be a part of this strange universe.

But you are Jessica Stone, says that voice in the back of my head, and I wish I could shove it into a box and bury it. *There is no universe where this exists.*

But then the other half of me, the part that remembers the look of all those Amaras through the camera lens, the contagiousness of Dare's enthusiasm before each take we filmed, the passion behind Imogen's eyes when she talked about saving Amara . . .

The view of letting go. Of being yourself.

That part of me whispers, *Or this could be the best idea of your life.*

"Imogen," she says quietly, and goosebumps prickle up on my skin because, even though it's not my name, she means me. The real me. Not the me behind the veneer of Jessica Stone. I like the sound of it.

And I like the sound of us.

My phone dings, and at first I try to ignore it. But then it dings again.

"Are you going to get that?" she asks.

"It's just Twitter," I say dismissively, and then I snap out of my daze.

It's Twitter.

I pull my phone out of my back pocket and check the notification. Oh no. I think I might just vomit.

The thief posted another screenshot of the script.

@starfieldscript337
I'm happy you guys are loving this. Tomorrow, we'll show you how legit it is. ✌ #ExcelsiCon

GENERAL SOND lifts CARMINDOR'S chin. CARMINDOR struggles against his bindings. A video screen comes to life behind them.

                    GENERAL SOND
          That is Velaris Six, one of
          your colony planets on the
          edge of the Federation.
          About six million people,
          wouldn't you say?

A beam of black and purple light hits the
planet. Then Velaris Six fractures apart.

CARMINDOR stares at it in shock.

                    CARMINDOR
          NO!

                    GENERAL SOND
          And now there are none.

The Council politely applauds.

                    CARMINDOR
          You killed them all of
          them.

                    GENERAL SOND
          Every one of them. Their
          leaders refused to conscript
          to the Path of the Sun, and
          so I gave them my judge-
          ment. This will happen,
          again and again, thanks
          to the powers given to me
          by the Black Nebula -- no,
          gifted to me. Every planet
          that refuses to conscript
          will be terminated.
                    (pauses)
          Unless the Federation
          Prince shows them the way.

```
            CARMINDOR
    You want me to become a
    mindless follower?
```

GENERAL SOND smiles, and it's so deceiving
because it is earnest.

```
            GENERAL SOND
    I merely want to save you,
    my Prince, because no one
    else will.
```

My hands are shaking. Somehow it feels like a threat. No, I *know* it is. And this time there's no clues, no signifiers. It's just a cropped photo of the script. Whoever the thief is, they're learning—and that means I have even less chance of finding them.

I'm ruined.

Harper lays a concerned hand on my shoulder. "Imogen, are you okay?"

I look up and I want to scream that I'm not Imogen. That I'm about to be no one, the girl who leaked the *Starfield* sequel script and no Hollywood studio would ever work with her again. My career will be over.

But I can't tell her that because she thinks I'm someone else.

She says softly, surprising me, "Are you hungry?"

"I don't have any money with me," I reply tightly. I can't look at her.

"Lucky for you I am also very, very broke. C'mon, we haven't had dinner yet."

She takes my hand—her fingers folding between mine—and drags me in from the balcony and out of the Stellar Party, knowing before I even said anything that I was trying not to fall apart.

HARPER FISHES AROUND IN HER BACKPACK for her keycard and lets us in. We aren't even in the same hotel anymore, but one adjacent to where I'm staying. It's a modest room, like most are, I guess; there are two double beds and a minifridge and a pretty outdated TV on a dresser. I can tell from the suitcases strewn across the room and the bathroom full of shampoos and straighteners and toiletries that she's rooming with three other women, but they're all gone.

"I hope you're hungry," she says as she dumps her purse in the doorway and walks over to her suitcase.

I don't exactly know what kind of food is supposed to be in a suitcase until she unzips it to reveal a jumbo-pack of those ninety-nine-cent ramen noodle cups. She asks me to fill the coffeemaker carafe—after washing it out—so I do that while she pulls the desk out from the wall and sets it up as a table, the edge of one of the beds serving as a bench.

My mind is still buzzing with the new script leak. I don't want to think about it—can't think about it. If I do, I fear I may lose all hope.

This is impossible. Why am I here? Pretending to be Imogen? It doesn't make sense anymore. I'll never find the thief. But I don't want to be Jess again yet.

I pour the water into the coffeemaker and turn it on.

"Make yourself at home," she tells me, but I'm not exactly sure how to do that. I feel like strange sharp edges right now, catching on everything I rub against. So I just sit down at the table that she prepared. "Do you want anything to drink? We have . . . " She pops open the minifridge and assesses the contents. "Bottled water, sparkling champagne—but oh, you're underage, aren't you? Seventeen, right?"

"Nineteen," I say without thinking, and then bite my lip. I shouldn't have corrected her. I should've just said yes, but . . .

"Oh!" She laughs and shoots me a look. "Eighteen."

"Really?"

"Yeah, but it's weird. Since I'm so, you know, internet famous quote-unquote," she says, "because of my trash Tumblr, everyone expects me to be thirty or something. It's like we can't be successful young."

"Or if we are successful young, it's through a fluke or luck or happenstance and not hard work—and yeah, some of it *is* luck or a fluke, but not all of it. You have to have at least a little talent, too."

"Unless you're a Kardashian," Harper deadpans.

I snort, having met the youngest of them. "I'll have a Diet Coke if you have one?" I say instead.

She hands me one from the minifridge. The coffeemaker begins to hum and drip hot water into the pot. She tears open the noodle cups and picks out chopsticks and a plastic fork from her bag, arranging them on the table in front of me. She's so thorough. I could watch her for hours.

I pick up a teal teddy bear, one of its eyes missing.

"Oh, that's November. I never go anywhere without him," she says. "He's my travel companion."

"We always need one of those. Mine's—" I catch myself before I say Ethan, because Imogen doesn't have Ethan, Jess has Ethan. "Mine's a good book," I finish lamely.

She laughs. "Different ones or the same?"

"Same. It's my favorite. Dog-eared and spine cracked. What kind of books do you read?"

"Manga mostly, some French comics. There are some great webcomics out there—I'm also a sucker for a fanfic. There's this one General Sond fanfic that I shouldn't like but *starflame* do I ever. The author, ThornyRose, is ridiculously good."

"I can't say I read much fanfic."

"Really? I could've sworn you said you read her."

"I mean, not lately," I quickly deflect. "I've been busy, you know. With the Save Amara stuff. Do you always bring ramen to the con?" I try to change the course of the conversation, shifting uncomfortably on the edge of the bed.

Harper laughs. She didn't notice. Good. "Do I ever! Con food is way too pricey, and I'm a poor starving artist so I don't have money for all the fancy restaurants around here. My friends say I make the best hotel ramen in the world, and I had promised you I'd make it for you if we ever met in person, and here we are."

"Here we are," I echo distantly, trying not to feel upset that it wasn't a promise made to me, but to Imogen. Why am I upset over something like that? I try to wrestle control of my feelings. I am a professional *actress*. I'm fine. "You know, that's pretty high praise. I've had a lot of good ramen."

She holds up a finger. "But you've never had *my* ramen. Passed down from coupon-savvy Hart to Hart, we have perfected the art of the ninety-nine-cent ramen. Observe!"

With a flourish, she takes the carafe and pours steaming water into both cups, closes the lids, and puts our chopsticks on top to keep them down. Then she sets her phone timer for seven minutes.

"Seven minutes in heaven," I murmur aloud. *Aloud.* I slap my hands over my mouth, mortified. "I didn't, that wasn't what I—"

Harper laughs, and her eyes crinkle, and my heart flutters. "It'd definitely kill some time."

I can feel my ears getting red, heat and mortification rushing to them. "I—I didn't mean it. That just reminded me, is all."

She tilts her head. "My first kiss was a seven-minutes-in-heaven thing. I was at a birthday party in middle school. It was . . . terrible."

"My first kiss was . . . " On the set of *Huntress Rising*, but I can't tell her that. "He was older and I was, like, fifteen. His stubble was scratchy and it gave me a rash—and he smelled like weed. He'd been smoking all day."

"Ugh, that sounds awful."

I look down at my hands, picking at the cuticle on my thumb. "It definitely wasn't what I had in mind for a first kiss." But it was my job, and I didn't have a choice. That I chose not to tell Harper. "It doesn't really matter. I've had a few good kisses since then." Including Dare. He was one of the better ones, actually.

Harper tilts her head when she looks at me. "You know, Imogen, you're nothing like how you act online."

My heart jumps. *Oh no.* "How so?"

"You're just not," she says as she sits down beside me, folding one leg under the other. She smells like lilac body lotion, and I try not to breathe too deep and drown in it. "It's almost like you're a different person."

"Maybe I am."

And she smiles at that, because she thinks I'm being coy.

I swallow, staring into her dark eyes, the color of angry clouds and midnight skies, and I find myself threateningly close to liking them a little too much. I shake myself out of it and clear my throat, averting my gaze to the cup of noodles. "So, why seven minutes?"

"Because ramen is best al dente," she notes, still giving me the same look that makes my skin hot and cold at the same time, "and seven minutes is the perfect amount of time. What would you do in seven minutes?"

"In heaven, or here?"

She grins. "Here."

Oh—*oh* I am in trouble.

Because I think I have a crush on this girl with curly dark hair and ink smudges on her brown fingers and trouble tucked into her maroon-colored lips.

Her cell phone beeps. The seven minutes are up. She takes off the lids and stirs the noodles with her chopsticks, and I do the same.

"Bon appétit," she says.

IMOGEN

My relationship with He-Who-Will-Not-Be-Named ended this way:

He didn't call, he didn't text, he didn't even say, "Sorry, babe! I lost my keycard and got stuck in an elevator and I had to fight off some Hydra agents with nothing but a shield and my superior good looks!" Although we both know I wouldn't have believed him. The point is, Jasper didn't even make the effort to do any of those things. He just didn't show. He ghosted me hard—and I don't think he even felt bad doing it.

I hate it.

I think what I hate more, though, is that I'm lying here on the soft carpeted floor of Jessica Stone's hotel suite, looking at the clock on the nightstand as it turns ten o'clock.

Screw it, I think as I push myself up and onto my feet. *I'm not going to stay in here.*

I want to say I don't feel super incredibly foolish that Vance hasn't called but . . . I do. Of course he wouldn't call. He has better things to do, with parties to go to and hot people to meet, and I was that lousy girl who fell for his *I'll call you later?*

Ugh.

I'm so freaking *mad* at myself I could cry. Because a part of me knows that I'm here in this suite because Jess told me I couldn't be anywhere else, and the only other place I could be, as myself, is with my moms down the hall as they do their nightly unwind with wine and *Buffy*, or with my brother down at the Stellar Party . . .

Grabbing my Converses out of my bag, I put them on, grab the keycard so I can get back in later, and leave the room. I'm not supposed to go out because I still look like Jess. I haven't taken the wig off, and my eyeliner is on *point*, but I don't want to be in here, either, waiting for Ethan to come back. It's been three hours.

He's probably with Jess.

I don't really know where I'm going, but I avoid as many people as possible as I head through the hallway. Music pulses from the rooms with the parties, rattling the light fixtures on the walls. I pass hotel rooms hosting old-school LAN competitions, fan meetups, and revelries with no theme at all. I quickly duck away from them—but not fast enough.

"Hey, Jessica!" someone shouts.

I glance over my shoulder, but I can't tell who's calling Jess's name, and I don't want to know either. Whoever it is, it can't be anyone I should talk to.

So I dodge around the corner, into the emergency stairwell and out through another door. It leads to the rooftop pool a few stories below Jessica's hotel suite. It's not actually on the rooftop—which is still a few floors above me—but it is on *a* rooftop, I suppose. It closed at ten o'clock, so the place is quiet.

I can barely hear the traffic in the streets way down below.

Even in Jessica Stone's makeup and clothes, I have the baggage of Imogen Lovelace underneath, and there is still that little voice in my head telling me that I am nothing, that I'm just someone in Milo's shadow who won't amount to much—and everyone else already knows it but me.

I don't want to listen to that voice.

Especially now, when it's closer than ever to being right. Because General Sond is the next villain.

Because no one cares about Amara. Not really.

Shut up shut up shut up! I say to that disembodied voice.

Even as Jessica, I can't seem to get Imogen out of my head. The highs from earlier are a dull throb in the back of my memories. How come the negative thoughts sound so much louder than the good ones?

With an aggravated noise, I wrench off my wig, tossing it behind a planter with my keycard, slip off my shoes, and run toward the pool.

The water is fresh and cool, and it shocks all the thoughts out of me—my mind is finally, miraculously void of everything. I swim a lap, letting Jess's designer dress tangle around my legs. It's a salt-water pool, so I know it won't get ruined. I just needed to swim.

Besides, swimming in a pool disguises crying fairly well.

Not that I'm crying.

Because I'm not.

On my third lap, I hear someone calling my name, and I think it's the security guard asking me to kindly get out of the pool. I pop my head up from the deep end and see that it's—

Ethan.

Standing there at the other end with his arms folded over his chest, one eyebrow so archedly raised it would make my mother Minerva so freaking proud. My heart leaps into my throat before I realize that him being here can't be anything good.

Crap, what does he want? What did I do wrong now? I sink down to my nose and bob there, as if I'm hoping he'll just go away. I'm glad my makeup is mostly waterproof, and that I stopped crying two laps ago. I hope my eyes are mostly dry by now and not red-rimmed and gross.

"What on *earth* are you doing?" he asks in a hushed and very exhausted tone.

I pop my head out of the water long enough to say, "Swimming," before I half-submerge my face again.

He sighs. "I can see that. You weren't in the room, so I thought . . . Anyway, I saw you swimming down here and came to inform you that the pool's closed. I'm going back up to the room. To *bed*."

"What about Jess?" I say, and instantly kick myself for asking.

Surprised, he tilts his head. "I suppose she's with your friend Harper. Why?"

"I'm surprised you two aren't hanging out." Ugh, why am I being so petty? It's like my mouth can't stop it. "I mean, unless you two already were."

"The panel ran over and I stopped to get dinner. There's Chinese takeout in the minifridge if you want any."

He doesn't *seem* to be lying. I swim halfway across the pool until my tiptoes can touch the bottom. The pool area is dark. The only light comes from dim lamps in the corners of the deck and the bright fluorescents in the sides of the pool, turning everything a whimsical, unearthly blue. Like being underneath an ocean.

His expression is curious. "You know Jess and I aren't . . . we don't like each other like that. If that's what you're insinuating."

I roll my eyes. "Right. Like anyone can resist the pull of the beautiful Jessica Stone."

"You're also beautiful," he says. But before I can ask whether that's in response to my statement or it's a compliment, he adds, "when you're not being an absolute pain in my ass. What if someone checks the security cameras? Sees you swimming out here?"

"I took off the wig outside the camera's view," I reply.

He scowls and pivots to leave, and I realize that I don't want him to go. Mostly because I've been alone all night, and I guess even his company is better than none. "How did you meet, then?"

"Who?"

"Jessica."

He hesitates, but then he turns around and sits at the edge of the pool. "Honestly? She's my godsister. Our mothers met way back in college." As he says this, he rolls up his trousers to just below his knees, takes off his shoes, and sticks his feet into the water. "I've known her my entire life. We've done everything together."

"Wait, so you're like twenty-something? Really?"

He blanches. "Do I look *that* old? I'll be eighteen in December. I just finished high school. I'm taking a gap year, and Jess needed an assistant, so here I am."

"But you wore a *suit* today!" I reply, flabbergasted. "And you're always on this high horse of 'oh look at me I'm so superior to you.'"

"I do *not* sound like that."

"Oh you so do. You called me a rapscallion."

"I will never live that down," he mumbles, more to himself than to me, and rubs his hand over his face.

"So." I slowly migrate toward his side of the pool, doing the numbers in my head from what I know about Jess and now what I know about Ethan. "You two are like five years apart? Jess is twenty-three, isn't she?"

"Actually . . . no."

"Older?"

"She's nineteen."

"Nineteen," I echo. "But the internet says she's definitely older."

"The internet's wrong, surprisingly. She lied when she was fourteen to get the part in *Huntress Rising*. She told the director she was almost eighteen. After that she just never corrected anyone." He shrugs. "She'll do just about anything to make sure she succeeds. She needs to. It's like there's this dial in her head that's constantly turned up to eleven. She's *intense*. She's always thinking one step ahead—or three."

He talks about her in such a tender tone, like he really does admire her. He might say he doesn't love her, but maybe he just doesn't realize it yet.

"Sounds like she means a lot to you," I say.

"She does—she's like a sister to me."

"Well, she's doing better than me. I'm no one," I reply. "I mean—Jess is smart, and she's gorgeous, and she's talented. She made a fantastic Amara. She's amazing, and I . . . I guess I can do cool voices?"

Ethan studies me with those dark, dark eyes, and I feel myself shifting uncomfortably. "Imogen," he starts—and the way he says my name, like it's somewhere between a lullaby and an exasperated sigh, makes my stomach flip all the same. "Why did you want to trade places with Jess?"

The question takes me by surprise. I turn my eyes toward the water, watching my dress float and ripple around me. The reflection of my pink hair creates a rosy halo around me. "Don't you already know? You sleuthed me out, Detective. I want to save Amara."

"But you could've done that a myriad of other ways—you *are* doing that, it seems, at least by your online presence."

"As if that's enough," I sigh, resting my hand just above the ripples of the water, watching the lights from the pool dance across my skin. "You know, I really love Amara. I relate to her. She was able to make mistakes and still come back from them—she wasn't *ruined* because of them. She learned, and she grew, and she became stronger." Because Amara is the type of character who always screwed up—like me, trying to do the right thing but never doing it the right way. Like the online petitions, the Twitter hashtag, the movement itself—it's all fine and good, but it wasn't the right way because . . . "I'm no one, Ethan. I haven't done anything. So I guess that's why I wanted to be Jess, so I could be someone. So my voice would matter."

"Imogen, that's not—"

"Oh, it's true," I interrupt. "My brother's a year younger than me and he's vice president of his class, *and* he'll probably even be quarterback. He's just so talented at everything, I feel like . . . like I'm letting everyone down because I'm not good at anything. And it's not because I don't try," I add before he can suggest it, because people *always* suggest it. "I've tried out for the debate team, but when I had to debate a guy over women's reproduction he told me that women are too fragile to have control over their own bodies. I got kicked out of the club for kneeing him in the nads—"

"Whoa, really?"

"—and I tried to join the track team but I'm about as good at running as I am at algebra, so I couldn't join the math club, either."

"Imogen," he tries to stop me, but I'm just getting started on the Great Failings of Imogen Lovelace.

"I suck at grammar, even though I love books," I tell him, beginning to count my shortcomings on my fingers. "I'm in the book club, and the anime club, and I started a sci-fi club for the sole reason of getting after-school credit for watching reruns of *Starfield*. I'm still very proud of that."

"Imogen."

I begin to pace from one side of the pool to the other, half floating, half moon-walking. "But it's not like the sci-fi club will turns heads on a college application. I don't even know where I want to go, or what I want to do, and I'm a *senior* now. Milo's basically already accepted to any school he sets his sights on and I—"

I don't realize that he's slid into the water until he catches me by the shoulders with his large hands and turns me around. He didn't take his clothes off, either, abandoning only his glasses on the edge of the pool, and dampness is slowly bleeding up his starched button-down shirt. He sinks down and looks me level in the eyes. *Starflame*, is he handsome. Long eyelashes and warm brown eyes and expressive brows that crinkle together a little as he says my name for what feels like the millionth time, and I'm still not tired of it.

"Imogen. You started an online movement that has over fifty *thousand* signatures to try to save a character from a television show you are fiercely passionate about."

I quickly look away. "Yeah, but anyone can do that."

"I think you're wrong—and I certainly don't think just any-one can step into Jess's shoes as well as you have."

"But that's only because I look moderately like her with a wig on and I can imitate voices pretty well."

"Not everyone can do that."

"Look moderately flawless?" I joke.

"Imogen," he says, and I kind of just want him to shut up and keep saying my name over and over again until I get so sick of that name that I want to change it to something else, and then I want him to say *that* name, and then the next one, and then— "you might not be now, but you're learning how to be, and someday I know you're *going* to be amazing."

My bottom lip begins to tremble. *Starflame*, now why did he have to go and say that? Why couldn't he just laugh at me like Jasper did and tell me how he loved my *passion* in that tongue-in-cheek way that really wasn't a compliment at all? His hands begin to loosen from my shoulders the longer I'm quiet, because I'm not sure what to say.

What *do* you say to something like that?

He opens his mouth again and I am *incredibly* afraid of what's about to come out, because I know it'll only stir up feelings I definitely don't have about this boy who is secretly in love with Jessica Stone but doesn't know it. And I really, really don't want to be the Other Girl in that situation, because I've seen Jess's life—I've lived it!—and I've seen his devotion to her, and I know where I'll be at the end of all of this:

On a curb outside of the ball, waiting for a Prince Charming who'll never come.

So I do the only thing I can think of—

I splash him.

Like, not just one of those pansy splashes, either. I grew up with a brother, so I had to learn to deal some real damage whenever we visited the community pool. I splash Ethan so hard it's like a tidal wave of pool water coming at him. He sputters, drenched, the gel finally loosening his hair from its meticulous hold.

"You did *not* just do that," he says, offended, as he wipes his eyes.

"You talk too much, anyone ever tell you that?"

He scoffs. "Like I'm the only one!"

He proceeds to rake his arm across the surface in revenge. Water gets into my eyes and my nose, and blindly I shove water back at him. But he's way taller than me and, not surprising, has longer arms, so he has full advantage in pool warfare. I try the doggie-paddle maneuver, but he comes back with a fan of water that drenches me, and the tides turn and I'm on the losing end of this battle, like the *Prospero* pitted against a fleet of Noxian horde ships. I try in vain just to stay above the surface.

But then he does the unthinkable.

He puts his massive hand on my head—

And pushes me under.

I barely make a sound before he dunks me, and when I come up for air, gasping and blinking salty water out of my eyes, he's already starting for the stairs. "I win," he says over his shoulder. "Now get out before someone calls Security—"

"Never surrender!" I cry, and take off after him—which in the water, you know, is basically slow-mo running in real time. I grab him around the middle and use the only move that ever works on Milo—I knock his legs out from under him and I suplex his body into the deep end.

Turns out he's a *lot* heavier than I thought, especially for a beanpole. And his torso is very solid. And are those *abs* I feel?

Oh sweet baby Daleks, please don't tell me Ethan actually has a nice bod.

That would just be too much.

He pries my arms from around his waist and comes up for air first. I'm right behind him, coughing the water out of my lungs.

"What're you trying to do, *drown* me?" he sputters as he paddles to the edge of the pool.

I wipe the water off my face, half coughing and half laughing, and grab on beside him. "Add *that* to my resume. World-champion splasher. Another useless talent of Imogen Ada Lovelace."

"You flipped me back!"

"Is your pride wounded?"

"A little," he admits.

He could make for the stairs again, but instead he lingers near me, and I think we both realize at the same time how close we actually are, and there are flecks of gold in his eyes I haven't seen before and that is *so freaking* cliché I kind of adore it. Not him. But his eyes. I have to remind myself that I can't like him, but it's so hard when a droplet of water beads at the end of a lock of raven hair in front of his face, and falls on his cheek, and rolls down his cheek slowly, languidly, like I want to run my finger down his jawline. It's like there's no one else but us in the world, and his eyes navigate steadily to my lips.

I should've exfoliated them earlier. A sugar scrub or something. I should've packed a cute bathing suit instead of jumping in wearing Jess's dress. I should've done *something*—

NOT THAT THIS IS ANYTHING.

BECAUSE IT'S NOT.

It can't be.

But then he migrates closer, closing the gap between us—the snippy remarks and the snark and the circumstances—until the heat from his skin burns against mine without even touching me, and the cool blue of the pool reflects across our faces like ripples in the ocean, and I think I might be—

I think this is—

"Ethan," I whisper, and it's my voice—my *real* voice—that breaks the spell.

He jerks back as if he's forgotten that I'm me. Then his look morphs into mortification. Because it *is* me. And he wants Jess.

"I should, ah . . . I should get out of the pool. I—I'm sorry."

"Oh, of course," I murmur, trying to keep my voice steady.

"It's not you. It's just, I'm only here to keep a lookout for you for Jessica, so you don't r—" But then he stops himself. "And you seem fine at the moment. You're not masquerading as her. So."

He pushes off from the edge and swims toward the shallow end.

I don't say anything until he's halfway to the stairs. He stands, his wet button-down clinging to the cordlike muscles of his back. Dammit, he *does* have a nice body. And it kind of just makes me angrier. I don't know why.

"So that's the only reason you came out here?" I ask. "For Jessica?"

"That's not—"

"To make sure I'm not ruining her career? Was that what you were going to say?"

His lips press into a thin line. He can't meet my gaze.

Oh, I'm right.

I scoff. Of course I'm right. Why would he ever want to just be nice to me? "Don't worry Ethan, I won't screw up your *precious* Jessica Stone's career."

"You think that's all I care about?" he asks, clenching his fists.

"Well, the writing's on the wall, isn't it?"

"You don't know the first thing about Jessica—or me—and here you are coming in to our lives thinking you know everything. Thinking that you can just mess with Jess's life—play in it like it's this funhouse ride. It's not, Imogen. Jess's life is real."

I purse my lips. "If it's so *important,* then why let me mess in it to begin with?"

"Because Jess needs to—" But then he stops himself, and looks away. "She just needed this."

"So I'm important enough to pretend to be Jessica, but I'm

not important enough to know the real reason why," I infer, and he doesn't correct me.

He just folds his arms over his chest, looking more uncomfortable by the moment. Finally, he says, "You should get out before security comes by."

"You mean before I can screw up Jess's career?" I mock.

"It's not like you can screw up your own," he snaps cattily, but then realizes what he said. "I didn't mean it that way. I just meant—"

Oh no, he's said enough already. I push myself up the side and out of the pool. I grab the keycard and the wig I'd stashed behind the potted plant. "No, I get it. Don't worry, Ethan," I snap as I leave, and he just stands there helplessly. "I won't *screw up*."

I clutch the wig to my stomach as I make my way through the lobby, where con-goers mingle with friends, some with their costumes slowly melting off them, others in pajamas. No one glances at me, no one looks twice, even though I'm sopping wet and my dress leaves a liquid trail behind me. The people who do notice me probably just see a mess of a girl, waterlogged, with runny makeup and pink hair stuck up in a spiky crown around her head.

Don't cry, I think, unable to get Ethan's words out of my head. Why did they make me so *angry?*

I think I'm angrier at myself more than anything. Because I actually thought—

I let myself think—

Because he's so freaking *insufferable,* I actually—

I elbow my way through the crowds, breathing deeply so I don't outright cry, and reach the elevators. There is a difference between loving someone and stanning someone. I can stan Darien Freeman and Vance Reigns and Chris Pine and Cole Sprouse all I want, because at the end of the day I know it's a one-sided affair.

Yeah, I freak out over movie stars. I think they're hot or cute or SUPER ADORABLE I MEAN COME ON.

But *loving* someone? That's expecting them to love you back. I don't expect love at first sight. That heart-crushing, soul-melting, foot-lifting sort of fairy-tale romance that *The Princess Bride* sells you. But liking would be nice. A nice warm like that assures you that you won't be left out on the curb during a fairy-tale ball night without a Prince Charming or a pumpkin carriage.

In the universe of Imogen Lovelace, however, that's an impossible thing.

I push the palm of my hand against my eyes, willing myself not to burst into tears as the elevator doors glide open.

"Monster?"

The familiar voice makes me look up, and there are Milo and Bran. My brother must recognize the look on my face because in one long step he's out of the elevator and drawing me into his arms. I press my face into his chest and he smells like the Stellar Party—vape juice and Oh No—and I try really hard not to cry.

"Let's go get some food—I'm thinking burgers," Bran says, and I nod against Milo's chest, and they lead me out of the lobby and down to a diner at the end of the street.

JESS

As it turns out, I was starving—but for more than just food. For company. For a quiet moment like this. Harper and I laugh and talk about all of the things that I never talk about with anyone: the latest trash mag gossip, the perfect eyeshadow palette, that YA rom-com that had the most adorable kiss. We talk about her family—it's big and loud—and we talk about our favorite bands and childhood crushes.

I want to tell her everything about me. I want to tell her about my parents, and how since I became an actress they live in a big house in Nashville, and they come to visit me as often as they can, and my dad is a computer tech and my mom works with charities. I want to tell them about our dog, and about Ethan, and about how lonely it sometimes is in that posh LA apartment my agent found for me. I want to tell her how I miss going for hikes with my dad, and I want to tell her about that red carpet stumble, and what it was really like on the set of *Starfield*.

I want to prove that Jessica Stone is not the aloof, cold robot everyone thinks I am. I am not a serial dater. I simply never cared. It was so easy not to care because I'm not built that way.

I'm not built to take a random person into a bedroom, I'm not wired to want those things, and so it made all those dates and chaste kisses with celebrities so easy. It never went further than that. It was never falling in love—it was never even falling into like.

It's a part to play, and so I played it.

What I *am* built for is falling in love slowly, page by page, like reading a favorite book. I am built for the nearness of someone, the quirk of their lips, the sincerity of their smile, the dreams just underneath their skin. I fall in love moment by moment, collecting who they are, who they were, who they want to be, into a kaleidoscope of colors.

I have only fallen in love once, and she left a hole in my heart the size of the universe. So I know the feeling, the strange beast in my stomach that shifts and growls whenever Harper laughs, whenever she says something snarky, whenever she calls me Imogen, because in my head I hear her calling me Jess.

I know this feeling, and I try to shove it down because this is *not* who I am. She is falling for nobody. For a girl who will be gone in the blink of an eye.

And I guarantee she will not like Jessica Stone.

" . . . And I *swear* to you," Harper says with a laugh, telling a story about the ExcelsiCon ball last year, "it was like the *entire* place just canceled her. The girl went running out of the ballroom so fast, she tripped in the lobby and fell flat on her face. It was hysterical!"

"I kind of feel sorry for her. I didn't know Darien could be that mean."

"She was mean, too. Right down to the bone. Sage told me the whole story. If anything, that girl deserved what she got. She's the reason Elle Wittimer's called Geekerella. She wanted to be a beauty vlogger or something, but she's working at her mom's nail salon now."

"It's funny how sometimes we don't end up where we think we will," I remark.

Harper turns her dark gaze to me. "What would you do if you could do anything? Doesn't matter if you're talented at it or not."

I don't even have to think. "An astronomer."

"*Really* now."

"I love stars," I say earnestly, and she bursts out laughing, which makes me smile sheepishly despite not knowing whether she's laughing at me or—no, no it's definitely *at* me. "Listen! I'm not kidding. I love everything about stars. I love proton stars and neuron stars and cosmic phenomena. If I could, I'd get Stephen Hawking's equation describing black holes tattooed on me. That's how much I love space."

She wipes the tears from under her eyes. "You're really serious, aren't you."

"Of course!" I jerk to my feet, taking her hand and pulling her up with me. She grabs her keycard as I pull her out the door, not even bothering to put on shoes. "Where are we going?"

"I'm showing you some stars," I reply, and punch the elevator button for the top floor, where we head for the stairwell.

"Oh my God, we're actually going up," Harper says.

"I'm being totes serious right now."

"Then you need to work on your fresh-from-Azkaban cosplay."

"Or my drought-bringing-dog-star cosplay," I reply.

"Ugh, *nerrrdddd*," she drawls.

But it's playful.

"I gladly take that compliment."

"*Neeeeerrrddddddddd!*" she cries, her voice echoing down the stairwell as we climb to the top.

Most rooftops I've visited haven't had alarmed doors, so I'm counting on this one being accessible when I shoulder it open and wedge a cement block so it doesn't lock us out. The almost-midnight Atlanta skyline sparkles brightly around us, the city lights reflected off glass buildings that twist up like titans frozen in a dance of steel.

It's so much quieter up here. I let go of Harper's wrist and breathe in the humid air. Because of the light pollution, you can't see as many stars as you can on my grandfather's patch of land in Tennessee, where the sky is so wide you can almost fall into it, but this is a good enough view, for good enough people, on a good enough night. There are no trolls yelling in my mentions about how I'm not enough, no people dissecting how I play a character, or the way I say a word, or why I will never—no matter what I do—be good enough.

I think that's why I dislike Elle just a little bit. She was one of those people. She tore into Dare without even knowing him, knowing how big a fan he is, or how passionate he will always be about *Starfield*. The internet makes it easy for us to forget that there are people on the other side of those characters, and whether you like us or not, we're people too. So your hot take shouldn't dehumanize me, or tell me that I'm wrong, or that I'm worthless, or a slut who slept on some casting couch for the role.

Because I'm none of those things. And it's so, so hard to remember that when the internet just keeps echoing it back to you.

But up here there are no echoes and no trolls, and I am just a girl wearing her heart on her sleeve, staring at the sky, asking the universe—just for a moment—to be enough.

I orient myself and point to one of the brighter stars. "See, there he is. The Dog Star. And there's Mars over there. And over here . . . " I spin around, not really noticing where I'm going—

—and collide with Harper.

She's smiling, and looking up at the sky, too. "You know, most *normal* people don't go looking up at the sky."

"I never claimed to be normal," I reply.

In the nighttime air, with buildings towering around us, thirty stories up and far above car horns and gossip and chatter, I look down—just briefly—to her, and she's looking at me. In the darkness, her eyes look like pools of ink I could dip a pen into and write a ballad about the way she's looking at me. My heart trembles as she takes my hand and laces her brown fingers through my pale ones.

"I think I finally see you, Imogen Lovelace," she says.

It's important to see that people like us exist. Her voice echoes in my head, along with Imogen's.

But Princess Amara is dead, and she isn't coming back.

Not even if I want her to.

And I don't.

Do I?

I don't have to wear that galaxy-glitter dress that pinches me under the arms. I don't have to run in heels or dye my hair that god-awful red. Or actively ignore most social media because of the trolls. I don't have to eat an inedible catered salad. I don't have to listen to Dare complain about his uniform not being the right shade of blue. Or watch Amon act out a fight scene and stub his toe on a prop.

And I probably won't meet Harper at another con. As Imogen, or as myself.

It was an accident that I met her here.

Almost impossible—

Impossible.

Things that would never happen in real life. A fangirl with wicked stepsisters and the actor she despises falling in love. A fashion designer and Geekerella's stepsister finding each other.

Colliding with your look-alike in a con bathroom at the edge of the world and falling for her internet friend.

Impossible.

I'm not Imogen Lovelace, I want to tell her, and now is the perfect time, when the stars are bright and the sky is wide, but the words catch on my tongue as I remember all those Instagram comments. The Twitter notifications.

What if she's one of them?

Or what if she gets mad that I've lied to her this whole time and never wants to talk to me again? Is this how Dare felt when he had to confess to Elle? How did he get up the courage? I don't know much about Harper, but I want to, and I'm afraid of all the things I'll never get to know if I tell her who I am.

So like the scene in *My Best Friend's Wedding* when the ship goes under the bridge—the moment passes and there's no going back.

In reply, because I don't know how to reply, because replying will break her heart, I squeeze her hand tightly and point up to a star and tell her its story because I can't tell her mine.

Just a little while longer, I pray to the impossibilities. *Let me be Imogen for a little while longer.*

IMOGEN

FOOD HELPS MY MOOD, AS DOES watching my brother inhale an All-Star Breakfast in five minutes flat. I swear to God he's a black hole. Even Bran is slightly disgusted at the sight. There is nothing quite like it. Milo doesn't ask why I was wet, or why I smell like a pool, or what happened to make me cry. He knows I'll tell him, or I won't. But then he says:

"So, Jessica Stone, eh?"

I look up from my coffee and involuntarily shiver. We're sitting in a Waffle House, and my hash browns are cold because I only picked at them, and the coffee is warming my hands. "Um . . . what . . . about her?"

Bran, sitting beside me, picks up the wig on the seat between us. It looks more like a dead rodent right now, rather than Jess's long and lustrous locks. He arches an eyebrow. "We know."

"You . . . know what?" I try to play dumb, pretending that there's a coffee ground floating in my cup. "I don't know what you're talking about."

"She was at the Stellar Party," Milo says, finishing off his fried egg in a single swallow. "So we know about it. Well, kinda. She was with Harper."

I wince. "Has Harper found out?"

"No." Bran shakes his head. "She thinks she's you, and I *think* there's something going on between them."

"What do you mean?"

"Like I think J—" But he's cut off when Milo kicks him under the table. They give each other a meaningful look, as if I didn't just witness that. Bran clears his throat and says, "I think Jess is having a great time. Being you, I mean. And she isn't half bad."

That's a relief, anyway. "I'm glad."

"And you being Jess . . . she's not worried you're going to," Milo makes a motion with his fork toward me, "you know, the Save Amara stuff?"

Of course he'd ask. He's like the sixth member of the Scooby gang, looking for clues to the murder of my life. I breathe in through my nose and then smile because I've found that I lie easier when I'm smiling. "Nah."

"Then why *are* you impersonating Jessica Stone?"

"She asked me to. She said she wanted to take a break for a while."

Bran almost spews his coffee. "You don't believe her, do you?"

"Of course not, but she hasn't told me the truth yet, either. And I haven't really been looking. I'm just, you know, enjoying the ride. It feels nice being seen." The last part kind of slips out, and all three of us fall silent.

Somewhere near the kitchen, someone drops a coffee mug and it shatters on the tile floor and someone else calls for an order of hash browns scattered and smothered. I grab the ticket from the table but then hesitate when I realize I don't have my wallet. Bran plucks the bill from me and scoots out of the booth.

"I'll get it. Finish your hash browns, though," he adds as he walks over to the register.

I sit quietly with Milo. He studies me with those dark green eyes, and I pick up my fork and start shoveling the cold, congealed potatoes into my mouth so I don't have to answer whatever question I know he wants to ask. We're siblings, and we're close. I've told Milo everything over the years, and he's told me everything, too. I was the first person he came out to in his freshman year of high school, although with our parents it didn't really matter.

"But I wanted to tell you first," he had said. This was back when he was scrawny and a little shorter than me, and I could still suplex him splendidly in the community pool. "Because you're my best friend, Monster."

"You're mine, too, bro," I had replied, and scrubbed his curly head.

But how could I tell him that I can't live up to the example he sets? That I'm just not built that way. That I'm afraid of being nothing in his shadow.

He sets down his fork, a frown tugging at the edges of his mouth. "Monster . . . "

I chase the hash browns with a gulp of coffee. "Let's not talk about it, okay? And don't tell anyone about me and Jess—not even our moms."

"Of course not, but why do you think—"

"Okay." I slide out of the booth to end our conversation, grabbing the wig as I go. Helplessly he lets the topic drop and we wait for Bran to pay, and they escort me back to the hotel before hitting up another all-night showing of *Galaxy Quest*. I wave goodbye from the lobby and head inside.

The problem is, I can't get into my own room without my

keycard, and guess who shockingly forgot to take it? Along with my phone, credit card, and bag. I've got no choice but to shuffle up to Jess's suite.

I barely insert the key into keylock before the door jerks open.

Ethan towers in the doorway, vibrating like a human-looking sock puppet full of angry bees.

Uh-oh. That's *definitely* not a happy face.

His fists are clenched, his shoulders jarringly straight, his mouth set into a thin line. He glares down at me from behind the shadow of his glasses. He's changed into dry clothes, sweatpants and a loose tee, although with one look I remember the sight of his wet shirt clinging to his shoulders and chest. I quickly put those thoughts out of my head as fast as I can. His hair is kind of wild and dry, not gelled like it usually is, and he has a cowlick on the right side that I never noticed before. A part of me wants to lick my palm and try to flatten it, but he looks like a tower of angry cats and I fear for my hand. The way the muscle in his jaw throbs, I think he might just want to strangle me.

I clear my throat. "Ethan . . . um, hi. I, um, left my stuff in here."

He breathes in through his nose, and a little of the tension melts. He sidesteps so I can slip past him into Jess's hotel room. It's just like when I left it. I grab my bag that I'd thrown on the couch and loop it over my shoulder.

"I think I'm going to go back to my hotel room for the night. So, tomorrow morning . . . "

And that's when I notice all of the freshly ironed shirts hanging in the bathroom doorway. An ironing board stands just behind the couch, the iron giving off a soft hiss of steam.

He was . . . *ironing*?

"Where have you been?" he asks, closing the door with too-measured gentleness. His voice reflects his true feelings: quietly controlled rage.

Oh. It clicks.

"You *iron* when you're worried," I say, hazarding a guess.

"And fold laundry, and mop floors, and hem pants—and don't change the subject. Where have you been?" He folds his arms over his chest, a finger tapping agitatedly against his biceps.

"Out," I reply. "Why do you care? I wasn't being Jessica."

"You went off on your own!"

"Of course I did! Aren't I allowed to? You obviously don't care what happens when I'm me, only when I'm being your *precious* Jessica."

"Imogen—"

"And you know what? I get it. She has everything! She's not living in anyone's shadow! Don't worry. Jessica Stone's intact. I didn't tell anyone her secrets. Besides I'm no one. I'll always be no one. It's my lot in life, right?" And then I do something I know I should not do. I adopt Jessica Stone's perfect lilt and I purr, "But I think your love for Jess might be a bit *unrequited*?"

A muscle on the left side of his jaw twitches with annoyance.

I know I'm being nasty and cruel. But he was nasty and cruel, too, and I'm too tired and emotionally compromised to reel myself in.

So is he, apparently.

He rakes his fingers through his thick black hair. "Forget it! You know why I was mad? Because of this." He digs his phone out of his sweatpants pocket and hits a contact. He puts the call on speakerphone and my stomach drops into my gut when I read the name.

IMOGEN LOVELACE.

He even spelled my name right.

Although he's calling it, my phone doesn't start ringing, and shame eats at the edges of my ears because I remember I put in the number for my favorite pizza joint back home. It rings three times before one of the co-managers answers, "Junie here, and you're calling the Roman Pizzeria, what can I get for you—"

He stabs his thumb on the END CALL button, his dark eyes seething at no one but me.

I swallow hard.

Oh.

Right. I forgot about that.

"Is this some *game* to you, Imogen?"

I clench my jaw and look away. Okay, I hadn't really thought that plan through. And all of the little things are starting to come together. Him ironing, calling my number, being angry with me— it means that, whether it's because I'm Jessica or not, he was worried about me once I'd stormed off. And that makes me feel just a little worse for yelling at him.

"You can't be Jess forever," he says, his voice thin and brittle, "and those people out there? The ones who cheered for you? The paparazzi who called out your name? They care about Jess, and no matter how much you want or try to be her, all you'll ever be is a copy."

His words feel like a Kamehameha wave come to incinerate me, stinging deep below the makeup and the pretty designer dress. Tears pool at the edges of my eyes, burning.

"Is that what I am to you?" I ask quietly.

His eyebrows furrow and he looks like he might say something, but he never does. The silence is all the answer I need. I duck around him and head for the door. "I'm going to my room. Have a good night."

I slam the door behind me, leaving like a companion from the Tardis, because the doors close exactly the same, abandoning me in the universe.

Alone.

DAY THREE

SATURDAY

———

"You were warned about me, *ah'blen*."

—Princess Amara, Episode 54, "Nox and Forever"

JESS

I PULL MY—WELL, IMOGEN'S—BADGE OVER my head as I hop on the escalator and head up to ExcelsiCon. The showroom floor doesn't open for another ten minutes, so that means I have time to grab coffee from the hotel café and find Harper's—and my? Imogen's?—booth. My cheekbone is still a little sore, but concealer has covered up most of the gross bruising. My face should hurt more and I should feel much sleepier than I do, but honestly bliss is the best pain reliever.

The last few hours feel like a waltz across the stars. I never want to come back down.

Harper and I stargazed until just after midnight, when she had to go check on the Stellar Party, and I ended up falling asleep in her bed before she returned. This morning, I woke up to her in bed with me, looking at me from where she lay on her pillow, the distance between us like one star to the next—lightyears traveled in a single breath. She smiled and I burrowed my head into the covers and tried to stop my heart from beating so fast.

Harper's room was not quite as stocked as my suite—they didn't even have coffee filters—and so she tasked me with a coffee run while she began setting up the booth.

That gave me time to hurry up to my suite in the other hotel and grab an extra pair of clothes; I didn't want to wear Imogen's again. I found Ethan asleep on the couch, his phone on the floor. I picked it up and put it on the coffee table and covered him up with a blanket.

Imogen probably stayed in her room for the night. If I'd been in her shoes, I would've too.

Without waking Ethan, I took a quick shower and slipped into a pair of jeans and a black hoodie I'd reserved for the plane ride home; I put on a pair of comfortable flats and tucked my hair into my SPACE QUEEN beanie. As I quietly left the suite, I slid Ethan's glasses back on, the feeling of anonymity settling over me like a soothing balm. No one looked twice at me in the lobby; the morning was cool, the convention halls empty.

Maybe I don't hate ExcelsiCon as much as I thought.

I decide to take a shortcut across the showroom to the café, thinking that I haven't even gotten a call from Ethan yet, which is glorious. The Twitter leaker hasn't posted again either. Everything is so calm.

And I am so, so happy.

Not even the towering Nox King on the corner of the aisle can ruin my mood.

"Monster!"

My feet slow to a stop. It's a voice I don't recognize—not Bran or Milo or any of the people I met last night. I glance behind me.

Approaching me is woman with long black hair, dressed in a lacy black evening gown with butterfly sleeves and thigh-high boots. Her nails are like cat claws, her eyes dark with thick make-up. And then those dark eyes widen. "Oh, I'm sorry, you're someone else."

I blink at the woman and then, remembering the warning, I look to the Nox King statue. Then back at her.

This must be one of Imogen's mothers.

Cursing, I quickly angle my face away and fold my arms over my chest to hide my badge. "Um, it's fine."

When I begin to leave she adds, "Your aura is very troubled. Come to Figurine It Out and we can—"

"That's great, goodbye!" I hastily escape the aisle, grateful that she doesn't follow, and breathe a sigh of relief. That was *much* too close. Harper said that Imogen's parents were fun, but that was just bizarre.

I shake off the encounter and grab our coffees, arriving back at Artists' Alley right before the floodgates open and con attendees rush inside. I slip behind the table just as people emerge from the escalators, on their way to panels and signing lines and meet-and-greets. I sit with a relieved sigh and hand Harper her coffee.

"The nectar of the goddesses," she says, and sighs happily. "You know, there's something lovely about coffee in the morning when you're running on four hours of sleep."

"Four hours? You should've gotten at least six."

"Well *someone* kept kicking me out of bed."

"Well there was an entirely *other* bed that your roommates didn't use last night."

"It was cold in the room. We needed to sleep together for warmth," she points out slyly.

"Save Amara!" I cry, thrusting a pin to a passing Caine Wise, who takes it and goes on his way. The convention is slowly filling again with people, browsing across the showroom floor and into Artists' Alley. I push my glasses farther up my nose, hoping Harper will change the subject because, despite how much I truly and deeply want to flirt with her, I am walking a tightrope of time.

The thief hasn't posted another part of the script since last night, and I'm beginning to wonder why they've been silent for so long. Any one of these people could be the culprit—any of the costumed heroes and antiheroes and secondary characters that pass by the booth. They might've even taken a Save Amara pin, for all I know.

And I hate to think—I'm dreading to dwell on—the realization that I'm not really looking forward to the next tweet. Because that means I'll be one step closer either to finding the thief or to the thief outing me, and either way that is another step farther along the tightrope away from Harper.

There have been so many chances to tell her the truth and yet . . .

"Save Amara!" I call to a passing Spider-Man, and he takes the pin with a nod.

Harper finishes setting up her side of the booth, various art prints and stickers and enamel pins laid out across the table, and then opens her sketchbook to work on commissions. We sit in comfortable silence as she draws and I hand out pins, asking people to sign the petition, even though it goes against everything I want in my career.

I'm doing it to keep in character, I convince myself as I clip a pin onto a small Amara and watch her toddle away with her mother.

"Your brother's trying out for quarterback, right?" Harper asks as she sketches the face of Obi-Wan Kenobi, Space Daddy (the commissioner's request, not my words).

"Um . . . yeah." I think she's talking about Milo. Imogen doesn't have another brother, does she?

"Has he heard anything yet?"

"Um, I don't think so."

She nods, looking up from her sketch, and her eyebrows furrow in uncertainty. "Um, Imogen?"

"Hmm?"

My name is Jess, I should say.

"Would you . . . would you want to go to the ExcelsiCon Ball with me tonight?"

My breath catches and I swallow hard to keep the answer from rising up out of my throat. I hesitate because I'm not Imogen, and I am standing on the edge, and this is very, very bad—

"Or not," she adds when I don't say anything. "I mean, dances are stupid anyway."

"No, Harper, that's not—"

A familiar ringtone breaks out from my back pocket. At first I think I imagine it—but no, it's definitely the *Pokémon* theme song.

Only one person is assigned that ringtone.

"Excuse me," I apologize, and slip out of the booth. I retreat to the outer corner of Artists' Alley, near where the pretzel man set up shop. It's a little quieter here, and it gives me space to shrug out of Imogen's character without anyone noticing. I check my phone.

I have a missed call and a text from Ethan.

ETHAN TANAKA (12:02 PM)

—*Jess, another tweet is up.*

—*[Link]*

—*I think you need to call Darien.*

I click on the link, even though I already know I don't want to read it. The dreamy haze that has danced in my head all morning crystalizes with a cold burst of dread.

CARMINDOR DIES, the tweet reads.

It feels like a rubber band that has been wound and wound and wound around me pops. I sink to the carpet, staring at the excerpt. There are no clues this time who this person is or where they are—just the barest edge of a leather sofa. But I'm not sure if I really care all that much who is leaking the script.

I don't know what I thought I wanted to find in the sequel.

I don't know how I expected to feel.

But it isn't . . . this.

I pull up Dare's number, but I hesitate to call. It's noon, and the cast has a panel at noon.

The news broke during the panel, I realize, and my stomach twists into knots. I hope Imogen doesn't do anything stupid.

Ethan won't let her. Will he?

IMOGEN

A PHONE DINGS IN THE AUDIENCE—*Starfield*'s communication tone—and then another ding in the front row. Then a hundred dings in succession.

My smartphone vibrates on the table.

Darien and I, the only two of us on the panel (Amon, our moderator, is late), look at each other. We're supposed to be talking about what it's like to play opposing forces. "Star-Crossed in *Starfield*" is the name of the panel, and, you know, I was feeling pretty good about bullshitting my way through it.

Another phone dings.

Now I shift in my chair, apprehensive.

A murmur sweeps across the crowd.

My phone vibrates for only two things right now: my mothers texting me or another leak of the script.

I don't know what to do—should I read it like everyone in the audience is obviously doing? My eyes stray to the front row until I realize that Ethan isn't there. I left the hotel without him this morning. I didn't go to Jess's room to see if he'd escort me to the convention, and I did well by myself. The paparazzi greeted me outside the con and I gave them Jess's best smile as I breezed past.

I don't need to apologize to Ethan—he was out of line last night, too. Way, *way* out of line. Although, I barely slept a wink in my hotel room, my traitorous brain writing and rewriting apology texts to him that I never sent.

Not that I would apologize.

Not until he apologized first.

Darien makes the executive decision to check his phone, and the warm look that he'd fixed on his face grows stony.

And then distant.

I check the notification, too. My breath catches in my throat. Oh, *starflame.*

@starfieldscript337
CARMINDOR DIES. LOOKS LIKE WE'RE IN FOR A NEW HERO.

PRINCE CARMINDOR hears AMARA's voice in his head, but it doesn't matter. He can't control his body anymore, and his mind is fading. He keys in the code to drop the shields to the Federation's Commissary. The last stronghold.

He knows he must welcome GENERAL SOND. The Path of the Sun is the only way to find salvation. To find AMARA.

> AMARA(V.O.)
> You don't want to come find me yet, *ah'blen*. You have work to do.

> PRINCE CARMINDOR
> (talking to himself)
> I will always look for you.

                         AMARA (V.O.)
                    But you will not find me
                    here.

          He keys in the last number as the door to the
          control room opens behind him. He hears his
          name, but it's too late. Everything is muted. He
          has lost too much blood from the wound in his
          side.

          CARMINDOR collapses to the floor and does not
          get back up.

My hands begin to shake. Just as I thought: Carmindor will be conscripted, and the only person who can save him is dead, and they haven't written in another character who can. From the corner of my eye, I watch as Darien gently sets down his phone. His Adam's apple bobs as he swallows, and his gaze drifts up to mine.

And suddenly, I can see it in his eyes—how he wishes that I were Jess. The real Jess.

My hands close into fists.

The low murmur in the audience grows louder the longer we sit here, unsure of what to do. Do we acknowledge what just happened or press on with the panel? In all my nervousness, I realize I'm biting my thumbnail.

Jess doesn't bite her thumbnail.

I force my hands onto the table and lean over to whisper to him, "What do we do?"

He shakes his head. "I don't—"

"Sorry I'm late!" Amon jumps up the steps, rushing onto the stage. He pats me on the shoulder as he passes. "Did I miss anything?"

Everything, I want to scream. *You missed every—*

Amon sits down at the end of the table and scoots his chair up to his microphone. "Hello there. Thank you, everyone, for coming to our panel. We're going to start with some easy questions—"

Someone in the audience jumps to their feet. Because of the stage lights, I can't see who it is, just a dark shape in a sea of shadows. "Is it real?" they shout.

Amon smooths a smile over his face. "I'm sorry, is what real?" he asks, but Darien leans in close to his microphone, shaking his head.

"No, it's not. It can't be."

"Isn't it?" I whisper.

Another shadow asks, "Are you dying, Carmindor?"

"No! I'm not!" Darien's voice is sharper than it should be, and then he adds, quieter, as if wondering the same thing, "Of course I'm not."

"Don't lie to us!" another person shouts. "Are they killing *Starfield*?"

My nails dig into my palms.

"Get a better Carmindor!" someone else shouts. "Reboot it again!"

"Kill it!"

"Bring back David and Natalia!" another person cries to more shouts of agreement.

Beside me, Darien's face begins to pale. He sits back in his chair, but his shoulders are bunched together as though he's getting ready to spring from the table and leave. Other people shout slogans I've read on Tumblr and Twitter, more obscene things that I'm sure Darien has read before but never experienced in person.

There are dark sides of every fandom. The pockets filled with a certain kind of nostalgia where everything is sacred and shouldn't be tampered with. Where new things are always trash, or judged too harshly, or not up to some unknown holy standard. Where new people with new ideas can't touch an old sinking ship even if it'll repair it—make it better than before.

This is that toxic side, bubbling up, boiling over. It's the side that I've had the pleasure of staying far away from because it's so small and inconsequential. But now, sitting up here on the panel, that sludge of toxicity is pushing right to the edge of the stage.

Jess is always so much closer to it than I ever was. Is that why she hates *Starfield*?

Is *this* all that she's seen of it?

By now, my fingernails are leaving crescent-shaped indentions in my palms. This is my chance to tell the haters off. To make my argument that Amara should be saved—that she deserves to be saved and—

And in saying that, would I be any better than these people shouting that they want Natalia and David back? These people arguing that Jessica Stone can never live up to the dress she slipped into? Haven't I, too, done that in a certain slant of light? For better reasons—good reasons, I daresay—but I don't think my heart has been in the right place. I think she holds an important place in the *Starfield* fandom, but that isn't why I want her back. I want to bring Princess Amara back because she has become a reflection of my own self-worth.

And Jessica Stone—the girl I'm supposed to be playing, the actress in this Greek tragedy—never wanted that.

Because the fandom never gave her a reason *to* want it.

Oh, *starflame*. Now I understand, and it took almost three thousand manbabies to show me.

I set my jaw, my thoughts loud over the roar of the audience as a shouting match breaks out between new and old viewers, hardcore Stargunners and casual fans, shippers and antis, and it's all a mess. Darien forces back his chair and leaves the stage in long, angry strides and I quickly follow him down the stairs and through the side door into a hallway. I don't know whether to stop him, to comfort him, or . . .

I don't know.

But I have to do something.

So I grab him by the sleeve to stop him. "Darien, do you want to talk about—"

He doesn't look at me, his dark eyes trained on the ground. "Jess calls me Dare," he says softly. "People will start noticing if you don't." Then he wrenches his arm away and stalks down the hallway out of sight. I clench my fists again. We fans of Amara have been living with the knowledge that she dies for years, since before I was born, but Darien is just now coming to terms with the fact that he might be dead, too.

I look down at my badge. JESSICA STONE. VIP GUEST. And the button beside it, so small I doubt anyone in the audience could read it: #SAVEAMARA.

I could have done what I wanted to do up there on stage. I had the chance.

But I didn't, because it wasn't my place. Because I'm messing with Jess's life, and because Ethan's right—I *am* nothing more than a clone, merely playing in her star-studded world. It wasn't me those fans came to see, but her. It isn't me they love, but Princess Amara. I just happen to look like her with a little makeup and a lace-front wig.

"You didn't do it."

Startled, I turn toward the soft voice.

Ethan is leaning against the wall a little ways behind me, his arms folded over his chest in his usual old-man pose. He looks tired. His raven-black hair hangs shaggily around his face, and his dark eyes behind his glasses look strained. He's wearing a crumpled button-down with dinosaurs on it, unbuttoned enough to reveal a white shirt underneath, and blue jeans, definitely not in the state of dress I'm used to. Not pristine. Not *Jessica Stone's assistant*. He looks like the eighteen-year-old boy he actually is. He pushes his fingers through his hair.

I feel my spine straighten, like it always does around him. "Because you're right." My voice cracks. "I'm nobody."

"Imogen, you're not—"

"It's Jess right now, remember?" I turn so he can't see the tears filling my eyes and start to walk away. "I'll see you at the meet-and-greet thing."

And I leave before I give him the satisfaction of seeing me cry.

JESS

I SLAP MY HAND OVER MY MOUTH to stifle a gasp, but the pretzel man notices me anyway and looks at me worriedly. I quickly turn my back to him.

Oh, poor Dare.

I don't know how he feels, but I know what it's like.

When I initially read the *Starfield* script, for the first reboot movie, Princess Amara did not die. It's a little-known fact. But then Amon wanted to stick with Amara's original arc from the television show. He wanted to make the diehard fans happy, even though so much else was changed, and he thought he could do that by killing her off.

"We want to give our older fans something to recognize," he had said. "It'll look odd if you live."

He hadn't even asked me what I thought about the script change. He just handed it to me one day during filming—the day after Dare did his building-jumping stunt—and told me to read through the rewritten ending and memorize it.

So I did. The difference was, Amon had told me in *private*. I didn't have to learn about it out in public—in front of a crowd of thousands of people. I could process it before the rest of the world found out.

Dare deserved better.

Being an actor is weird sometimes. You get so attached to your character, some plot twist that takes you by surprise. But this is different. I was just a girl who was told that her character, to whom she connected, would die. I'd be lying if I said I wasn't happy when he told me. It wasn't a guaranteed out, but I had been naive. Dare ... Carmindor had been a dream gig, a fanboy's dream, and now ...

I try calling him for the third time but he's not picking up. I begin to pace in Artists' Alley, and the pretzel man's gaze follows me the whole way, though honestly I can't bring myself to care at the moment. I know that the panel ended abruptly but I can't parse how, and my Twitter notifications are pinging faster than I can mute them. What in the world *happened*? Is Dare okay?

I get so many Twitter comments that the app freezes, so I log onto Instagram instead. I wish I hadn't. A mind-blowing amount of comment notifications pop up. So many more than usual. I haven't checked my feed since arriving at the convention, and after a few days the comments usually taper off because of the app's algorithms. (Ethan once tried to explain all this tech stuff to me, but most of it soared way over my head.)

Before I can tap into the comments, out of the corner of my eye I see a pair of familiar sneakers and look up—there is Ethan with his hands in his jeans pockets. Alarmed, I turn to him. "Where's Imogen?"

"You got the text."

"Of course I did, and my social's crashing because of all the comments." I try to control my voice, but panic eats in at the edges. "What happened, Ethan? What's *happening*?"

"Well," he says calmly, pushing up his glasses, "Darien found out on stage that his character's dying, and he didn't take it well."

Of course he didn't.

My eyes are beginning to burn the longer I think about Carmindor dying. Something in my chest is tight and wrong, and it's so uncomfortable, but people are watching us, even in the back of Artists' Alley, so I can't freak out. *Breathe.*

"I should be happy, right? Carmindor dies, and because of that I'm sure Amara's not coming back. I'm free. Even if I don't find the thief who stole my script—I'm free." My vision blurs and my voice hitches. "Why aren't I happy?"

Ethan takes his hands out of his pockets and pulls me into a hug. "Because you love it, Jess."

The hairs on my skin stand on end. I push away. "Love it? Ethan, *Starfield* was the worst thing to happen to my career. It almost killed it!"

"Jess, I know you, and you're always so focused on the future. On what's ahead of you. You never looked around and saw what you had already."

"What I had?" I scoff, pressing my palms over my eyes, for once glad that I'm not wearing makeup that would smudge. "What I *had* was a dead-end contract—"

"Then why aren't you happy that you don't have to play Amara anymore?" he interrupts, his voice like flint. "I know you're not."

"I-I don't know! This convention has messed everything up in my head." I try to keep my voice low, but a person buying a salted pretzel is eyeing me curiously. The pretzel man waves them on and I continue in a hushed voice, "I only have a short window in my career—shorter because I lied about my age when I was fourteen—and I refuse to be known as that dead space princess. There are no awards for that."

"There's the Razzies."

"That's not funny, Ethan."

He exhales through his nose. "Look, Jess, I love you and you are my best friend, but you are so hardheaded sometimes I could scream. What movies do we remember the best? Do we remember the film that won the Academy Award in 1977 or do we remember the low-budget space opera from that same year that—"

"*Rocky.*"

"What?"

"*Rocky* won Best Picture in 1977."

He falters. "That was a bad example. You were supposed to say we remembered *Star Wars* the best."

"It was a great year for movies," I add. "*The Omen* won best score—"

My phone dings. It's not a text message but a news report from a celebrity gossip blog that I follow. Tagging me with screenshots of my own Instagram photos—and all the comments underneath.

Death threats. Violent threats. Comments making fun of my hair, my weight, me.

A chill crawls down my spine. They were bad before, but now they're a torrent of the exact nightmare I never wanted. It's coming true. It's finally coming true.

"What did Imogen do?" I whisper, and look up to Ethan, but his face is an impasse of emotion. "What did she *do*?" I repeat, my voice louder, and I show him the article.

"Jess, she didn't—"

"*Didn't* she? They're saying it's my fault—mine!—that Carmindor's getting axed. Because I'm not there to save him. Imogen said something, didn't she? On the panel. I should've *never* let her be me."

Ethan's shaking his head. "It's not what—"

"Isn't it? This entire thing was pointless. There's no way for me to win—none! If I get the script back, it won't matter because they'll blame me for killing Carmindor, and if I don't get it back and everyone finds out it's mine, I'll be the actress who killed *Starfield*!"

"Jess, *please* stop for a second." Ethan tries to grab me around the shoulders, but I brush him off. It doesn't matter what he has to say.

I've seen enough from my comments on social, and the buttons I had to hand out, and the moments on the panels when she almost did the unthinkable, and I've already made up my mind.

"Go—leave!" I snap, and slip into the crowd as quickly as I can, dodging between a group of Jedis in training, hoping to lose him. But when I look back I realize that he didn't even follow.

Ethan's wrong—I never could have liked *Starfield*. Or Princess Amara. Or this fandom.

Because the fandom will never like me.

IMOGEN

TOWARD THE END OF THE MEET-AND-GREET, the camera dies and the volunteer, a cheery girl with purple hair, excuses herself to go get a new battery. While she's gone I shake out my nervous energy, my limbs buzzing with excitement. I can't remember all of the people I've taken photos with, or all of their names—although I know I asked every one of them what it was. Whatever toxicity that was in the panel hadn't made it here, thank goodness.

Ethan finally slips into the photo-op booth. He hesitates, then looks at me, as if seeing that I'm still in one piece and not, you know, torn apart by fans. No, I'm still intact. I'm still playing Jessica Stone.

"Is everything all right?" he asks.

"Why wouldn't it be?" I clip in reply, but instantly regret it.

He nods quietly and sits on a stool in the corner, pulling out his phone to ignore me, or to pretend as though I don't matter. I know he's only here for Jess's sake, but I wish he wasn't.

The air is thick with tension. Like Jabba the Hut thick, so thick I'd have to wrap my chains around its neck and strangle it just to make it go away—and I'm not even wearing a metal bikini to do that in.

Out of the corner of my eye, I see a guy saunter into the booth. He doesn't even glance at Ethan, who just got a text and is replying with furious punches. Ethan doesn't notice him either.

He isn't supposed to be here, this guy. That much I can tell.

And when he looks at me, my blood freezes.

It's Jasper.

I would notice him from a football field away, the way he holds himself when he walks, and he grins as we make eye contact. Brown hair and green eyes. Oh how I wish he had looked at me when we dated the way he looks at Me-as-Jessica-Stone now. Then I might not have ended up bawling on the curb at last year's con.

I instantly get a bad feeling in my gut.

"Amaraaaaah!" Jasper cries, arms wide. He's wearing a Joker and Harley Quinn T-shirt and jeans, and one of his YouTube filming lackeys is somewhere close by, I'm sure of it. "You broke the internet today!"

I did . . . ?

How?

When I don't rush to embrace him, his smile falters.

"What, too good for a hug?" He says it jokingly, but my skin prickles.

He doesn't recognize me?

No—he thinks I'm Jess.

I smile thinly. "Of course not."

I'm just being paranoid. We hug. His hands slip low.

I push away from him so fast, it takes him by surprise and he stumbles backward.

"What the heck?" he yelps, and then breaks into another laugh. "What's wrong, Jessica?"

Jessica. He has the nerve to call me by my first name—well, by Jessica's first name—when he doesn't even know her. When he just touched my butt like it was absolutely nothing?

I don't remember Jasper ever doing that to me.

But it's becoming increasingly clear that I only knew the Jasper in my head—the Jasper I wanted to know—not the one who ghosted me at the ExcelsiCon ball last year and broke up with me over text messages.

He outstretches his hand, the one that touched my butt. "The name's Jasper Webster. I'm a pro gamer. Got about four million followers. Can we get a vid together for my fans?"

"Do you have a ticket?" I ask.

"I just"—he makes a slick slicing motion—"cut in line a little. Don't worry, I'm sure you don't mind."

He's talking to me like he didn't just grab me. Like I overreacted for nothing. No, he knows what he did was wrong and he's just acting as if it doesn't matter.

He notices the button pinned to my lanyard. "Save Amara? That's really cute."

"What do you want?"

He flicks out his cell phone and starts recording. "I just want to congratulate the girl who ruined *Starfield.*"

The confusion must be written all over my face, because he laughs and asks, "Is it true you didn't want to be in the sequel, so the director cut you at the last minute in the first movie?"

"*Excuse* me?" In my surprise, my voice slips out of Jessica's drawl and into my nondescript crisp one. It's a little lower than Jess's, a little less sweet.

"Now Carmindor's dying, and it's your fault."

That was about the most absurd thing I'd ever heard in my entire life—and I was raised in fandom. I look at the video camera, and then at Jasper, trying to gauge how he wants me to react, so I don't give him the satisfaction—

Suddenly Ethan is there, yanking the phone out of his hand and deleting the video.

"What the hell, man?" Jasper snarls (but he definitely doesn't say *hell*).

Ethan tosses back the phone, his eyes like onyx. "You're done. Get out." At his full height, he's a head taller than Jasper. His expression is cold and impassive, the kind of look reserved for people about to snap someone else's neck. The only clue that he is the least bit agitated is the quickened pulse beating at his throat.

Starflame, Jessica doesn't need a bodyguard when she has *that*, I realize.

Jasper laughs off Ethan's unspoken threat and raises his hands in a surrender-like motion. "Dude, look, step back. We're busy."

Then he tries to come at me again, but Ethan puts a hand on his shoulder.

Jasper whirls around, fists clenched, ready to swing. I don't have time to shout to Ethan that a punch is coming before he raises a hand and deflects the blow with his lower arm, grabbing Jasper by the shirt and pull-throwing him out through the nearest curtain. The panels of black fabric fly apart just wide enough for me to watch Jasper trip and fall on his face onto the retro rug, right in front of a line of fans waiting for the next star, before fluttering closed.

I look at Ethan wide-eyed, and he seems just as surprised as me that his move actually worked. He opens his mouth to say something but the volunteer pops back into the booth, fixing her glasses that keep falling down the bridge of her nose.

"I am *so* sorry! That took way longer than I thought," she says. Then she asks if I'm ready to finish my meet-and-greet.

There are only ten fans left, so I smile and pose and ask their names, just like before. But this time, their names stick with me—though not for the reasons they should. Because they don't try to feel me up, because they are nice, because they are decent human beings.

And I hate that some of the dickwads in their midst are not.

After the last photo, I rub my arms, feeling dirty and miserable. Is this what Jessica has to put up with all the time? Harassment like that? Is that all she's ever seen of the *Starfield* fandom in the month the movie's been out? Nothing but provocation and disapproval and people shouting how she can never live up to Natalia Ford?

I leave the booth as quickly as I can. I don't know where I'm going, but somewhere away from people.

Somewhere I can stop and peel off my skin.

"Hey," Ethan calls after me.

I push through a GUESTS ONLY door that leads into a hallway. It's vacant, but not far enough away. A few moments later, the door opens again. Ethan's gaining on me with those ridiculously long legs. I take another corner.

My mind is frazzled.

I'm shaking.

I thought Jasper wasn't that kind of guy.

I'm so mad at myself. Why did I clam up? I saw what was happening. Why didn't I yell at him to take his hands off me? I shouldn't have let him hug me in the first place. Was it my fault? Did I—

"*Imogen.*"

Ethan grabs me gently by the forearm to stop me.

"I'm fine," I say, and his impassive face twitches in agitation. He knows I'm lying. I grit my teeth. He hasn't cared about me so far in this charade. Why should he start now? "I don't need you to protect me—I mean, Jessica."

His eyebrows furrow, and he drops his hand from my arm. "Of course."

How often does that happen to Jess? I want to ask, but I'm also a little scared to know. I curl my fingers around the sides of my blue dress so Ethan can't see them shaking. "I had it under control. I didn't need you to come to my rescue. I was fine."

"Imogen . . . "

"I'm *Jessica* right now," I snap, "and I said I was fine."

"You were *not* fine."

I am vibrating with anger. "WHY DO YOU CARE NOW?" I scream. "I'm just some stupid peasant pretending to be a princess. A nobody who isn't worth your time."

I hurt him just then, I know I did, but hurting him feels like scratching a sunburn when it itches. It feels awful, but it's a relief, too.

"Excuse me," I mumble, and I don't even wait for him to argue. I escape down the hallway and through another set of doors, and he doesn't follow. I'm not sure where I'm going—I'm heading in the direction of the Green Room, but I don't want to go there. I want to rake my fingers across my skin and peel myself back, or drown in a marathon of *Starfield* and forget about Jasper, or—

"Jessica?"

I blink and realize I'm outside the Green Room, my hand on the doorknob. I let go and turn toward the voice.

Vance Reigns smiles around a toothpick, and it's disarming and sincere and he doesn't know what I've just been through. He's oblivious to it. In his perception of the world, it never happened.

"Is something the matter?" Vance asks gently.

I fix on a plastic smile, and I hope he doesn't see it slipping.

"I'm fine. What're you doing here?"

He shrugs and hoists a black backpack higher on his shoulder. "I *was* going to watch your panel earlier but . . . "

"It didn't quite go as planned."

"Are you okay?" he asks.

"Of course—why wouldn't I be?"

He pulls his hand through his gorgeous blond hair. "I tried to call your hotel room last night after I got in from a dinner I had to go to, but you never called me back. It was late, though. I'm sorry."

Late. He must have called while I was in the pool, or at the diner with Milo and Bran. But he'd called. I hadn't even thought to check the answering machine when I went to grab my bag, but then again I doubt Ethan would've approved. He'd said as much about Vance Reigns.

Which is funny, because Vance has been nicer to me than Ethan will ever be.

"It's okay," I reply softly. I begin to walk around him, but he grabs my arm to stop me.

"Whoa whoa whoa, Stone. Where're you heading?"

"Hotel, probably."

"How about not?" He smiles again, and the last few moments with Ethan wash away. Vance loops my arm into his like a new Doctor claiming his companion. "Wanna go grab a bite with me, Jessica Stone? I feel like you might need a break."

I hesitate because that *does* sound nice. A bite to eat away from the convention. A quiet place to think and regroup.

With Vance Reigns.

I might be a ball of confliction, but I am not dead.

"*Please,*" I reply, trying not to sound too desperate.

JESS

As I make my way back to Harper's booth, I can't help but take stock of the damage that's been done. The comments on my social are only getting worse.

Every time I delete one, two more take its place. Calling me names, critiquing my body, and my bones, and my career. This is just the thing I didn't want. Just the thing I tried to stay out of. But really, I should've known it would come to this. Because I'm not just a woman in Hollywood, I'm a woman in fantasy/sci-fi Hollywood. Not only are the roles less prestigious, they're subject to the criticisms of trolls who are dissatisfied with my accomplishments, my looks, my talent, my *breast size*—and who blame me for anything and everything they find wrong. What's worse, I know this is just a small portion of them, because I am white and straight-passing. Actresses of color get mobbed for merely existing.

"I hate this," I whisper, and quickly shove my phone into my pocket. I want to rake my hands through my hair but I can't because I have this stupid beanie on. The convention is so loud, I can't hear myself think. People stare at me even though I don't want them to. Nothing is private. There's nowhere I can escape.

Ultimately, my feet find their way back to Harper's booth. She looks up from her Obi-Wan commission. "Something up?"

Another chance for me to tell her the truth. That I'm Jessica Stone. That I've lied to her, and I'm sorry, and my life is falling apart and I'm not even present to watch it crumble.

And deep down, I don't want to be.

"No," I lie.

"Well, whatever is *not* up," Harper tries to soothe me, "it'll be fine. There's a quote that I like to always remember—"

"'It's fine'?"

She scowls good-naturedly. "I find your lack of faith disturbing."

"It is a leaf on the wind—"

"'You are not alone, *ah'blena*,'" she says, quoting a line I know all too well. It's what Carmindor says to Princess Amara during one of the Nox King's infamous galas. Two-thirds into the movie, before the Black Nebula ruptures and the princess has to sacrifice herself to save the galaxy.

And it's the exact quote that makes my lips wobble. I push up my glasses and look away.

Harper closes her sketchpad in alarm. "There *is* something wrong."

"You won't understand."

"Try me."

"I can't," I reply, pushing my fingertips under my glasses to wipe away the tears I am definitely not shedding right now. *Keep it together, Jessica. Keep it together.* "You won't understand."

Harper exhales an aggravated sigh. "You're right—if you don't tell me, I'll never understand. I don't know what's come over you these past few days, but you definitely aren't as happy as you seemed to be, and I know something's wrong."

Oh, was Imogen that much of a ray of sunshine?

I shake my head. "Do you know what it's like to put every-thing you have into something—like a project, or a character—and it's just never enough for anyone? Knowing that, no matter what you do, you'll never live up to the expectations in other people's heads?"

"That's a tough spot to be in," Harper says, cocking her head and taking a moment to consider her response. "I think you should just live up to the expectations in your own head first, because you're always hardest on yourself. At least that's how I feel when I'm trying to write my comics."

I fidget uncomfortably and chew on my bottom lip. "It is?"

"I think it's bullshit that the only meaningful stories are the ones that are deep and pondering and boring, saying all this non-sense without ever saying anything, and you're supposed to, like, read meaning into the yellow wallpaper or something." She rolls her eyes. "You know what I think? I think sometimes the stories we need are the ones about taking the hobbits to Isengard and dog-human dudes with space heelies and trashy King Arthurs and gay ice-skating animes and Zuko redemption arcs and space princesses with found families and galaxies far, far away. We need *those* stories, too. Stories that tell us that we can be bold and brash and make mistakes and still come out better on the other side. Those are the kinds of stories I want to see, and read, and tell. 'Look to the stars. Aim. Ignite'—*that* means something to me, you know?"

No, I don't. But . . . I want to.

Harper takes my hand and squeezes it tightly, giving me the courage I need. "Harper, I need to tell you something—"

"Jessica Stone?" a voice interrupts.

I glance up, and on the other side of the booth table is that interviewer from my first day at this con—the woman with the candy-apple-red glasses and the off-script questions. The journalist who made me humiliate myself in front of Natalia Ford. I quickly push my glasses up on my face. "I think you have the wrong—"

"You are! I'd know that face anywhere. What're you doing here?" Her eyes grow hungry as she drinks me in like her next paycheck. She's starting to attract the attention of other people in the aisle.

"Dude, I think that's her," a Deadpool says to another Deadpool. "Look at the mole on her left cheek!"

I quickly jump to my feet, covering the mole with my hand. Really—*now* is when people notice it?

The journalist presses on. "Aren't you supposed to be at a meet-and-greet?" Then her eyes slip to Harper. "And who's *she*?"

"Imogen?" Harper asks, giving me a strange look. "What's happening? Who's this woman?"

"I'm sorry," I whisper, and my eyes burn because I'm on the verge of tears, and this is not how I want to be seen in public. This is not how Jessica Stone is seen in public. My chest begins to tighten as I stumble out from behind the booth. "I'm so sorry—"

The first phone camera flashes and I flinch.

I can barely breathe. *No,* I think. *No, this isn't how this is supposed to happen.*

"Excuse me," I mutter, forcing my way through the gathering crowd, leaving Harper at her booth, surrounded by the chorus of my name.

"Jess! What do you think of the script?" someone shouts.

"Isn't she at a meet-and-greet?"

"Can I have your autograph?"

"I LOVE YOU JESSICA STONE!"

But all I can hear are the Instagram comments, and all I can see are the Photoshopped images from trolls online. The crowd begins to follow me, and even more people turn to watch. My brown hair is slipping out of my beanie, and I don't have time to push it back up again.

I break into a run—and they follow.

Please stop, I beg. *Stop following me.*

Turning down the last artists' aisle, where the plushies are, I mutter a plea for forgiveness before I toss the entire rack onto the floor in the hopes of blocking the crowd from pursuing me—or at least slowing them down.

The girl in the booth looks up from her smartphone just in time to see me knock over the rack and squawks, "NO!"

But the plushies tumble across the floor, and I sprint toward the emergency exit twenty feet away. The art-deco carpet swims in my vision, and I can't seem to catch my breath.

If I'd never thrown away that script, if I'd never thought of this foolish idea to have Imogen impersonate me, if I'd just breathed and kept to myself and pushed my feelings down beneath my toes and not fallen for Harper Hart, then I wouldn't be in this situation.

But I can't get the look on Harper's face out of my mind, the confusion morphing into betrayal as she realized who I was. The kind of person I am. How long I've lied to her. Oh God, I lied to her and that's unforgivable and I can feel a bit of my heart breaking because I remember how she looked this morning as the sunlight poured through the curtains, her face inches from mine as we whispered to each other, "Good morning."

And it hurts.

It hurts so much because I was—

I was—

I was *happy*.

And now I am unraveling stitch by stitch.

I don't stop running until I shove open the hotel doors and stumble out onto the sidewalk. It's pouring rain outside. My flats get soaked the second I step into a puddle, but I can't stop because a few people are still following me. Haven't they gotten the hint?

Just leave me alone!

I wrap my arms around myself as I bound off the curb and make my way across the street to my hotel—

A car horn blares.

I jerk toward the sound, headlights blinding, tires squealing. The burning smell of tires punctures the scent of muggy rain on asphalt as a black car screeches to a stop just inches away from me.

I stare at the car.

The back passenger door opens and out steps Natalia Ford, her gray hair pinned into a bun atop her head. She's wearing a shirt covered in a pattern of tiny artistically rendered middle fingers and a blood-red ascot.

I swallow the lump in my throat.

A clash of thunder rumbles overhead, reverberating between the tall buildings. Behind me, a few fans and the journalist burst through the doors in search of me.

Natalia tilts her head and steps back into the car, which I take as a sign to join her. I round the car, open the door, and slide in. The car drives away before my fans realize which way I've gone; I watch them disappear in the rear window as we take a side street out of downtown Atlanta and away from the convention.

"You know, I've heard rumors that you dislike conventions," Natalia says, "but sweetheart, tossing yourself into traffic isn't *quite* the best way to get your point across." She crosses one leg over the other and I notice Stubbles perched in her lap, staring at me with jaded green eyes.

"I wasn't looking," I reply. I don't realize it at first, but I'm shivering.

Natalia turns up the heat. The windshield wipers knock back and forth, the constant thrum of the rain dampening the sound of my chattering teeth. Her white-goateed driver faces forward, wearing a slick black suit. There are rumors that he's also her, um, boyfriend, which reminds me a little too much of *The Princess Diaries*—except with Julie Andrews replaced by Meryl Streep from *The Devil Wears Prada*.

"Thank you, Ms. Ford," I say after a moment.

"For what?" She slides her hazel gaze over to me. It's just as sharp as her tongue. "I merely almost ran you over and then you decided to get into my car."

Oh. I clear my throat and reach for the door handle. "You can tell your driver to stop anywhere and I'll get out—"

"Don't be silly. We're going much too fast. Plus there's a paparazzo trailing us."

I glance behind me, and sure enough a black SUV with tinted windows is following us a few cars behind. "I didn't even realize. How did you know it was there?"

"I might be an *ancient* Hollywood actress who has no career to speak of, but I have dated enough starstruck manbabies to sense a camera from a hundred feet away."

"I honestly wasn't thinking when I said that in the interview," I say, but she waves me off.

"Don't apologize. If you apologize for everything, then your apologies will never mean anything. That woman was drilling you terribly hard. What did you do, interrupt her flirting with your costar?"

Is she . . . joking? Is Natalia Ford trying to crack a joke? I can't tell. Talking to her is like playing poker with the Godfather. "I . . . might have. Or I said something wrong. Or any number of things that I can't really remember doing—jeez, this convention is driving me insane. I'm not usually like this. I'm cool and composed. I don't flub interviews. I don't offend other people . . . How did you do it?" I ask, looking over at her. The leather seats are warming up, and I'm not shivering anymore. "How did you survive all of this? All of the fans hating you?"

"When I played Amara, there were barely message boards on an old dial-up computer. I didn't have to worry about the general public giving me an earful of critique I didn't need. But now all you young people are socially connected to everything. Your fans have you at their fingertips. It must be a nightmare."

Her hairless cat slinks over to me and curls up in my lap, purring like a contented pet. Gently, I drop my hand down to pat it, but it hisses and swipes at me with claws out. Mixed message received.

"Nostalgia's a hell of a drug," she says after a long pause.

"And the greatest *honor*," I add wryly, "a female character can have is death. Especially a useful one."

A spark ignites in Natalia's eyes, and she turns to face me. Her cat slinks over into her lap again and begins kneading her legs with its long, lethal claws. "Yet it isn't an honor at all, is it?"

"No—and it's not just *Starfield*. Even after this, if there is an *after this* for me, in the next film I'm either going to be fridged, or I'll be cast as a forty-year-old actor's love interest, or I'll become that quirky secondary character. Or I'll just be nothing. That's all I'll be. That's all *Starfield* will ever be."

"Then change it."

"Change it?" I want to laugh, and the cat's ears airplane back because my voice is high and brittle. "You're kidding, right? What can *I* do? I just want to make a difference. I just want to be part of movies that mean something—"

My voice catches in my throat as I remember Harper's words: *Sometimes the stories we need . . .*

Natalia gives me a keen look.

"I have to find Imogen," I whisper, and I order the driver to pull over. I'm somewhere in the outskirts of Atlanta, I can call a taxi to take me back to the convention, but Natalia motions for her driver to keep going. "Ms. Ford, I need to get back to the convention—"

"I would suggest you check the diner on the corner of the next street."

I look at her blankly.

She produces a smartphone from her purse and turns it on. She shows me a gossip site—and its lead photo.

Imogen and Vance Reigns.

"I think you need to save her."

"*Starflame!*" I hiss, and before the car even stops I've shoved the door open and am hopping out. "Thank you!" I call over my shoulder, and she waves dismissively until I close the door and the car moves on.

I can already count three of those cockroaches encroaching on the diner, and from the look of it, Imogen has no clue. Of course she doesn't. I should've told her to stay away from Vance Reigns. That bloodsucking social climber will do anything to get ahead.

It occurs to me a little too late that I never prepared Imogen at all for being me, because though she might look like me and can imitate my voice, she doesn't have the years of accumulated knowledge of who to trust and who to steer clear of. And she definitely doesn't understand how to handle these sorts of situations.

But Jessica Stone does.

I whirl around to the paparazzo who had been following Natalia's car and motion for them to pull over. I have an idea—it's an awful one, and Ethan would definitely not approve, but I don't have time for a better plan. The skies have brightened and it's only drizzling now, and the city has become so humid that the air sticks to me like a tongue.

The paparazzo pulls over and a window rolls down to reveal a woman in her midtwenties, her hair swirled up into a bun atop her head. She pops her gum and lowers her heart-shaped sunglasses. "Miss Stone, you know I only park illegally for you—"

"Can I ask you a favor?"

"I'm sorry, did you just say you need to ask me for a favor?"

"I'll give you an exclusive. A photo no one else'll get. I just need you to help me out." I glance over to the other paparazzi. "Can I get in?"

She gives me a once-over before she pops her gum again and smiles. "Yeah. Get in, loser. We're gonna get some photos."

IMOGEN

To GET OUT OF THE RAIN, VANCE AND I dip into a small diner a few blocks away from the convention and slide into a booth. We're only moderately wet, and we're laughing from our mad dash into the restaurant. The is the second time in twenty-four hours I've been within touching distance of Vance Reigns. My heart should be about ready to explode, but I can't stop thinking about the glare Ethan gave Jasper at the meet-and-greet.

He looked about ready to kill him.

I shouldn't have snapped at Ethan like that. He was only trying to help.

Yeah, but he's a burnt Hufflepuff, I try to reason with myself, *and you're getting food with a Gryffindor.*

A clap of thunder rumbles overhead, and lightning reflects off the skyscrapers around us. We made it to the diner just before the storm hit in full swing, and I shake off errant water droplets on my arms.

The diner is red-and-white checkered, with neon signs glowing in the windows and the smell of greasy fries and sweet ice cream hanging in the air. I sit on one side of the booth, assuming

Vance would go for the other, but instead he slides in next to me, stretching his arm across the back of the booth behind me.

He smells like a mixture of motorcycle exhaust and some sort of expensive cologne, and sitting this close I can see stubble on his cheek. This feels really, *really* cliché, straight out of a '90s rom-com starring a rough leathery bad boy and a chaste good girl.

Oh, if he knew me—the real me—he'd realize I am *not* that good at all.

"You looked upset earlier. Is everything okay?" he asks softly, as a preppy waitress comes over and hands us two menus.

"I'm fine. A strawberry shake, please," I say before I can think of what Jessica would order. I'm too tired to play that game.

"Um, yeah, chocolate malt. Thanks," he adds, giving the waitress a dashing smile before turning his gaze back to me. She stares at him, blinking, for another moment, realizing that yes, it *is* Vance Reigns, before she hurries off to tell the other waitstaff.

"Are you sure you're fine?" he asks. "Is there anything I can do?"

I toy with my words, arranging them in my head, before I say, "Do you ever have a little voice in your head that tells you that you aren't good enough? And you've never done anything in your life, so you begin to think that maybe that little voice in your head is right? That maybe you *aren't* smart or talented or pretty enough—"

"Pretty? Jess." He angles himself in the booth to turn his full attention to me. "I think you're beautiful."

It's a phrase I've never heard in my life. At least, not directed at me. Not while some utterly gorgeous guy stares into my eyes, his gaze curving down my cheek, resting on my mouth. He knows what beauty is—he must, because he *is* beautiful. The way his shoulder-length blond hair is twisted back into a bun while wavy locks escape, framing his chiseled face. The intensity of his icy blue eyes makes it a little hard to breathe, and a lot hard to think.

He called me beautiful.

VANCE REIGNS.

CALLED ME.

BOOOTEEF—

"I-I do?" I stutter. "I . . . I am?"

"Of course. Why do you seem so surprised?" His thumb trails down the side of my neck.

Gooseflesh prickles my skin before I can remember that I'm Jessica and not Imogen, and Jessica is told that she is beautiful all the time. She lives in a land where she's probably never been told anything else.

She's probably reminded that she's beautiful every day of her life.

I love my Kathy and Minerva—they tell me I'm pretty and special and so Gryffindor I probably need a disclaimer, but it's not the same. My moms love me to the moon and back, but they're my family.

A stranger has never called me beautiful until now. Not sincerely.

All my life I've thought that maybe if I didn't rush in, if I grew my hair out, if I put on makeup or liked *Gossip Girl* or sports or anything besides *Starfield* and animes, maybe I would've been asked to study sessions or proms or football games.

Maybe Jasper wouldn't have bailed on me at ExclesiCon last year.

And yet, when I slip into playing Jessica, people take notice. I'm interesting as Jessica—I'm smart and talented, and this boy I barely know just called me beautiful.

Then why does it feel weird, and wrong?

"No one has ever called me beautiful before," I say softly.

Vance laughs, deep and rumbly. "Now I know you're lying. Everyone knows you are, Jess. It's part of the package."

That word gives me pause; his hand rests on the side of my neck and he leans in close. I ease backward a little. "The package? Like I'm some made-to-order special on QVC?"

"It's just a saying, Jess. You're gorgeous," he says and twirls a finger through my hair. I really hope it's human hair and not, you know, fake, but he doesn't seem to mind either way. "And you're mysterious, and not easy to take out on a date, that's for sure."

"A . . . date?"

"Isn't that what this is? You finally agreed to go out on a date with Vance Reigns."

Oh sweet baby Carmindor, he just referred to himself in the third person.

"And *I* finally get to go out with one of the most elusive girls on the market." He lowers his face as if to kiss me—

NO HE IS COMING TO KISS ME.

I plant a hand on his chest and push him away.

"Whoa, we barely know each other, Vance."

He scoffs. "Barely? Jess. We run in all the same circles. You dated that cad Darien Freeman, and we both know I kiss much better than him."

Oh no.

I've made a grave mistake.

The Vance in my head, the one who is kind and charming and puts a finger down to "Never have I ever had a crush on Ron Swanson," is dying in a blaze of bad acting.

He goes on, even though I really would just appreciate him shutting up. "We'd look great together, don't you agree? General

Sond and the dead Princess Amara. The tabloids'll go *nuts*."

"You . . . want to date me," I fill in.

He rolls his eyes. "Duh."

"But what if we aren't compatible?"

"Jess, we're not on the market for what's inside."

"On the market?" There it is again. Those words.

The waitress comes and sets down our shakes and quickly scurries away. Warning signs flare up in every corner of my brain because this is *not* where I want this conversation to be going.

Vance takes out his phone from his back pocket and pulls up the camera.

"I'm sorry to lead you on," he says, sounding not very sorry at all, "but honestly, you play the game too, don't you? Go on a few dates, call a few paparazzi, pretend something scandalous is about to go down."

"But what if I . . . "

He gives me a peculiar look and the charming set to his face is no longer charming at all, but arrogant. "What? You actually thought I—? Oh, Jess." He *tsk*s and takes a selfie of us, even though my face is already beginning to fall. He turns his head to me, our shoulders touching, and he is so close that I can smell the mint gum on his breath and see the individual strands of bronze in his hair. His lips part into a strange toothy grin, more beast than prince, and he says, "Princess Amara doesn't have a happy ending. I thought you knew that."

"*What?*"

"And you'll never get a second chance." He runs his thumb along my jaw. "Stop looking at me like I'm talking nonsense. Why couldn't you act this swell on screen?"

"This was all a stunt? You—you invited me here for a *photo*?"

"They're worth a thousand words." He shrugs away from me and takes out his wallet, tossing a five-dollar bill onto the table. "You can pay for the rest, yeah sweetheart?"

Sweetheart.

The word pulls me out of my stupor.

We aren't sweet—he barely knows me. And I've seen enough BBC *Doctor Who*s to pick up on the sarcasm in his brilliant British accent.

I can handle a surprise selfie. I can handle figuring out that he's a douchebag supreme with a side of dumbass.

But what I *can't* handle?

I am the daughter of Kathy and Minerva Lovelace, and I am no one's *pet name*.

I plant my hands on his chest and shove him out of the booth so hard, he flops onto the ground. He stares up at me from the tiles, because clearly he's never been put on the ground by a girl before.

"Don't call me sweetheart," I snarl, "you two-faced nerf-herding hobgoblin!"

He stumbles to his feet, shaking out his leather jacket, vibrating in anger. "I'll see you on the front pages!" He jabs a finger toward the window, and for the first time I notice the paparazzi outside, peeking from behind parked cars. He sneers. "Good luck getting off them."

He called the paparazzi, I realize, and a flash of anger jolts through me.

Then—just to add insult to injury—he reaches for his shake. Oh no, sir. No you don't. I snatch it away and toss it at him, melted ice cream spilling across his shirt and precious leather jacket. He gives an anguished cry, as if I've torn his favorite Blue-Eyes White Dragon Yu-Gi-Oh! card in half.

Oh, he hasn't even *seen* what I can do yet.

I grab the other milkshake, glad that it's strawberry, which goes so well with chocolate. I stand on the booth's bench and hold it menacingly over his head.

He looks up in disbelief. "Stop! What the hell—"

And then, I dump it.

He slushes around, wiping strawberry milkshake from his eyes, calling me all of the most colorful names in the book, and then he storms out of the diner on squeaky shoes. The paparazzi train their lenses on him as he leaves.

The waitress returns, handing me a handful of napkins. "Your insult was way better."

"Thanks. I'll help you clean up," I offer, and take the mop from her hands. I'm glad I'm in motion so that when the paparazzi turn back to take more photos, they don't see Jess's hands shaking.

But it's strange.

They don't turn back to me.

They don't click their cameras.

There's a woman shooing them away from the window—

The bell above the diner door dings and my skin prickles, thinking it's Vance, come back with the paparazzi. I summon all of the best insults I can think of. I launch into my tirade: "Coming back for seconds? Good, because you haven't even *seen* my Angry Feminist Rampage yet. Jess?" Her name comes out as a squeak.

Jessica Stone is standing in the middle of the diner, her SPACE QUEEN beanie in her hands and her soaking wet hair pulled back into a ponytail. She leaves a puddle on the ground around her. "Angry Feminist Rampage? See, the trick is," she replies, folding her arms over her chest, "to *always* be angry."

"Jess!" I jab a finger at the people with cameras. "They'll see!"

But she waves her hand. "Don't worry about the paparazzi," she says, and I notice they're not pointing their cameras at us. She levels a look at me, "I think I need to tell you the truth."

JESS

As Imogen finishes mopping up the milkshake, she says, "So let me get this straight: you accidentally threw away the *Starfield* sequel script that some asshole then found in the garbage and started posting on Twitter, so you asked me to switch with you in hopes that you could find the thief before they revealed that it was yours?"

"That about sums it up." I tap some hot sauce onto my fries.

"Huh."

Most of the paparazzi have left us for Calvin (I gave them his hotel name and room number, so I make a mental note to buy him a sorry-you-were-bait bouquet later), but a few hang around in the diner, watching Imogen and me from a distance. They aren't taking photos, though, because I promised them a better op later. The paparazzi aren't *all* soulless cockroaches. They just go where the money is, and I've never given them a reason not to trust me. They're more like—what're those things called? The birds that sit on a rhino's back, picking bugs off its skin? They're more like that.

There is an ecosystem in Hollywood that I know well. It's just the rest of the world that I don't quite get. Especially the internet.

Imogen leans on the mop. "And you still haven't found out who took the script?"

"It's a big convention. I was stupid to think I could do it alone."

"Then that makes two of us," she replies with a sigh. "Listen, Jess, about the whole Save Amara thing—"

"Why does it mean so much to you?" I interrupt, picking at my basket of fries. "Why does *she* mean so much to you?"

She. Princess Amara.

Imogen winces, her lips pressed into a thin line. She picks at the rough handle of the mop, as if I had asked her to explain solar combustion. Now that I finally have a good look at her, I much prefer her with a pink pixie. She looks a little too much like me in that brown wig and drawn-on mole, and I'm really not all that surprised she pulled me off so well. In any other life, she could've been me.

There is a theory of parallel universes—or a *multiverse*— much like String Theory's extra dimensions of spacetime. It's the speculation that there are other parallel universes running along-side ours with different pasts and different futures—where one choice you make splits off into another parallel world. So, per-haps there's a universe out there where the impossible happens and I'm not *Starfield*'s princess.

Perhaps there is a universe where a girl with a pink pixie is.

"Princess Amara is brave," Imogen finally says, and her voice is soft and timid, like she's telling me a great secret not many peo-ple understand. "And resourceful and she's the kind of princess who rescues herself, you know? She wasn't made to be someone else's character arc. When I first saw *Starfield*, I *knew* her. She wasn't perfect—and that's what I needed. She's constantly in her father's shadow, or Carmindor's—but she tries so hard, constant-ly, to cast her own. And in the end she does by becoming the best version of herself. That's why Amara means so much to me. She taught me that I can make mistakes, and own up to them, and be better because of them. So . . . I want to apologize—I didn't know what you'd gone through. Or I mean, what you *go* through."

I snap my gaze up to her, and she quickly looks away, but it's too late. I know that tone. "What happened? Did something happen?"

Her mouth thins, and she sits down on the other side of the booth in silence. The waitress refills my glass and, seeing that she's interrupting something, quickly hurries away. Imogen refuses to meet my gaze.

I don't know Imogen very well, but I know that when she's quiet, there's something incredibly wrong. "*Imogen*, what happened?"

"It's stupid. I mean, it's done now."

"That doesn't tell me what happened." Then I add, "It wasn't Ethan, was it? I know you two got into a fight last night but . . . " I reach for my phone in my pocket and pull it out to call him. "I don't know what's come over him but—"

"NO!" She almost climbs over the table to stop me from texting him. I stare at her, startled, and she melts back into her seat in embarrassment. "No—it's not him. It's really not that big of a deal, okay? During the meet-and-greet today, a guy I knew came in. He just—his hand 'slipped' and he—you know—sorta copped a feel," she says hurriedly, her cheeks burning.

Oh. Oh *no*.

"It was *mortifying*," she adds quickly, "and before you ask, he didn't recognize me. He thought I was you."

Wait—she thought that I'd be *mad* at her? I'm furious, but not at her. I exhale through my mouth, the one thing I can do to keep myself calm as I process this. "And *you're* okay?"

"Me?" She gives me a surprised look. "I want to punch his teeth in, I'm so mad."

"You and me both," I reply, and on my phone I pull up the email for the con's management team.

"Do you know this asshole's name?"

"I don't know if he's going under his real name or his You-Tube name, but I'm supposed to meet him tomorrow after the con anyway. He wanted to tell me something. Me, Imogen. Not you," she clarifies, and with a relieved sigh, she stands to put the mop back into the bucket. "I can really pick 'em, you know."

I send off the email. "Well, if you meet him tomorrow, I just told management—although I'm sure Ethan already has, too—to tell security to come by so you won't be alone."

"Pff, I don't need backup." She puts up her arms and flexes them. "I got these deadly weapons."

I bite the inside of my cheek to keep from grinning. "Do you always resort to jokes during serious conversations?"

She lets her arm flop down and sighs. "Yeah, it's kinda a natural defense."

"You must be great at funerals."

"Oh, I'm dead serious," she says with a straight face, and for a moment I can't tell if she's joking, but then she snorts a laugh and shrugs. "I'm just silly. I can't help it." She glances back at the booth where she and Vance were sitting. "Trying to be you was a lot different than I thought it'd be."

That amuses me. "Because my life is so perfect?"

"As *if.*" Then she slowly turns her eyes to mine. "Because you're a real person."

Oh. I quickly look away.

A group of *Starfield* cosplayers comes in and sits down at the opposite end of the restaurant. They barely even glance over at us, chattering about the latest *Starfield* news and the leaking script, discussing rumors about Amara's return—and lack thereof.

"I don't think I want her back," says the Carmindor cosplayer. A genderbent Euci glares at him. "Don't start again."

"I think she's whiny and too perfect. I mean, she can pilot a Starkadia without any training *and* resist General Sond's conscription? Come on," he scoffs, "she's a Mary Sue. She doesn't even do anything, and the actress who plays her isn't even hot."

"Shut up, Mike," says a General Sond cosplayer, snapping open his menu, "and stop being a sexist asshole."

Imogen watches them thoughtfully, and I wonder—what were the odds of running into Imogen in the first place? What were the odds of meeting Harper? Of stumbling on that Princess Amara meet-and-greet? Running out in front of Natalia Ford's car?

Maybe *this* is the impossible universe after all.

"You know, I thought I could hashtag Save Amara all by myself," she says, pulling me out of my thoughts. "I mean, I did everything. I started petitions, I made buttons, I spearheaded the movement, I collected all the signatures. I even thought that if I were you, I could actually change things . . . " She shakes her head. "But, after everything that's happened, I realized that I never stopped to wonder why you *didn't* want to be Amara anymore. I never realized that the only part of *Starfield* you ever saw were the bad parts—and I'm sorry. I was looking at my fandom through rose-tinted glasses, and in the end I was kind of more the bad part, wasn't I? To you, at least."

I shrug. "Lot of fans want to save their favorite characters or TV shows."

"Usually the actors also want to, you know? I didn't even

think about why you didn't. If it's because of fans like the guy in the meet-and-greet . . . I can understand why you'd hate Amara."

"Mo, I don't *hate* Amara," I clarify. I drop the fry into the basket and wipe my hand on my napkin. Then I log into Twitter and turn on my phone to let her read the comments.

Slowly, her mouth falls open.

"I once told Dare that as actors, all we can do is embody a character for a while and play them as best we can. I remember like it was yesterday—we were sitting on set and he was so incredibly nervous to play Carmindor." I grin at the memory, drawing stars in the condensation on my glass of water. "He looked up to the fictional Federation Prince. I didn't understand why then, but I do now. Sometimes the best heroes are the ones in your head—but that doesn't make them any less real. I remember telling him that it didn't matter whether you were the Val Kilmer Batman or the George Clooney Batman, you were still valid. Sometimes it's hard to remember that."

Imogen turns off my phone, and there is a crease between her brow, a little like worry and a little like anger. "Oh Jess . . . I didn't know it was *this* bad. I'm so sorry."

"Me, too. I'm sorry I lied to you at the beginning. The truth is, I messed up pretty badly too. I was so intent on not being Princess Amara that I didn't stop and look to see what I had right now. Just because Natalia Ford has a dead-end career doesn't mean I will."

Imogen's eyebrows furrow. "Dead-end? But . . . she went on to do other things, you know. She's—Natalia Ford is one of the most prominent TV showrunners in Hollywood. If a network needs a series course-corrected, they bring her in. She's won three Emmys for her work."

I blink. "No, she hasn't."

"Yeah. She *definitely* has."

"Then why haven't I head of her?"

"Well, she goes by N. A. Porter—"

I give a start. "As in *Blades of Valor* N. A. Porter? *The Sunrise Girl* N. A. Porter?"

"Yeah, Jess. You didn't think she made all of her money from syndication, did you? They got paid peanuts for *Starfield*," Imogen scoffs.

This information settles into the soft matter of my brain like pebbles at the bottom of a pond. When I complained about being typecast, about always being a foil, Natalia Ford told me to change things. Like she had as N. A. Porter.

She told me to change things because it isn't as impossible as I'd thought.

Imogen slides out of the booth to return the mop to the bucket and then rolls it over to the waitress before coming back to sit down again. She takes off the brown wig, her pink pixie sticking up every which way, and steals one of my fries.

"Oh *starflame*—HOT!" She gasps as the hot sauce zings right to her nose. She grabs my water and chugs half of it. "Are you trying to kill me?"

I shrug and pop another fry into my mouth. "It doesn't bother me."

"Oh that's going to burn for a while," she says, fanning her open mouth. "All right. If we're going to find this script, we need to figure out who stole it."

"We?"

"You don't think I'm going to let you do this alone, do you? We've still got time. There's three hours until our last panel at ExcelsiCon, and what better place to reveal who the script belongs to if not at that panel?"

"I can't ask you to help me—"

"I want to. Friends help each other, yeah? I mean, I've lived in your shoes for almost forty-eight hours, I think I know you better than I know my brother." And Imogen smiles at that, because she knows Milo better than she knows herself, I think. "So, tell me everything you know about this thief."

"Well, they're at this convention, and they always seem to post when some big *Starfield* thing has happened or is about to happen."

"That makes me think it's someone associated with the film. Another actor?" Imogen leans back in the booth and frowns. "But then wouldn't they have their own script?"

"No. My agent said I had the only one."

"So, it has to be someone on the inside, someone who doesn't like you. A fan wouldn't know things that are going to be revealed, and the thief posted that General Sond excerpt before Vance was announced. *Starflame!*" She gasps and jerks ramrod straight, the color draining from her cheeks. "Right before I shoved Mr. D-Bag out of the booth and poured two malts on him, he told me that Princess Amara doesn't have happy endings and that I'll never get a second chance—*because he already knew.*"

She looks me dead in the eye, and we say together:

"Vance Reigns."

I push my fries aside, my appetite gone. A waitress comes to take the basket, but Imogen snags one with as little hot sauce as possible and eats it. I say, "It makes sense. No one in Hollywood likes him because he'll do anything to get ahead. He even pitched a fit on the set of *Blades of Valor*. His poor PA quit after that. No one likes working for him. He's hungry for fame. If he frames it so that he finds out I'm the one leaking the script . . . "

Imogen nods. "That would definitely boost his standing in the

Starfield fandom. Girls are already ovulating over him—have you seen the shitposts on Tumblr? Some of those people need to be hosed down they're so thirsty. And Vance is staying in our hotel. So he could've been the one to fish your script out."

I don't want to get my hopes up, but my heart is beginning to beat in my ears. It must've been Vance. I just didn't recognize him because I'd never seen him outside of awards shows. I didn't think he would be a suspect.

But honestly I'm not surprised.

"All right—yeah—okay. So what now?"

"Now," Imogen says, grabbing her bag and scooting to the edge of the booth, "we have to prove it. What do you say, partner?" She sticks out her hand.

I smile and accept it, and she pulls me to my feet. "This might sound a little weird," I say, "but I feel like I know you. Aside from the whole we-traded-lives part."

At that, she smiles widely and says, "Welcome to the fandom life, where you never know anyone but you always know everyone."

"Like Harper," I say before I can stop myself. "Which," I look away in embarrassment, "you might have to explain some things to her. I kind of ran out of the convention when she figured out that I wasn't . . . that I'm . . . And she's so great and nice and perfect—she didn't deserve all of the lies I told her."

Imogen crosses her arms over her chest and studies me, as if I'm some plot twist in a story she hadn't expected to like, and then she leans in and asks, "Do you like her?"

"W-what?" I sputter, and a blush spreads across my face. I grab the receipt and hurry to the cash register, and she follows me like a Baskerville hound.

"You do!"

The cashier rings up the order. I dig around in my purse for exact change and hand it to her, my cheeks so hot they're searing. "I—it's—"

"Then you don't like Ethan?"

I nab my receipt and whirl around. "*Ethan*? Oh God no. Wait—" I narrow my eyes, cross my arms, and imitate the same scrutiny she gave me, which causes her to lean backward a little. I don't even have to ask the question before her ears begin turning pink and she whirls to hurry out of the diner.

"*You* like *him*!" I accuse, following close on her heels. "Rule six! It was a rule for a reason!"

She shoves open the door and steps out into the muggy Atlanta afternoon. This is the photo I promised the paparazza, and I put on a smile as she snaps pictures while Imogen and I make our way down the street. Imogen is so flustered and lost in her own head that she doesn't even notice. "I thought you made the rule because, well, you liked him."

"I definitely do *not*. I just didn't want to see him getting hurt, especially since you're so cute in all the ways I'm not—and in all the ways he likes." Her ears are growing redder and redder, and she can feel it too; she quickly arranges her hair over them. I catch up to her as we cross the street, leaving the paparazza behind. "You didn't hurt him, did you?"

"Not on purpose! And you hurt Harper!"

"I didn't mean to!" I say defensively. "But I want to apologize. I screwed up."

"Yeah, me too."

Ahead of us in the streets is a parade—all types of people dressed in cosplay sashay down the avenue to the tune of every fantasy and sci-fi theme the marching band behind them can play. There are Vulcans and mechas and Jedis and Labyrinth goblins, anime demons and zombie pirates and dragonborns and sailor scouts and dark elves—heroes and villains and everyone in between. Whatever apologies we were about to make to each other for messing up our friendships fall away as we're caught up in the magic. I'm filled with the memories of stargazing on hotel rooftops and singing the *Starfield* theme off-key with a bunch of strangers I didn't know but understood and seeing all of those radiant Amaras through the viewfinder of a camera—

And all of the stories I want to tell.

Only when the parade has passed and the street clears do I turn to the girl who could have been me in another impossible universe, and I say, "I want to save Amara."

IMOGEN

WHILE JESS IS GROVELING TO HER ASSISTANT, since he clearly will *never* want to see me ever again, I fix my pink hair—wig no longer needed—and march straight into ExcelsiCon to gather reinforcements. The moment I flash my badge, *my* badge, to the attendant and ride the escalator up to the showroom, I feel like myself again, and I breathe in the con stink as if it's fresh air.

I need to find Milo and Bran. They're the only ones who can help me with two parts of Jess's plan, which rides a little on the side of batshit but, to be fair, some of the best ideas do.

"If we're going to save Amara, we need to prove she exists," Jess had told me.

I didn't expect the plan she laid out next. It will take an impossible amount of luck to pull it off, but ExcelsiCon has always excelled at the impossible. I just hope it can work its magic one more time.

At some point I also need to text Harper and tell her the truth. I don't know if she'll ever want to be my friend again—especially after I purposefully hoodwinked her into hanging out with someone else—but I can't not try. Harper and I have been internet friends for years. She's the one person who believed in my Save Amara initiative when no one else did, and I've been the ultimate crappy friend to her.

I just hope Milo and Bran are at my moms' booth and not at some movie screening. There isn't enough time to hunt them down, and with my luck they'd be missing.

Instead, when I turn the corner, I find Harper at the booth talking to Milo. They both notice me at the same time—my pink hair does kind of stand out—and their conversation instantly dies.

Welp. There's nothing quite as uninviting as ruining good conversation.

My moms are on the other side of the booth, by the Funko-Pop throne, assisting a customer buying that gorgeous Nightwing figurine—you know, the one with the *really* nice butt?—and I hurry over to Milo and Harper sporting my best apologetic smile.

Harper watches me wearily as I approach. "So, you're Imogen."

"Hi, Harps," I say painfully.

She doesn't look as surprised as I thought she would. Even worse, she looks disappointed. "So the other person really was . . . "

"It's a long story. I'm sorry—"

"*Sorry?*" she interrupts with a scoff.

I wince. "I know. But trust me, we didn't think—" But I realize that whatever excuse I have doesn't account for how long we lied. "I'm sincerely sorry, Harper. But it's so nice to see you in person."

She sighs. "This is so messed up. Because I . . . " But then she trails off and shakes her head. "It's just messed up."

"So why're you here and not Jess? Did she get bored?" Milo asks.

I sneak a look at our moms. "Can we go behind the booth for a moment?"

From the back of the booth, Bran pops his head out. "Ooh, are we about to learn some secrets?"

"You deserve the truth," I say. "All of you." I look at Harper, and she nods decisively.

While our moms are distracted, I corral Harper and Milo into the storage space with Bran. Milo has to hunch over to squeeze inside the small space, and we all barely fit. I take a deep breath, and then I tell them what Jess told me. About the script, and the thief, and the internet comments trolling her mercilessly.

"Why are they saying it's her fault that Carmindor dies?" Harper asks. "That doesn't make any sense. Amara died—*ohh-hh*. They're blaming her for dying, which is why Carmindor is dying."

"That makes about as much sense as their usernames," Bran says. "LukeSkywanker69. Huh. Nice."

"*Babe*," Milo chides.

I take my phone out of Bran's hands and deposit it in my back pocket. "So will you help us? Jess and I need to track down the thief who's posting these excerpts. We think they're going to post who the script belongs to and out Jessica during the panel in two hours."

Bran shakes his head. "That isn't a lot of time."

"We *think* we know who it is—Vance Reigns—we just need to prove it. That's where you come in. We were thinking, Bran, that since you're our tech wizard genius, you could hack into the thief's Twitter account and then hack into the phone, and when we give you the cue, make the phone light up or something and—"

"Imogen, I appreciate that you think I'm a tech wizard, but I'm not *that* magical," he interrupts. "And that's illegal."

Well, crap.

Everyone's quiet.

Then Harper asks, "Can you hack into the account?"

"I mean, that's the easy part," he replies. "Still illegal, but yes."

"Then could you get the phone number linked to the account and call it?"

"Oh yes, I can definitely do that."

"Harper, that's genius," I say and then turn to my brother. "And now for the other part of the plan . . . "

Milo quirks a bushy eyebrow. "There's another part?"

"Jess needs your help to steal the Princess Amara dress from the exhibit. That's going to be the hard part."

My brother blinks and then leans in to me. "Excuse me, what did you just say?"

"You are going to steal the one-of-a-kind, ultra special, super important Princess Amara ballroom gown on display in the exhibit. With Jess."

"Oh, okay. That's what I thought you said."

"And Harper's going to help too," I add, nodding to my friend, who doesn't seem too keen on the idea. She will, won't she? She's been with Jess this whole time, so I'm sure she won't mind. I put my hand in the middle of us. "Okay, who's with me!"

Milo and Bran exchange a look—communicating in a second that this plan is about as bulletproof as Princess Amara driving a spaceship into the Black Nebula—but they put their hands over mine anyway, three-fourths to completing our friendship circle.

"Harps?" I say, glancing to the last person on our team.

Her brows crease, and she sighs and shakes her head. "I'm sorry. I've been pulled along in this scheme long enough. I gotta get back to my booth. Good luck, Monster."

Then she pushes herself between Milo and Bran and heads back into the showroom, and my stomach sinks. Of course. I want to run after her and stop her, but what right do I have to do that?

If we were really friends, I wouldn't have lied.

I shouldn't have.

I can't think about that, I tell myself. I'll apologize later. I'll tell her the whole story.

That is, if she ever wants to talk to me again.

"So, Monster, tell us how to get in trouble," Milo says. "You were always the best at that," he adds, not unkindly.

That makes me smile despite my probably-ruined-friendship with Harps. I clear my throat and say with Princess Amara's saccharine ruthlessness, "It is one of my most glorious qualities," and I ask him to follow me.

JESS

My phone buzzes as I head down the hallway to my hotel suite. It's from Imogen. I actually decided to trade numbers just in case something goes wrong. I don't think she'll be posting mine to any lewd websites.

> IMOGEN (4:47 PM)
> —Harper isn't going to help us.
> —I'm sorry, Jess.

I am, too. It's because of me that Imogen lost her friendship with Harper, and I lost . . .

How could I lose something I never had? We shared ramen and stars and stories, and maybe that's all that two people are, sometimes.

We're just satellites that fell into each other's orbit for a breath and then traveled on.

I slip my keycard into the door and shove it open.

"Ethan, I know you're in here!" I call as I sweep into the

room. *The Great British Bake-Off* is blaring on the TV, and that can only mean one thing. I turn it off and call his name again.

It means he's utterly smitten by Imogen Lovelace.

I knew it.

"Ethan!" I call. The door to the bathroom is closed, and there isn't a single sound coming from behind it, but I know he's in there. He has already stress-ironed all of his shirts, hung up all of my dresses—oh brother, what did Imogen *do* to him? "I'll keep screaming until you come out of there! I'll tell everyone that you wear Superman boxers and—"

There's a clatter on the other side of the bathroom door, and he wrenches it open in nothing but his jeans and a towel around his shoulders, his face half shaved and shaving cream still sticking to one side.

"*Shush*!" he pleads. "And they're Batman boxers, thank you very much." But then he blinks and takes me in—me, Jess, his friend, is standing in her own hotel room again. His eyes go wide. "Oh no, did something else happen? Did that monster of a girl—"

I hold up a hand and he quiets down. "I think you need to apologize to her."

"Me? To *her*?"

"I know you, you dolt," I remind him. "You like her."

"*Her*? Why on earth would I like that—"

"Ethan."

His shoulders sag. There are plenty of things Ethan Tanaka can do. But the one thing he can't do is lie to me, his best friend. And I can't lie to him. "Come here," I mutter, and I pull him into a hug even though I only reach up to his chest. I tell him about the plan Imogen and I have come up with to get my script back—or at least to expose Vance for the thief he is—and Ethan nods quietly as I explain what he has to do, which is also very important.

"You need me to . . . work the lights," he clarifies.

"Elle will distract the tech guy and you, wearing a black shirt, will just squeeze into the booth and hijack the lights."

"But I don't have a black shirt," he says helplessly. He begins to scratch at the side of his face still covered with shaving cream and then stops himself.

I hurry over to my suitcase, pull out a black shirt, and hold it up to his torso. It's a women's medium, so it should easily fit over his scrawny shoulders. "It might be a little short, but it'll have to do."

"Is this punishment for being mean to Imogen?"

"Yes," I reply happily, shoving the shirt into his chest, "it is. Now finish shaving and go change."

IMOGEN

THIS IS THE LAST TIME I WILL EVER BE Jessica Stone and, *starflame*, am I going to make it count. The panel is about to begin, and I'm pacing back and forth in the small space behind the curtains that block the audience from our waiting area, chewing on my thumbnail because, *screw the rules*, I have pink hair. You know, under my wig. Hidden.

It's still pink, okay?

This is it. Our moment of glory. We're on the edge of it. Just waiting.

On the other side of the waiting area, Vance Reigns flirts with one of the volunteers, and I restrain myself from losing the fries I ate back at the diner.

I check my phone. Three minutes before the panel. I'm trying not to hardcore freak out but honestly? It's much harder than I thought it'd be. One, I'm playing with my new friend's career, and two, I *really* hope things go according to plan.

I should've warned Jess that my plans usually fall spectacularly to pieces.

Nah.

"Something eating you?"

I jump at the voice and look up from my phone. Darien is standing in front of me, all glorious black curls and long eyelashes and warm brown eyes. I wait for my fangirl senses to kick in and freak out but . . . they don't. Ethan's eyelashes are much longer.

What am I doing? This isn't an eyelash-length competition. Weirdo.

I put my phone away and clear my throat. "Well, um. You know, just the usual."

He nods. "Uh-huh."

From across the room, I hear Vance chuckle at something the volunteer says. It's smooth like honey and makes my entire body go rigid. I can't believe I fell for that—for him. How naive could I be?

Darien glances over his shoulder at Vance and then back at me. "You know, he disguises himself pretty well for a bag of dicks."

My eyes widen. "*Darien.*"

"I can say it," he replies, and takes a bottle of water offered by a volunteer. "He's a piece of trash. He shouldn't have tricked you like that."

He's in on the plan, too. After apologizing to Ethan, Jess's second order of business was to find Darien because we couldn't pull this off without him. Jess shot him a text, and we reconvened in Jess's suite so she could freshen my makeup. By the time we made it back to Jess's suite, Darien and a girl with crimson hair were waiting outside her door.

She had grinned at us—that kind of troublemaking grin I recognized from the gossip news proclaiming her Geekerella—and brandished a box of red hair dye. "So who needs to become a princess?"

And that is how I met Elle Wittimer.

If I ever shipped people in real life (which I don't, because it's weird to me, unless it's me and someone really hot and it's only in my head), then she and Darien would be my FOREVER OTP. But I totally don't ship real people.

. . . except maybe them.

"I just hope this plan works," I mutter to Darien, eyeing Vance as he and the volunteer break out into a flirtatious laugh. "I'm kinda mostly afraid that Bran won't get his phone number in time. And . . . "

I hesitate, because this part I hadn't really wanted to say out loud. I don't want to jinx anything.

"And even if we do expose him, Jess will still take the blame for throwing the script away in the first place. And even though she said she wanted to take the blame, I don't understand why she *would*."

Darien nods. "I know. But let's trust her, yeah? She's not the brightest witch of her age for nothing."

I gasp, fake-shocked. "Darien Freeman, did you just refer to something *other than* Starfield?"

"I know, right? It's like I'm multidimensional or something."

"*Shocker*."

Then he checks his phone. "Oh gosh, look at the time. It's distraction o'clock!"

He winks at me and hurries to the exit of the waiting area. A volunteer stops him, but when he says he has to go to the bathroom, she lets him escape into the hallway.

I quickly text Jess.

IMOGEN (5:55 PM)

—*The Carmindor is in motion.*

JESS

THERE IS SOMETHING TO BE SAID WHEN the actress playing the new Amara in the reboot devises a plan to steal the original Amara's gown from a coffin case while half of the con watches.

Although I don't know what that something to be said would be, honestly.

I guess I'm about to find out.

The dress is located in the center of the exhibit, beside the original Carmindor's uniform, which is, as Dare once pointed out, the *perfect* shade of blue. A hue that matches the swirls in Amara's dress exactly.

There are three booth attendants patrolling the exhibit, orbiting one another in bored rounds. Fans take photos in front of the cases, posing beside their favorite uniforms. There is a constant crowd in front of Amara's dress that I had hoped would ebb as it grew nearer to the big *Starfield* panel—where they're supposed to announce the title of the sequel—but the crowd doesn't seem to be letting up at all.

I share a bag of popcorn with Imogen's beefcake of a brother while we watch from the edge of the showroom. Bran is back at the booth, hopefully hacking into the Twitter account. It's just a few keystrokes, he assured me. Just ask for password retrieval, get a glimpse of the characters in the Twitter profile's phone number, and go to work on a phone directory site. He stressed that there was a program to test out hundreds of thousands of phone numbers—or whatever. I'm not even going to pretend to understand it. I had half a mind to ask him to purge the entire account—delete every tweet until no trace remains—but that won't help my narrative.

No, people already know that Amara is dead and Carmindor dies. What they don't know is the ending to the story, and that is something I do not intend to give them. At least not yet.

Endings can always change.

Amara's dress is the last piece of the plan. This part was my idea, actually. I don't just want to expose Vance as the the insufferable jerk he is. If I'm going to back Imogen and save Amara, I need to convince the fandom that Amara needs to be saved.

Not only that, but I know that I would look like perfection in that dress. The new Amara in the dress she could never live up to. And in it I will prove to everyone that there are stories yet to tell, and stars to cross, and shipper wars to wage, and if a fandom can't shift a narrative then nothing can.

At the beginning of all this I was against #SaveAmara, but now I realize that Imogen and I are on the same side. We both want meaningful narratives, less flavor-of-the-week female characters, more legitimacy as a genre. We want to save Amara—but we want to save our future, too.

"So what've I missed?" Dare asks, jogging up beside me. He has on a pair of Ray-Bans, as if that *really* disguises him in the crowd. People are doing double-takes the longer he stands beside me.

Imogen's brother gapes at him. "You . . . you're . . . "

"'Sup, my man," Dare says coolly, and gives Milo the finger guns.

"I think I'm going to die," Milo whispers.

Nerds. The lot of them.

I toss another piece of popcorn into my mouth. "Cause a distraction while Milo and I get the dress. You think you can do that?"

"Can I do that," Dare scoffs and looks at me from over his Ray-Bans. "I was born ready." He wiggles his eyebrows and saunters out into the hallway, opening his arms like, *Ladies.*

Honestly.

But it seems to work. The first girl who notices him screams and comes running, and then another and another, until he's surrounded by fans asking to take his photo and pose with him. He treats them all so graciously, I'm kind of a little annoyed.

It doesn't work for long, however, and by the time Milo and I get to the case, a volunteer appears, red-faced and panicked. "Mr. Freeman! You're on a panel, like, now!"

Oh, no.

Two of the booth attendants are beginning to separate from the crowd, and neither Milo nor I have even opened the case yet. I mutter under my breath and work my hairpin into the hinges. The first screw pops out. I start on the bottom one. Imogen's brother blocks me with the hulk of his body, but that isn't going to help if the booth attendants look over and see me unhinging the door to the case.

"Um," I hear Dare say to the volunteer, "I mean—I'll be there in a—I have to—can we wait a few—"

Ugh. I forgot how Hufflepuff he is. Pushover.

But then another voice cuts through the crowd. I recognize it, but I can't put my finger on where exactly I've heard it before. It's rough and gravelly. Definitely an older gentleman.

"Skipping out on a panel? In my day, I'd never do such a thing."

It sounds like the pretzel guy. Henry or whatever.

I look around the case to the commotion. It definitely is Pretzel Henry, but without his pretzel stand and no longer wearing his pretzel smock. He stands across from Dare, wearing a tropical shirt with a white undershirt peeking out and beige trousers, his face is clean shaven and his graying hair is pushed back over his head.

Imogen's brother makes a strangled noise in his throat. "Holy George Clooney's bat nipples. That's . . . "

Oh.

Ohmygod.

That's where I recognized him from!

Now that he and Dare are in the same spot, the likeness is almost uncanny. Dare's nose is a little bigger, and his eyebrows are much more expressive, but the two of them could be cut from the same cloth. Natalia Ford and I look a little alike, but this is like that scene in the new *Star Trek* where the new Spock, Zachary Quinto, meets the old Spock, Leonard Nimoy. This is probably the single strangest unscripted thing I have ever seen in my life.

I don't think they've ever been in the same room before, although Dare knew he was here. David Singh hasn't been in the spotlight for years. According to what I've read, he's done humanitarian work supporting disaster relief and charities across the world. And, apparently, he's been here. At ExcelsiCon. As . . . a pretzel guy.

I watch as Dare stares, unabashedly, at the elder Carmindor. "I'm . . . you're . . . sir!"

"Skipping out on your panel, you should be ashamed," Pretzel Henry—I mean, David Singh—says, shaking his head. "That isn't very princely of you, Mr. Freeman."

"I—but I wasn't—I'm not—"

David Singh turns his gaze ever so briefly to Milo and me and then back to Dare. He knows what we're doing. He's . . . *distracting* them for us? Dare darts his eyes from us, to David Singh, and then back to us again as if trying to piece together this hectic turn of events. But all I can give him is a helpless shrug because this is not going as planned. *Come on, Dare, improv a little.*

He swallows thickly and, apparently finally making up his mind, straightens his spine and sticks his hands in his pockets in a very jerklike way. "I was merely giving my fans some one-on-one time, unlike you. You haven't been seen in years."

"I prefer anonymity in my retirement, but maybe I should've come back and taught you some manners, kiddo."

"Manners? Like I could learn anything useful from you, old man," Dare bats back.

The crowd is growing, and now everyone is most definitely interested in this showdown. They don't even notice Milo and me.

Imogen's brother pats me on the shoulder, and I hurriedly wiggle my hairpin into the bottom hinge. It pops off and the glass door falls open. Milo catches it, and I grab the dress on the metal mannequin, folds of spun silk and taffeta, and pull it out of the case.

In the next blink, we're gone.

IMOGEN

"So, where's your boyfriend, Princess?" Vance's oil-slick voice purrs behind me. "Darien got cold feet?"

I resist the urge to shove my fist of fury right into that smug jawline of his and instead whirl around to him and feign shock. "Oh look, a wild nerfherder appears!"

His blue eyes narrow. "You look nervous, sweetheart."

"And I've told you not to call me that, supercreep. What, are you done flirting with the volunteers? Were you *lonely*, Vance?" I say, trying to keep my voice in Jessica's range, but after using it constantly these last few days, my vocal chords waver in and out.

He smiles at me and begins to say something, but then Amon bursts through the doors, clapping his hands loudly to get our attention.

"All right, crew! Let's—wait, where's Darien?" he asks, taking a frantic headcount of the panelists. "Where's our Carmindor?"

I clear my throat and say in Jess's sweet accent, "He went to take a piss."

"*Now?*"

I shrug. The lights on the stage begin to rise.

Amon glances at his phone, and his lips curve down into a frown. Vance nudges his chin toward him. "What's wrong, Boss?"

"Nothing—it's nothing. Everyone, gather round!" He motions to bring us all in, and Calvin and Vance circle up with me. "Here's where we get to announce your hard work and the title."

Calvin thrusts up his fist. "Heck yeah! Beating that leaker to the punch!"

Amon's phone begins to ring, but he quickly silences it.

"That too. Are you ready, team?" He sticks his hand out into the middle, and everyone puts their hands on top of his. "Jess, I know you're off in your own world, but are you with us?"

I blink out of my thoughts and put my hand with theirs.

"Look to the stars!" he starts. "Aim!"

"Ignite!" we cry, and break the circle.

Bunch of nerds, I realize. The lot of them.

Except for Vance. Vance can go take a hike off the nose of a Nova-class star cruiser.

The lights in the audience crash to black, and the *Starfield* theme comes on, so loud it vibrates my chest. Excitement races across my skin like electricity. Jess should be here experiencing this. She should be the one about to walk out onstage.

She'll be here, I remind myself, and I eye Vance for the umpteenth time. Bran should be taking over his Twitter account by now, getting his phone number.

Amon climbs the stairs to the stage first, and the rest of us follow into the blinding light.

The roar of the crowd is . . . *monstrous*.

Three thousand screaming fans, and even more watching the live-stream on the internet. With so much *Starfield* fandom gathered in one place, there's no way not to feel alive. Like every one of us is linked in some cosmic tapestry, all of our lives affected, in some small way, by *Starfield*. I close my eyes and listen to the crowd singing along to the theme song like it's their own heartbeat, and there's nothing quite like it.

There will be nothing quite like this ever again.

Amon introduces us. I try to squint beyond the glaring lights pointed at me, but I can't see if Jess is in the audience. I can't see Ethan, either. Wherever Bran is, he should be calling Vance's phone right about now. I glance down the table to the phone's screen but it's dark.

Please let this work, I pray to the impossible universe.

"So! Before we get into the questions, and as we wait for our Carmindor," Amon says into his mic, setting his phone on the table. The screen blinks on—someone is calling him.

And not Vance.

About a thousand expletives race through my head.

No way.

NO FRAKKIN' WAY.

"I want to give you all a surprise—the title of the sequel! Can we bring it up on the screen?" he shouts back to the guy operating the lights. But what he hopefully doesn't see is that the tech guy excused himself a few minutes ago after a fan—Elle, really—accidentally spilled an Icee all over him, and Ethan, cosplaying a techie in a too-short black shirt, quietly took his place.

I just hope Ethan knows how to operate the light board.

But the lights don't even flicker.

I watch Amon's phone light up as the number calls again, and again, but because it's set to silent, it doesn't vibrate. I begin to feel sick to my stomach.

Vance isn't even looking at his phone, which is also faceup on the table. He gets a text from his mom (SWEETIE U LOOK SO HANDSOME!!) but that's it.

Oh no.

Amon clears his throat. "Uh, tech guy? Hello—"

This time the lights flicker.

We need to stop this *now.*

The plan has become our worst-case scenario and I'm *really* regretting not telling Jessica about how unlucky I really am.

"Hey, is there a technical difficulty? I can show the title later—" Amon says, but he gets shut down very quickly by raucous booing fans. He quickly holds up his hands. "Okay, okay! We'll wait."

Vance glances over to me as if I'm responsible for this, and I give him a cheesy smile and wave, one finger after another, because yeah buddy we're in this. We're here for the ride. There's no way to stop Bran, and it's too late to call off Ethan, and the stage lights are crashing to black.

Besides, you know what they say:

Anything can happen once upon a con.

Everyone sits in darkness with baited breath. No one moves. No one speaks. It's as if a weighted blanket has been thrown over the entire room. The audience is looking expectantly at the screen behind us, waiting for it to display the title and logo of the *Starfield* sequel, when suddenly the back door bursts open.

The thump of heels on padded retro carpet is the only sound in the room. From the light leaking in through the open doors, I watch as the folds of her radiant dress billow around her like a swirling dark-purple nebula, rhinestones and glitter and starlight sewn into the seams. The original, stolen straight from the glass coffin it was kept in. The dim light sparkles against her golden tiara, inset with crimson jewels to match the blood-red of her hair.

Starflame, she looks like Amara.

She looks like our princess never died.

JESS

I'VE HEARD FROM MULTIPLE SOURCES, ALL of them named Darien, that if you watch *Starfield* in chronological order, Amara has a redemption arc to rival Prince Zuko's. She actively hates Carmindor in the beginning, she hates everything he stands for, she hates the Federation and the Intergalactic Peace Treaty. She wants to make her father proud.

In the second half of *Starfield*, she realizes that nothing can make him proud. There are lines she can't cross. There are things she doesn't want to do. There are things she does anyway.

And in the final episodes? She may not be nice—but she is *good*.

I am the best parts of her, and part of the Amaras I pass in the crowd—the gender-bent one across the aisle, the ten-year-old one with glitter in her hair, the Black Nebula Federation Princess Amara come back from the grave. I'm a part of every Amara at the con, every Amara on the screen—just as the first Amara is a part of me.

And we don't die quietly.

There are stories that you tell and stories that tell things to you; stories that win awards and stories that win hearts. Sometimes they're the same. Sometimes they aren't. Sometimes the stories you want aren't the ones you need, and the ones you need are the ones you never thought you'd like.

Perhaps this is one of those stories.

Perhaps *Starfield* is one of those kinds of stories to me.

With each step I take, the crowd grows increasingly restless. They begin to understand just what's happening. That the Jessica on the panel is not me.

Vance Reigns lays eyes on me for the first time. "You—*you're* Jessica? The real Jessica?"

I cock my head to him. "Are you the real Vance?"

He jabs a finger back at Imogen. "Seriously? This fake has been playing you? This whole time?"

At the end of the table, Amon tries to keep the panel under control. "There's probably a reasonable explanation for all of this. Jess? Whichever one of you is real?"

"We're both real," I tell him.

Imogen is shaking her head at me. Something is wrong.

"Then why don't you explain it and let us get back to our panel?" Vance replies, and if I didn't know better I would've thought he was being very amiable. Not about to lose his temper. But there's a muscle throbbing in his jaw. He doesn't like being taken for a fool. "This is *pretty rad.*"

"Of course, but don't you want to know the name of the film first? Friends?" I ask, looking back to the audience, and they cheer. I lower my hands and they quiet again. Wow, this kind of power is kind of addicting. "But I think Vance already knows it."

Vance laughs. "Yeah, I can take a guess—"

"No guesses needed. Because you're the one leaking the script." The crowd murmurs.

I see Imogen hang her head.

Vance's eyebrows jerk up in surprise. "I—what? You're kidding, right?"

"Don't play dumb, Vance. It's not becoming."

"Yeah, because I'm not. Bloody hell, I don't even know what you're going on ab—"

"Then show us your phone."

"What?"

"Show us your—"

Vance Reigns, General Sond, the villain, holds up his phone. There is a text from his mom—now two, now three—but no missed calls.

But if not him, then . . .

My eyes find Imogen's, and she has her arms crossed and is pointing (not so subtly) to the right. Toward Calvin and Amon.

And Amon's phone is lit up like a beacon.

Yeah, I'll just keep spam-calling him through an untraceable Google number, Bran had told us. *You know, to get the screen to light up.*

Ohmygod.

This entire plan just went supernova.

"What's the meaning of this, Jessica?" Vance asks. "Why do you think I'd leak the script? I don't even have it! How do we know you're not the leak? That it's not *your* script?"

My *trusted* director looks at me, and we lock eyes, because I had been wrong this whole time. I'm *not* the only person with the script. One other person would have it. In fact, he'd have it before everyone else.

Amon.

Was he just—was he going to let me take the fall? Let those fanboys and trolls have at me, make their lewd comments, scrape my career across their teeth? When the time came for someone to get in trouble for leaking the script, was he simply going to pawn it off on me because I was on the outs and leaving anyway? He gave me a script even though Princess Amara was dead.

He was so adamant not to have Amara come back that he wanted to frame me for a publicity stunt to ensure that I wouldn't.

He's the one who killed me off in the first place.

"It is," I say, never taking my eyes off Amon. "It is my script, but I wasn't leaking it."

Amon clears his throat. "We can talk about this later, Jessica—"

"No, we need to talk about it now. It was you."

Amon scoffs. "You just accused Vance, and now you're accusing me? Jessica, think a little. Why would I steal your script?" There's a patronizing note to his voice that curdles my blood. I won't let him talk to me like this. He never thought I was pretty enough on camera, he never praised my work while giving Dare and Calvin compliment after compliment. He made me *run in heels* when I obviously didn't want to, and Princess Amara never would have.

I ball my hands into fists.

"I lost the script, Amon," I say, "and I spent two days looking for it because I thought someone had stolen it out of the trash. At first it was so I wouldn't look bad in front of you, or any other director who wants to work with me in the future, but now . . . "

"Jess, come on," Amon groans. "Stop making a hysterical spectacle. You don't like *Starfield* anyway."

At that, I hear a few people in the audience chuckle. I feel their laughter crawling up my spine, mocking me.

"You're right," I admit.

The murmurs grow louder, and Amon sits back, amused.

"I didn't like *Starfield*," I go on, "but that was because I didn't know what it could be. I only saw a part of it. I only knew what it was like from the outside looking in.

"But I think I'm beginning to. *Starfield* isn't going to win any awards, and *Starfield* isn't going fix everything that's wrong with the world, but you know what? Sometimes the stories we need are the ones that can show us a happy ending and make us feel whole and welcome and loved. And that, I think, is the true magic of *Starfield*, of watching twenty Amaras through a small camera lens strike the same pose, of howling a theme song off-key, of debating its economy and its politics and its world-building and whether Carmindor's uniform is really the perfect shade of blue. That's the part of *Starfield* I never saw before, that magical, weird, and wondrous part that I now want to protect."

I turn to the audience and survey the three thousand shadows staring back at me. My doppelgänger sits behind me at the table, looking increasingly uncomfortable, but she shouldn't worry. The audience isn't looking at her. In the dark room, telltale flashes of cameras and lock screens set people's faces aglow.

"I only saw the parts of *Starfield* that didn't want me," I say, and that includes Amon. "I knew the niches who didn't like my acting, or my hair, or my breast size, or the fact that I even existed. They said that my mole *ruined* their princess. But that's the thing with Amara"—I look out at the audience, those shadowed faces staring back at me, unrelenting—"she belongs to no man, and no king, and she certainly doesn't belong to you." I look down at one of the girls in the front row; she's ten and dressed as Princess Amara. I take off my silver crown and place it on her head. "She belongs to us—all of us. She taught us how to be bold and powerful, and she taught us that we can make mistakes and be better. That we don't have to be perfect—we can just be *enough*. We carry her with us. And because of that, Amara will never die."

The ballroom is quiet and this is not how our plan was supposed to go, but this is how it went, and I am still intact on the other side. Whatever happens now is out of my control. Perhaps it always has been, but I like the thought of having tried to change it.

And then I turn, like a ghost, and return down the aisle whence I came, and behind me rises a tide of silence.

Amon stands abruptly and calls after me. "Jess! Jess, where are you going?"

"The horizon is wide," I say over my shoulder, my words spoken in the steady, even cadence of Amara, "and I have a girl to kiss."

Then I pick up the sides of my dress made of stars and wishes and impossibilities, and I run out of the room.

IMOGEN

THE BACK DOOR SWINGS SHUT, AND silence swallows us whole. No one moves as Jess's words sink in. No one breathes. It's like the silence after a rubber band, wound too tightly, suddenly snaps. The tension is gone. And then—

Vance glances at Calvin. "Did she just say a *girl?*"

Calvin gives him a crude look. "Don't talk to me," he says—I think—because at the same time an audience member stands, picking up her magical staff, and follows Jess. Then another. And then an entire row of people. Filing out in growing numbers until everyone is trying to cram out of the doors.

That's when it hits me—Jess is going to find Harper.

I jump to my feet and hurry around the table. Behind me, Amon shouts Jess's name, but I don't stop. That is not my name, and he definitely doesn't deserve mine.

Ethan meets me at the edge of the stage, with Elle right behind him, and takes my hand to help me down. "I think I know where she's going," I tell them.

"This way!" Suddenly, Darien flings the backstage curtains wide, beckoning us to hurry.

"Oh, so you've returned," Ethan says mildly.

Darien gives him a look. "You would not *believe* what just happened—"

"Let's talk and run, shall we?" I interrupt. "Follow me! I know a shortcut." There's a door on the side of the room that is always barred, mostly because it lets out to the next panel space, where the old guy from *Star Wars* is taking questions and—

"Does he sound like the Joker or is it me?" I ask.

Ethan rolls his eyes, and we cut into the next hall, and then the next, Darien and Elle following close behind. I know this convention center like the back of my hand. I know every nook and cranny, every shortcut and quiet bathroom, and soon I navigate us outside into the sticky Atlanta night.

Darien and Elle speed ahead, folding their fingers together, leaving Ethan and me to follow.

A stream of people follows Jess from one side of the convention to the other, trickling down into the street like the parade we saw earlier, and I can't help but smile like mad—because although it isn't a marching band, this is totally my new favorite trope. A bunch of nerds following a princess in a dress made of galaxies.

Beside me, Ethan lets out a long sigh. "So, now that you're you again, I think we need proper introductions. I'll start. Hi there, my name's Ethan Tanaka."

"That's a real smooth pickup line."

"That's a very long name you have, That's a real smooth pick-up—"

"Imogen," I laugh, offering my hand. "But my friends call me Mo."

"Mo, it's a pleasure."

We shake hands.

A block away, the crowd has stopped moving. I squint into the distance. "Is Jess trying to—"

He nods, looking as grim as ever. "Yep. She's climbing on top of that food truck. She always does things the hard way. There is an elevator. She knows there's an elevator." He sticks his hands in his pockets and sighs.

I grin at him, secretive and sincere. "I never got to thank you for helping me out with He-Who-Will-Not-Be-Named."

"Who?"

"The guy from the meet-and-greet. I knew him—well, *Imogen* knew him."

He pushes his glasses up the bridge of his nose, and the lenses flash in the street lights. "You're welcome. I'm sorry if I was a little . . . overbearing."

"You, overbearing?" I snort-laugh. "Whatever gave you that idea? But that move you pulled was really cool. What was it, karate?"

He gives me a blank look. "Mo, not every Asian guy knows karate."

My cheeks redden. "I didn't mean—"

"It was *Mortal Kombat*."

I blink. "What?"

"The game?" He explains: "I'm kinda a world champion *Mortal Kombat* player, so I guess my subconscious picked up Raiden's—"

"Okay, okay," I interrupt, and his lips twitch up into a smile. "Ugh, nerd."

"Ugh, fangirl," he mimics.

An impasse.

Down the block, Jess has finally climbed onto the food truck. The fans have gathered around her, and the *Starfield* song has somehow bled into the very fabric of the street. The street lights glitter off the tall buildings, green oaks lining the sidewalks beside lampposts and traffic lights. The streets are empty of cars. An older Luke Skywalker, peppery beard and shaggy hair, sitting on the shoulders of the tenth and eleventh Doctors, leads the singing, conducting the music with his lightsaber.

Jess grabs something from a green-haired girl standing on the hood of the food truck and hoists it into the air.

"Is that—? She has a megaphone," I deadpan.

Ethan takes his hands out of his pockets. "We should prob-ably stop her," he advises, and begins speed-walking toward his charge standing atop the Magic Pumpkin food truck. I follow this too-tall boy into the sea of people, cosplayers and fangirls and fanboys and geeks and nerds, people pretending to be other people and people just trying to be themselves, and it hits me as we edge closer to the princess in a shimmering galaxy dress atop a food truck—

I think I might like Ethan Tanaka.

And as he bobs and weaves through the crowd, moving far-ther and farther away from me, I realize that he'll be gone tomor-row, and I'll never see him again.

JESS

"Harper!" I shout up at the twenty stories of hotel.

My voice bounces back to me. I am too small and the distance is too large. I don't know what I was thinking, to be honest. That I'd just come outside to her hotel, *Romeo and Juliet* style, and recite my heart's feelings to her? And that she'd *hear* me?

I'd need, I don't know—

"Hey!" A figure stumbles out of the back of the food truck and walks over. It's the green-haired girl from the Stellar Party. Sage, I think her name is. She holds up a megaphone. "Wanna use this?"

"Yes!" I grab it and angle it up to the hotel balconies. "Harper!"

Her name booms across the hotel windows, ricocheting off the buildings in the middle of downtown Atlanta. I wince at the loudness. A few hotel guests open their balcony doors and stray outside to see what the noise is about, but not Harper.

Please, I pray. *If impossible things* do *happen here . . .*

I raise the megaphone to my mouth again to call her name—

On the fourth floor, a balcony door is shoved open and out steps Harper in her pajamas, a purple silk headscarf around her hair. "What are you doing?"

What am I doing?

I have absolutely no idea.

I hold the megaphone up to my mouth. "My name is Jessica Stone," I begin, because I am not sure where else to start, "and for a few days I pretended to be someone else. I thought I would just play a part, like I always do, and then move on, but . . . " I lick my lips, my voice wavering. There are hundreds of people gathering around me as I stand on top of this ridiculous food truck, the closest I can get to Harper. "I didn't expect to meet you," I continue, my heart thundering in my ears.

"You lied to me," she shouts down. "Why?"

"Because . . . " For a split second I think I might lie to her again. Take the easy way out and blame the script and *Starfield* and the fans. But I think I know her well enough to know that she'll see right through me. What kind of person would I be if I lied about why I lied to begin with?

She deserves the truth.

"Because I—at first I just needed to play the part of Imogen, but then, as I got to know you, I just became scared that . . . that you wouldn't like me once I told you who I was. People always expect Jessica Stone to be the person she's made out to be in the media and in magazines, but it felt so nice to just be me around you. And that was selfish and I'm sorry. I don't deserve a second chance, and I understand if you never want to see me again. But . . . " I gather my courage as hundreds of eyes judge me, wondering why I care so much about someone I just met.

And honestly, I couldn't tell them. I think there are people who come into your life, and you just know. For however long or short a time or however impossible it might seem—they're important. Like a guiding star amid a storm.

I take a deep breath and continue, "But I'm not lying now

when I say that I—I think I like you, Harper Hart. Will you go to the ExcelsiCon Ball with me?"

Four stories up, Harper doesn't say anything, and the longer I wait the colder my hands feel. My heart begins to pound. What if she'll never forgive me? What if this isn't enough? Will anything ever be? Could anything be?

Could *I* be?

Maybe we are like ships at sea, sailing in opposite directions—together and then gone. Maybe Harper loves someone else. But even if she does, I'll still have the memories of ramen, and stars, and how her lips twitch up when she's happy—folding them into a part of me I'll never let go, shaping me from the inside out. And I will carry on. Because, in the end, I am not a princess waiting to be saved.

I will do my own saving.

I am Jessica Stone. I am many things: a daughter, and an actress, and a fan of astronomy and the stars and the wide finite universe. I love strawberries on hot summer days and the way the moonlight shines so softly across Harper's face tonight. I am an explorer of my own sexuality. I am a kaleidoscope of hope and dreams and wonder in the shape of a girl. I am not a porcelain doll. I am not empty. I am worthy.

I am enough.

Harper leans over the balcony railing, and she smiles and tilts her head and shouts down, "Are you really *Romeo and Juliet*-ing this right now?"

I press the megaphone trigger and reply. "You bet I am. And if you say no I'll sing the *Starfield* theme until you come down and pry this megaphone from the fingers of my lifeless corpse."

"GOD PLEASE DON'T MAKE HER SING!" someone in the crowd shouts. Oh look, my legacy from last night's karaoke.

Even from way down here, Harper's smile is blinding. "Gimme a few minutes."

The crowd around me—which I had forgotten about—erupts into chaotic applause. I turn around and look down at the sea of people who followed me out of the convention hall, people in geek T-shirts and cosplay, toting art prints and nerdy collectibles, some of their phones aimed up at me. A Luke Skywalker cosplayer thrusts his green lightsaber into the air.

My cheeks begin to hurt and I realize that I'm smiling. Really, truly, stupidly smiling. So wide that the muscles in my face begin to ache. Because for the first time in as long as I can remember, I am happy.

Ridiculously, wonderfully happy.

In front of the truck, a familiar redheaded girl heaves herself onto the hood, followed by Sage. She motions to the megaphone. "May I?"

"Oh, sure," I say, and I hand it off.

Elle tests the trigger and then raises it to her mouth. "Attention, my favorite weirdos and nerds, thanks to an anonymous donor, each one of you now has a ticket to ExcelsiCon's notorious ball in the Grand Ballroom. Please check your lightsabers, spears, bows, and warhammers at the door. Now let's go party!"

The crowd erupts into another cheer and turns in the direction of the con.

Elle giddily turns back to me. "I've always wanted to use one of those!"

I laugh. "I take it Dare's the anonymous donor?"

Her grin widens. "Actually, it was Natalia Ford." The surprise must show on my face because Elle adds, "She was at the panel, and she told me to tell you that she has an offer for you. She said to call her later."

"And," Dare adds, coming up beside her, "Amon is on the phone with the executive producers right now." He's looking very intently at his nails. "They're having *quite* a discussion—"

"Jess!" someone shouts.

I quickly turn toward the sound of my name. Harper is waving from the entrance of the hotel. *Jess.*

She called my name—mine!

I hurry to the front of the food truck, where Sage helps me onto the hood and her girlfriend Cal helps me to the ground. Their chubby wiener dog sits in the front seat of the truck, pink tongue dangling, and howls at all the noise.

The crowd parts like a Rebel ship colliding with a Death Cruiser at lightspeed, and on the other side is an impossible moment. A girl with lightning-flecked brown eyes and a warm smile, wearing a sequined dress decorated with the *Starfield* logo, and I didn't think I could like her more.

Somewhere in the middle, Harper and I meet, and though I had words with the megaphone, they're all lost on me now and I don't know what to say. What can I say? How do I start?

So I do the only thing I can think of.

I give her the *Starfield* salute—*You and I are made of stars*—and I hope that's enough. She smiles and presses her hands to mine in the same pose, and then slowly, finger by finger, they fall together—

And she kisses me.

She kisses me and the world is too small and my skin is too tight and the universe is impossible and Harper Hart is *kissing me*. She tastes like cherry soda and maroon lipstick and stardust, and I lean into her like a sunflower to the sun. I want to memorize the shape of her mouth and the softness of her lips and the sound of the crowd humming *Amara's Waltz* from the movie.

And it is perfect.

And I am happy.

And I am enough.

Then she smiles and squeezes my hand. "Let's go dance our tiaras off, *ah'blena*," she says. And as Harper pulls me into the crowd of people I'll never know, geeks and fangirls and nerds and friends, I can't imagine anywhere else I'd rather be.

DAY FOUR

SUNDAY

———

"What a strange life we lead, *ah'blen*. I can't
say I'd change it for all the stars in the sky."

—Princess Amara, Episode 41, "Worse Than Death"

IMOGEN

I SCOOP THE REST OF MY #SaveAmara PINS into the cardboard box and close the lid. Slowly but steadily, the showroom is shutting down. In thirty minutes, the con will be empty, and everyone will wander back to their hotels, or to farewell parties, or home. My moms and I won't leave until tomorrow, when we pack up the U-Haul with all the figurines and hit the road back to Asheville, and by then all of this will have been a dream.

A pretty frakkin' sweet dream.

Every time I close my eyes, I remember the ExcelsiCon Ball—the colorful lights spiraling down onto the cosplays and nerd shirts, the music, the conga line that Milo and Bran started around the entire dance floor. The spectacle of Darien and Elle dancing, like legends returning from the depths of Reddit threads and Tumblr rumors, the *Starfield* waltz that followed. The moments Ethan glanced over at me, and took me by the hand, and spun me around to "Ramble On" by Led Zeppelin, laughing because I can't dance and neither can he, this strange tension radiating off us like Super Saiyan energy. It made my skin feel tingly and my heart flutter.

And then I blink and I'm on the couch in Jess's hotel room, with Ethan and Harper, sharing midnight pizza and watching the best Amara episodes of *Starfield*. I barely paid attention to the episodes at all—even my favorite ones!—because when Ethan shifted on the couch beside me all I could feel was the warmth of his elbow against mine and the way he slowly began to slouch until he fell asleep on my shoulder.

I quickly slide my box of pins off the table, trying not to let my embarrassment get to me.

This is the *worst* feeling ever. Knowing that Ethan and I wouldn't work—we're like a PS4 console and a Nintendo Switch controller. Incompatible.

Which is why I haven't seen him all day. I mean, we don't even have each other's numbers. I wish I hadn't given him the number for my favorite pizza joint instead of my real one. Stupid me.

But then, I guess it would hurt a whole lot more if I waited for him to text me and he never did. I don't think I could go through that again.

Attendees make their final rounds through Artists' Back Alley, and I hand out a few last pins. Harper's phone buzzes on the table, and she reaches for it and smiles.

"Jess?" I ask, although I already know.

Harper responds to the text. "She's in a meeting."

"*Another* one? Because of what happened yesterday?"

"Something like that."

"I hope she isn't in trouble," I murmur. I'd feel bad if she was, even though she did everything of her own accord.

Harper waves off my concern. "It'll be fine." Then she closes her sketchbook and stands, her arms outstretched. "Next time, don't send someone pretending to be you," she says. We hug tightly.

"Agreed." Then we release each other and I pick up my box. The pins rattle alongside all of the artwork I bought today. "How's your sister, by the by? Did she get into med school?"

"*With* scholarship," Harper replies proudly. "And your brother? How's the football thing?"

"We still haven't gotten word whether he's quarterback or not."

"Well, if I don't see you again before you leave, tell him good luck and I'll catch you on the internet?"

"Always, and safe travels! Oh, one thing. It's kinda been bothering me."

She begins to open her sketchbook again, but then closes it. She looks up at me. "Okay, shoot."

"Did you *really* think Jess was me this whole time? I mean, we know each other pretty friggin' well and, *starflame*, she's a world different from me and . . . Anyway, just curious."

She taps her mechanical pencil against her nose. "Yeah, totally."

Uh-huh.

I leave the booth. "See you next year!" I call over my shoulder as I make my way through the crowd toward the towering Nox King.

I would be lying if I said I wasn't scanning the crowd for raven-black hair and brown eyes and that insufferable disapproving frown, but the con is almost over and I'm beginning to realize that so is the magic. It must be the sleep deprivation, but my chest hurts a little at the realization that I'm just Imogen Lovelace again. And in the grand scheme of things, I'm not a part of Ethan's life.

When I get to Figurine It Out, Milo is slouched on the throne, and he sighs as I approach. Our moms are busy trying to sell as much stock as they can, knocking all of the prices down by thirty percent—which is a steal for some of the bigger pieces. They're helping a middle-aged woman as she tries to decide between two Sailor Moon poses.

"What's up, bro?" I ask, setting my box down on the foundation of the throne. "You look blue."

He gives me a long look before he says, "Just waiting for the rest of my life."

"Ah. Move over," I say, slapping his leg. He pulls himself to sit up and I squeeze in beside him, pushing the armrests out to make room. While the back and sides are strictly figurine boxes, the seat is just a hard plastic tub. It buckles a little with both of us sitting on it.

Together we look out over the closing showroom.

"You know, I don't think I'm all that perfect," he begins.

I groan and begin to pry myself up, but he puts one beefcake hand on my shoulder and easily pulls me back down. "*Miiii-llllooooooo*, I don't want to talk about this."

"I do, though. I need to. Because, I don't want to get sentimental or anything, but I've always thought I was in *your* shadow."

I give him a deadpan look. "Excuse me?"

"You're so smart, Mo!" he says, and begins counting my virtues on his fingers, "and you're funny, and you're good, and you bake the best chocolate murder cookies, and you're personable and you amassed *fifty thousand* signatures on a petition to save your favorite fictional character. Everyone loves you the second they meet you."

"But—but you—"

"What about me? I walk in and just try not to stumble over my own two feet. Everyone at school, all of our teachers, they take one look at my name and say, 'Oh, you're Imogen's brother,' because you leave a legacy so freakin' long that I've got little to no chance of the teachers actually remembering my name."

"Bullshit. You're a great football player! And you have the perfect boyfriend, *and* you're vice president and—"

"Yeah," he interrupts, rolling his eyes, "because that's the only way I can get out of your shadow."

I blink, my mouth opening and closing like a fish gobbling water, trying to think of some kind of comeback. Milo feels like he's in *my* shadow? I would ask if he's joking, but there's a crinkle between his brows that he always gets when he's being honest. It's so absurd that I begin to laugh, and so does he. I've been so bent on trying to get out from under his shadow, and he's been trying to get out of mine, that we just made everything impossible for each other.

"Okay, okay, let's make a deal," I say as I wipe the tears from my eyes. "Let's come to each other if we're feeling this way. And talk it through."

"Gross, like siblings who support each other?" He makes a face, and I punch him in the arm.

"*Yes*, like siblings who support each other—"

His phone begins to blare the *Power Rangers* theme song, and he digs it out of his pocket, checks the number, and shoots me a look of alarm. "It's Coach Evans."

"We'll finish this conversation later—"

"—or never—"

"Go answer it! Good luck!" I add as he scrambles off of the throne and closes himself in the storage area for privacy. I'm not going to say that I'm not nervous for him, because I am. I want him to get quarterback—I think he would be an amazing addition to the first yarn or whatever it's called.

I'm really hoping things work out.

"Is something wrong, Monster?" Minerva asks as Kathy

checks out the Sailor Moon customer. Minerva's wearing her hair in a fishtail braid that slithers like a stroke of black ink down her shoulder, blending in so seamlessly with her black lace dress that it almost looks like it's part of the outfit. "Your aura is very gray today."

"Earl or Dorian?"

She laughs and kisses the top of my head. "You know we're going to have to talk about what happened this weekend."

"Ah." I sigh. "Which part? The part where I impersonated Jessica Stone, or the part where I assaulted her costar?"

"You assaulted her costar? Which one?"

Kathy finishes with the customer and walks over to us. "We'll definitely talk about that later, but first we need to discuss this." She takes out her phone, which is open to Twitter, and shows me what I already know.

Early this morning, after I'd slipped out from beside Ethan and crept out of Jess's room, because I'm terrible at goodbyes, I deleted my Twitter as I rode the elevator down to my floor. The #SaveAmara initiative—everything. I'm sure it'll live on in other people's hashtags and other people's accounts, but I'm no longer the one spearheading it. I also deleted the online petition and its fifty-thousand-odd signatures (not before saving a copy, though).

I give my mothers a shrug, unable to look at either of them. "I think I've done everything I could, and the petition reached who it needed to. I don't want to be one of the people riling up the masses and spreading toxicity, and Twitter isn't the best place for nuanced conversations. I want to save Amara, but I don't want to do it at the expense of Jess, you know?" My last word wobbles, and I know it's because I'm on about four hours of sleep, so I bite my bottom lip to keep myself together.

"Oh, Monster." Kathy folds me into a hug. Minerva wraps her

long arms around us both, and we exist there while I try not to cry, sandwiched between the two people who love me most.

It's not so bad being Imogen Lovelace. I'm not a movie star, and I don't attract swaths of adoring fans, and my voice is tiny—but my dreams are big and I don't mind being me.

The fantastical is almost over, but it isn't over yet.

I have a boy to meet at the top of the escalators for one last time, and I have a bone to pick with him.

We break from our hug, and I dry my eyes and tell my moms I'll be back to help pack up after the floor closes. Milo's still in the storage closet talking to the coach.

I hope that's a good sign.

It's a quarter to five when I arrive at the escalators at the front of the showroom floor. I used to think that love was two people passing each other on these very escalators, heading off to different panels and different meet-and-greets, apart but together. Maybe we'd be cosplaying as Carmindor and Amara, and not Link and Zelda, and maybe we'd flash each other the Federation salute instead.

Maybe we could just smile at each other, and lock eyes, and not have to say anything at all.

Jasper slides past two cosplayers on his way up the escalators. He smiles in greeting, absolutely oblivious to the fact that he saw me just yesterday. He throws his hands into the air. "Mo! That was sick what you did on the panel! Impersonating Amara. Did she just tap you for that panel to do the stunt?"

I give him a once-over. Acid-washed jeans and his own logo on his T-shirt and messy brown hair. I can kind of see what I saw in him, but I much prefer guys in neat trousers with swept-back hair and dark eyes. "I was her for a few days," I reply.

"Ha! That must've been fun," he begins, and then his smile

falters. "Wait, what?"

"'What, you're too good for a hug?'" I recite the same agonizing line he gave me, and it finally clicks.

His eyebrows jerk up. "You . . . that was you, too?"

"You're a jerk, you know that?" I begin. "I don't even know why I'm wasting time on you. You used me, and when you found something—or someone, I guess—better, you tossed me away like I didn't mean anything. I waited for you for *three hours* at the ExcelsiCon Ball. I sat on the curb waiting—"

"Whoa, whoa, calm down."

"No, you aren't allowed to tell me to calm down. You're whiny, and you're selfish, and your videos aren't even funny. And you know what the worst part is? I actually thought that I deserved you, but I was totally wrong. I deserve so much better than you."

His face hardens. "Why'd I want to date some nobody like you, anyway?"

Maybe three days ago that would've hurt me, but now I just smile and step up into his face and say, "Because we both know that you're the real nobody. And oh? I almost forgot. I reported you for sexual harassment, so you'll never come to this con again."

"Are you kidding me? How will *you* get me to leave?"

And then, as if materializing out of the con crowd itself, appears Darien's ex-bodyguard Lonny and two of his security guards. Jasper sees them and hesitates.

"I suggest that you leave, Mr. Webster, and don't come back here again."

Jasper grits his teeth, jerking his gaze between me and the security guards about ten feet away, and then, with a last glowering look, he steps onto the escalator.

I breathe a sigh of relief as Lonny comes over to check on me.
"Are you all right, Imogen?" he asks, and I nod.

"I'm fine. Thank you."

He nods back, and then he and his security detail fan out into the crowd once again. I sigh in relief. I should've reported Jasper the second he touched me but at least now I know he won't be bothering anyone here ever again.

After he's gone, I stand there at the top of the escalators, rubbing my arms, trying to scrub the grossness away—

And then my phone buzzes.

> *JESS (4:57 PM)*
>
> *—#SaveAmara*
>
> *—[Link]*

My eyebrows furrowing, I click on the link.

Above me, the announcement for the end of the con booms over the intercom, and around me the world slows to a stop and everyone looks up as if the man speaking is the voice of a god. He's not—he's just the creator of ExcelsiCon, Elle Wittimer's father. He died about a decade ago, but it's become tradition to run his closing announcement every year.

I scan the article on my phone, and my heart rises, happy in my chest.

"Thank you for coming to ExcelsiCon! Safe travels across the universe, and we hope to see you again next year! As our friends in the Federation always say—Look to the stars!"

"Aim!" echoes everyone on the showroom floor, and I join in for the final word:

"Ignite!"

Cheers rise up across the con, and I close my eyes and relish it, because there's nothing quite like the possibility of another ExcelsiCon. I put my phone away and turn to descend the escalator for the final time this year, and that ride down is just as magical as the first one I ever took, the lobby of the main hotel spreading like a sea of fandom before me. It feels like leaving home for a little while, but knowing you'll be back.

That's when I see him.

He steps onto the up escalator, looking like he just ran a half mile, his glasses askew and his hair wild. He locks eyes with me, and suddenly there is no one else in the world. My breath hitches in my throat as we pass each other—

I turn around, trying to wrack my brain for something to say, *anything*, and he spins to me, too, and blurts out:

"I think I might like you, Imogen!"

I stand there dumbfounded as I'm carried down the escalator and Ethan is carried up. Then he jumps into action, scuttling down the up escalator, dodging past a Kingdom Hearts cosplayer and a sexy Dalek, taking the steps two at a time to meet me at the bottom, where he straightens himself, patting down the wrinkles on his airplane-patterned button-down and fixing his glasses.

We stand there, me holding my breath, him trying to catch his, and we are two sides of the same coin. Opposite and hopeless and—

"I think I might like you," he says again, breathless.

My mind is reeling. "Me? That's just because I look like Jess—"

"No, I like you as you are—as Imogen Lovelace. Not as Jessica Stone. I like that you chew on your thumb when you're nervous, and that you know how to braid even though you have short hair, and that sometimes you slip into strange accents when you don't mean to, and that you're bold, and you're courageous, and you're good, and—Look, what I said in the pool, I meant that, too. That you aren't nothing." He swallows and says, more softly, "Like Amara, you're going to be amazing."

"I'm not already?"

"*Starflame*, you're insufferable."

I take his face in my hands and pull him down to kiss me. He tastes like Cheerwine, his hands rising to cup the sides of my face. The mass exodus from the con bends around us like space-time around the *Prospero* at lightspeed. He smells so nice, like sandalwood cologne and crisply ironed shirts, and as I lean into him my heart flutters. Because he is kissing me. The disapproving, insufferable, maddeningly hot Ethan Tanaka is kissing *me*, Imogen Lovelace.

The best version of me. The only version. Kissing the best, dorkiest, most tall and wonderful version of him.

When we finally break apart, he takes out his phone and asks, "May I get your phone number? Your real one this time?"

"I think you've earned it," I reply, plucking his phone out of his hand, and kiss him again.

JESS

"IHM-OH-GEN-NE!" THE BARISTA CALLS.

I duck between two Sailor Scouts to snag my and Harper's orders and carry them to our table. My hair is pulled up into a beanie, but slivers of brilliant blood red escape and twist across my neck. People aren't really looking at us, probably because everyone is too tired to confront us, or my disguise is finally working, or because I told the barista Imogen's name at the cash register. Hey, we promised that we would switch back, not that I would stop using her name.

Although, it's hard to fool the paparazza sitting in her black SUV outside the café, but a girl can dream.

"Do you think Ethan found her?" Harper asks, taking a sip of her iced latte.

"I'm sure he did," I reply. He hasn't texted me saying that he didn't, and Imogen hasn't responded to my text yet, so *something* is keeping them both busy. "I think they'd be cute together."

Her curly hair is pulled up into a bun atop her head, wrapped with the same purple scarf from last night. "Long distance sucks, though."

"Well, I guess it would, but a few hours isn't *really* that far when you think about it." I nurse my dirty chai latte, and it hits the spot right where a good eight hours of sleep is missing.

She snorts. "A few hours? Jess, Asheville and L.A. aren't even in the same time zones."

"Who says I'll be in L.A. for the next few months? There could be a job that lands me here for a while. And then after that, who knows?"

Harper stares at me, blinking, before she figures it out. She lives here in Atlanta. It wouldn't be a few hours for us. She grins around the straw of her latte, and the glimmer in her golden-brown eyes is almost as intoxicating as the thought of starting something with her—something real.

A story that I get to tell.

"After all," I add flippantly, because I can't keep her guessing, "*someone* needs to save Carmindor."

"Indeed," she replies, trying to disguise her delight, but her knees are bumping under the table and she is not very good at hiding her excitement. "And you're okay with playing Amara again? Happy?"

I wish interview questions were this simple. Maybe from now on they will be. I lean over the table to meet her halfway, studying her perfect lips and her perfect eyelashes and the perfect curl of her dark hair. The paparazza in the SUV focuses her fish-eye lens on us.

Are you happy? my heart asks softly.

"Yes, I am," I reply, and I kiss her. I kiss her in front of the entire world, the first word on the first page of the rest of my life.

#AMARALIVES

By Elle Wittimer

[EXCERPT FROM *ENTERTAINMENT WEEKLY*]

It is a truth universally acknowledged that a fandom in want of a princess will save that princess. And sometimes it's the princess who saves the fandom.

At the twenty-fifth-annual ExcelsiCon in Atlanta, Georgia, this past weekend, it was revealed that the director of *Starfield*, Amon Wilkins, leaked the confidential script for the sequel. This morning, the studio announced that they have fired Mr. Wilkins from the project and replaced him with N. A. Porter—the directorial name of none other than *Starfield*'s original princess, Natalia Ford.

Following the shake-up, Darien Freeman has confirmed that he will reprise his role as Prince Carmindor, as will Calvin Rolfe as Carmindor's best friend, Euci. The villain in the sequel, revealed (in full costume) in an earlier panel during ExcelsiCon, will be General Sond, played by *Blades of Valor* actor Vance Reigns.

When asked whether the character of Princess Amara, incarnated so well by Oscar-nominated actress Jessica Stone, would make a reappearance after Ms. Stone's heartfelt speech on a panel late Saturday evening, the cast reserved their comments.

But they did tell us that *Starfield Resonance* will begin filming next month. And Jessica Stone will be there.

ACKNOWLEDGMENTS

EVERY STORY FEELS LIKE LEARNING HOW to write all over again.

But while the plot and characters are new (mostly), I'm so thankful to have constants in my life, like my agent, Holly Root, and my editor, Blair Thornburgh, and the amazing team at Quirk Books. I'm also thankful for my backbone, the smol group of friends who, without them, *Princess* would never have been possible: Nicole Brinkley, Ada Starino, Kaitlyn Sage Patterson, Katherine Locke, Savannah Apperson, C. B. Lee, Eric Smith—seriously, [in a Bette Midler serenade] *did you ever know that you're my hero?*

The past few years have been a little rough, and *The Princess and the Fangirl* is speckled with all of the things that became lights in the darkness for me—*Yuri!!! On Ice* and *Star Wars* and *Zelda: Breath of the Wild* and *Dragon Age: Inquisition* and *Critical Role*. But most importantly, I want to give a shout-out to *The Adventure Zone* and the McElroy brothers. Thanks, dudes, for giving me some ear-magic to listen to and a punch in the feels.

We find happiness in a kaleidoscope of stories: in books, in comics, in dance, in podcasts, in film and TV shows and video games. We find happiness in cosplaying as our favorite characters, and going to meet-and-greets with our favorite celebrities, and Dimension Door-ing onto the back of an Ancient Black Dragon, and finger-gunning Magic Missiles with our murder-hobo friends in a weekly session of *Dungeons and Dragons*. We all deserve to be happy, and love what we love, and be *unironically enthusiastic* about it. There is a magic in fandom that there rarely is anywhere else—where you can raise a TV show from the dead, and un-fridge a favorite character, and write fanfic that becomes canon. It is the kind of magic that brings our far corners of the world together.

So thank you, dear reader, most of all. I hope this story brought you a little happiness, a little feels, and a little love. Keep reading what makes you happy, and keep celebrating the content that makes you feel most alive, and carve out your spot in the universe, and write that coffeeshop!AU. Go on. I'll be over on AO3 waiting.

Look to the stars. Aim.

Ignite!

CARMIN...
GENERAL ... NEBULA
a dangerous ...

... the UCON... refuses it? Let the Noxian
... the Black Orbit, gives him

Your Highness, your treaty with us
is already thin.

CARMINDOR

The Black Nebula - what's happening to it?

The NOXIAN GENERAL draws herself up to full height. She
is unafraid of her answer.

NOXIAN GENERAL

It has opened again, unsurpris-
ingly. Looks like your princess
didn't sacrifice enough. Now get
out of my way.

...R's mood darkens. He stands rigid in the doorway,
...entinel. Just out of the NOXIAN GENERAL's line of
... two Federation officers. They have their hands
...stols, ready to draw.

...GENERAL notices them and she whirls back to
...ngrily.

NOXIAN GENERAL

You know this is war.

CARMINDOR
(to the Federation Offi-
cers)

Arrest her.

For a moment, it seems like CARMINDOR won't let her pass,
but then he steps aside and the General leaves.

EXCELSICON
4-DAY 2019
Jessica
Stone
VIP GUEST

#SAVE
AMARA